THE LAKE HOUSE

THEO BAXTER

INKUBATOR
BOOKS

Published by Inkubator Books
www.inkubatorbooks.com

Copyright © 2024 by Theo Baxter

Theo Baxter has asserted his right to be identified as the author of this work.

ISBN (eBook): 978-1-83756-383-8
ISBN (Paperback): 978-1-83756-384-5
ISBN (Hardback): 978-1-83756-385-2

PROLOGUE

He's acting funny again, I thought. Ever since he announced he'd taken a new job, things had been off. Not that they'd ever been on, not really. I was always suspicious of him, but this time... this time he'd gone too far. He'd moved us right next door to *her*.

I couldn't believe it when I'd seen *her* walking into the house on the lake next door to our new home. The beautiful home that I'd thought meant he was going to — for once — be happy with me and make a home, but *she* had to be here and ruin it all.

I *had* to find out what her game was. How had *she* enticed him to choose this place? I *knew* she was behind it. *She* was devious. Always trying to come between me and the love of my life. I would find out. That was why I was following her. I knew she was going to meet my love. He'd gone out this morning with no explanation. I knew it was to meet *her*.

I saw her leave her house, and rushed out of the house in my flip-flops to follow her. I then saw her enter the community mailroom, and sat down on the bench outside so I could see through the window.

Was this where she was meeting him? Had they planned this? I had to know. I peered through the window and saw her, but she was talking with another man, not my love. Was she trying to throw me off by flirting with this one? It wasn't going to work. I was onto her. I saw her moving toward the door, and grabbed the newspaper someone had left on the bench.

Holding it up in front of me, I hoped she wouldn't see me, but it didn't work. She turned and waved at me. *Waved.* Like we were friends. I stared daggers at her as she laughed with the man she was with. He put his arm around her and glanced at me, then whispered to her.

I knew he was trying to protect her. Trying to make me think she wasn't involved with my love, but I felt sure they were just playing a game. He was helping the bitch for some reason. She was probably playing him too. Stringing him along like she had been doing with my love. When they got about a block ahead of me, I stood up and sprinted after them. I should have worn different shoes. Flip-flops weren't the best for covert operations.

Where the hell did they think they were going? I panted as I followed them as quickly as I could. The bitch laughed as she glanced back at me.

I hated her.

I hated her so much.

She was going to pay for what she was doing to me.

For ruining my life.

For stealing my love.

I would make her pay if it was the last thing I ever did.

1

Have you ever had one of those moments where you want to run away, but it feels like someone has superglued your feet to the ground? Like you're caught in one of those glue traps for mice, and you're doomed to be frozen to the spot until someone picks you up, trap and all, and tosses you into a dumpster?

That was how it felt when I walked into my bridal suite to find my fiancé, Tony Ellison, and my maid of honor and best friend, Mary Casden, preemptively christening my marriage bed, on top of my crisp, white Vera Wang wedding gown. I couldn't do anything but stare as their moans grew louder in my ears. I must have said something or made a noise because they finally realized I was standing in the doorway. That was when the screaming started.

I often wonder what might have happened if I hadn't caught them. What if I had gotten back to my room earlier, or had stopped to speak to more than my mother? What if my hairstylist hadn't called to say she would be late, giving me just enough time to go up to my bridal suite and "relax" for a moment alone? What if I had bought the Monique Lhuillier bridal gown instead of going for the more expensive Vera Wang? What if that butterfly hadn't flapped its wings over the Pacific Ocean, causing the inevitable circumstances that led to me opening the door to my bridal suite and seeing the love of my life and the best friend I'd ever had screwing each other on top of my dress?

I supposed Tony and I would be married now, and they might still be carrying on their affair, or I would have eventually caught them, causing a very messy and expensive divorce. In a way, I'd dodged a bullet; I understood that now. But in that moment, stuck in a glue trap of my own making, I could only stare.

"L-Laura! What are you—" Tony stammered, trying to bend down to pull up his pants.

"Laura, get the hell out!" Mary screamed over him, covering herself with, of all things, *my* wedding gown. That was what woke me up, I think.

"Get your grubby hands off that!" I screamed back, grabbing hold of the dress.

Mary clutched the dress to her naked body, pulling it from my hands, and ran into the bathroom.

"Mary, get the *hell* out of that bathroom with my dress!" I yelled, ignoring Tony, and making a beeline for the bathroom door. He'd gotten his pants up by this point and came over to pull me away, but I just slapped him. "Get away from me. I'll deal with you after Mary gives me back *my* wedding gown," I screeched, pushing Tony away and turning back to the door.

By now we had caused enough commotion, and my bridal party had gathered at the door to the adjoining suite.

"Laura?" said my bridesmaid Celene Shelby, coming through the suite.

She couldn't see this. If she did, the whole town would soon know that Tony and Mary had been spread-eagle on my dress on the day of my wedding. Celene was the biggest gossip I'd ever known — harmless in general, but catastrophic in situations like this.

While I banged on the door, Tony ran out of the bedroom and into the suite next door. I could hear his charming voice telling Celene everything was okay, that I just had cold feet.

That wouldn't do at all. I turned my attention from Mary back to Tony, running into the suite and shouting at Celene and the other shocked bridesmaids, "Nothing is fine. I just walked in on Mary and Tony fucking on top of my $5,000 Vera Wang wedding dress." Tears started streaming down my face.

The bathroom door opened in the bridal suite, and Mary came in, still holding my wedding dress to cover her naked body. "We weren't *fucking*, we were *making love*," she corrected.

At that point, I couldn't stand any more. I knew Mary had a very romantic vision of the world, but her describing that encounter as "making love" broke me. I rounded on her with renewed anger. "You call that *making love*? Mary, you wouldn't know love if it smacked you in the face. Allow me to prove it," I said, as I smacked her across the face.

She dropped my dress in shock, then tried to grab it back. I got there first and threw it into the bedroom. Mary tearfully ran back in to get the dress, or maybe her own clothes, I didn't know. I was blinded by rage at that point and moved to chase after her.

Tony grabbed my arm. "Baby, just leave it. Please let me explain."

A couple of my bridesmaids ran past me into the bedroom to restrain Mary, who was putting on my wedding dress and crying about how cold it was without clothes on.

"Explain?" I asked Tony. "How are you going to explain what happened, other than telling me just how long you've been having an affair with my maid of honor?"

"You have it all wrong; it's just cold feet," he said. "I was in there looking for my cuff links when I saw your wedding dress, and it just hit me how scared I was because of how much I love you. I'm sorry."

He had me. Tony always did; he's a charmer to his very core. Luckily, the sound of my wedding dress being torn at the seams brought me back to reality as Celene tugged on it to get it off Mary.

"What are you doing?" Mary whined. "I could have worn it."

"When?" I asked, rounding on Mary. "When would you have worn *my* wedding dress?"

"Once you two split. Tony said it was inevitable," Mary cried, tears streaming down her face.

You'd think that *I* had somehow ruined *her* special day. I looked at the scene, Celene holding my now ragged dress, my other bridesmaids standing there in shock, Tony pulling my arm, pleading with me, and Mary sobbing naked on the floor, her grasping fingers still trying to grab what was once a gorgeous creation of silk and lace. The hotel's bridal suite, once so vast and opulent, had turned into a cramped room, with no room for air. I could barely breathe.

"I have to go," I muttered, turning around.

"You can't just go; we have to settle this," Mary cried out.

"You have to give me your blessing so I can be with Tony and we can get married."

"You can't leave, baby; we need to talk. You can't be alone right now," Tony said in his smooth voice.

I didn't answer either of them. Behind me, Mary cried out again, this time asking why Tony wouldn't stand by her, why he was spending time reasoning with that bitch (presumably, me). Tony dropped my arm and turned to Mary, giving me the chance I needed to get away.

I bolted out the door into the hallway, slamming the door behind me. I ran to the elevator, pressing both the down and up buttons before anyone had the chance to stop me. The elevator arrived just as Tony stuck his head out the door. I jumped in and pressed a random floor number, and then punched the "door close" button as many times as I could. The elevator doors closed in his face, and I was finally alone, zooming up to the penthouse floor.

I got out of the elevator and walked down the hall, trying to clear my head. It hit me that I was still wearing a robe that had "Bride" embroidered on the back. I started to take it off before remembering I didn't have much on underneath. When my hairstylist had said she would be over an hour late, Mary had suggested I go to the spa. I stopped dead in my tracks, realizing she'd probably said it so she could have a quickie with Tony. What a perfect opportunity for them. How stupid I had been.

I still didn't understand the kink behind doing it on my wedding dress. Was Mary that vindictive? Suddenly, it felt as if I didn't know either of them. Who were these people who had comforted me in my moments of sadness, celebrated my wins with me, and commiserated as I talked to them about my mother or wedding stress?

I wandered out onto the hotel's rooftop terrace. Luckily for me, it was early, and no one was around.

I heard a cell phone ringing and slowly came to the realization that it was mine and pulled it from the robe's massive pocket. I wasn't sure I wanted to talk to anyone right now, but I found myself answering anyway. The caller ID said Hotel Ritz, so maybe it was the hotel calling to tell me this was all an elaborate prank gone horribly wrong.

"Baby," Tony said.

I cringed. "Don't call me that. I'm done. I can't marry you."

"Why? Listen, I came to your room because I had cold feet, and I needed to talk to you. Mary was the one trying to seduce me. This was all Mary's idea. I love you more than anything. I need you. I didn't think you would ever overreact like this. Just come back, and we can get you something to calm you down. Laura, you don't understand what you saw, and I'm worried about what you're going to do right now."

I still didn't know what he said that finally made me wake up. Maybe it was because he'd told me I was overreacting. I had talked about it in therapy in the years since, and my therapist and I had never been able to pinpoint exactly what had triggered my wake-up call. In that moment, all of Tony's little white lies came rushing back to me, all the moments when I saw him flirting with Mary — or other women — and he told me I was reading too much into their interactions.

"No."

"What?" Tony asked. He wasn't used to me telling him no.

"I know exactly what I saw. I may not know how you two got there — though I can speculate — but I know what you were doing. If there was seduction going on, it happened long before I arrived."

"Laura, it wasn't me," Tony insisted.

"Tony, this is real life, not a nineties pop song. It was you and Mary and my wedding dress. I'm not one to kink-shame, but that is bizarre, even for you. I have cut you so much slack that I don't have any left for myself. You've flirted with every *single* one of my bridesmaids, as if you had some kind of sick fantasy of thoroughly embarrassing me on my wedding day."

"Let me explain," Tony whined.

"We both know exactly what kind of carnal instincts you have — not to mention the fact you used the most cliché adulterer's line in existence — so I think I can confidently say that you were screwing my best friend and *maid of honor* less than eight hours before you were going to vow to have and hold me forever and say, 'I do.' No matter which way you look at it, this wasn't the time or the place to engage in whatever exciting little game you have going on, and frankly, I would like to disqualify myself from playing. I don't want to see you — or Mary — ever again."

Tony was finally silent.

Then Mary's shrill voice came on the line. "Good. You don't deserve him anyway. You're so cold, and that's why you're going to be alone, Laura. You won't even listen to the man, who you said was the love of your life supposedly, explain why he's been so emotionally stressed. Why *he* needed a moment to himself on a day that isn't all about you. It's about the people around you, too. In fact, it was my day as well—"

I tuned Mary out after that.

Celene was the one who found me. I was sitting on a

deck chair, drinking a piña colada from the rooftop bar in my robe as I looked out over the skyline. As soon as I turned and saw her, I broke down in tears.

After the wedding fiasco, I thought I was invincible. Whatever you threw at me, nothing could possibly be worse than the day I caught my fiancé and maid of honor in the throes of passion and had to take a cab home in a silk bathrobe that said "Bride" on the back.

Or so I thought.

2

THREE YEARS LATER

Andrea Caldwell stared into the eyes of the man she'd hired to murder her husband. "You're sure this plan will work?"

"Lady, I've been doing this for a long time, and I've never been caught. You could say I'm pretty good at my job. I'll call you on this burner phone if I need anything."

The hitman, whose name Andrea would never know, disappeared into the night.

Andrea looked around her backyard, clutching her cardigan, making sure none of her nosy neighbors were at their window. It was highly unlikely at this hour. She looked back up at her own bedroom window, where she could see her husband, Ted, sleeping in their king-sized bed. Her body filled with fury, Andrea wanted to burst in and murder him then and there. Ted had cheated on her for the last time.

I stared at the blinking cursor on my computer screen, unsure of where to go from there. What was Andrea Caldwell going to do now, just crawl back into bed with her husband after sealing his fate with a hitman? I closed my laptop and stared out at the view of the lake, trying to use the serene vista outside my window to slow my racing heartbeat.

It had been three years since that fateful day. I had lost my ability to trust people, and the sight of Tony and Mary still haunted my dreams. I'd wake up sweating from the same nightmare at least once a week. In it, I have to sit through their wedding, wearing Mary's ill-fitting maid-of-honor dress, while I watch her wed Tony in my wrinkled, torn, and stained Vera Wang. If I let the dream go on long enough, the wedding usually ends in me attacking Mary and being hauled off to prison.

After *the incident*, Celene suggested that I start seeing a therapist. "You've just gone through a major trauma. You need more than a friend — you need professional help."

After I'd had a good cry, she made an appointment with Dr. Michael Delgado, one of the best psychologists in the city. It turned out to be the best relationship I'd ever had with a man. I spent most of that first year crying in his office as Tony and Mary flaunted their new relationship on social media, slowly converting all of our mutual friends to their "side."

Dr. Delgado translated my half sobs and ugly cries into healthy behaviors to help me move on. It was due to him that I was able to hold on to my job as an advice columnist at the lifestyle website *Goosh*. Every time a woman wrote in asking for advice about a cheating partner, his voice echoed through my brain, advising me *not* to tell that poor agonizer to "dump his ass and set fire to his car."

I *did* write that once. My editor, Lindsay, promptly emailed me to say: "While I understand and acknowledge what you've been through, perhaps you can channel thoughts such as this into other creative outlets?" Truly the nicest piece of criticism I'd ever received as a writer.

That was when I started writing Tony and Mary into my novels. My serial killers and victims were now imbued with characteristics of the happy couple, allowing me to kill them off over and over again, from novel to novel, and throughout the long editing process.

Was it healthy? Probably not.

Did it make me feel better? Absolutely.

If Dr. Delgado knew about it, he might even agree. After all, I wasn't *acting* on my violent thoughts, I was just *inspired* by them. I couldn't help it. While trying to get over the biggest shock and tragedy of my life, I also had to navigate Mary and Tony's demands that I forgive them, deal with my mother telling me that I needed to forgive Tony and fight to get him back, hearing from all of our mutual friends who suggested that *I* was the bad guy for not giving Tony and Mary some privacy, and Mary sending vaguely threatening "Dear Jane" emails to my *Goosh* column. Altogether, it was enough to drive anyone over the edge.

So after a year of living in a tiny one-room studio apartment in the city, I decided to move. I needed a major change, so I started looking for small towns. That was when I came across a brochure for Pine Lake. It was a small community a few hours outside the city, in the middle of absolutely nowhere. It attracted recluses and people looking for an escape — anyone who wanted to pretend the world around them didn't exist. In other words, it was the perfect place for a jilted bride who wanted nothing to do with her so-called friends, fiancé, and former life.

Celene, one of the few friends who remained by my side, helped me pack up and move. Of all the friends I'd thought would stick by me, I hadn't imagined Celene would be the one to do so, but I was grateful that she had. Not only had she stuck by me, she'd been my rock and become my very best friend. I made arrangements with Dr. Delgado to have the bulk of my appointments via video call and asked Lindsay for approval to work remotely.

Just like that, I picked up my life and plopped it into a small cabin on a secluded lake where no one knew about my dramatic past. I arrived at Pine Lake one year post-jilt, ready to write and move on.

Maybe it was distance, or maybe it was time, but my friends slowly started to come around. I talked to Celene pretty regularly — she still liked to gossip, and she said Tony and Mary's constant dramatics had started to wear everyone down and cause them to question the couple's story of star-crossed love. Great. I was glad to hear about it from afar — *very* afar. I was happy in my peaceful new life, where my biggest worry was whether it would be snowing when I decided to go to the community mailbox to pick up my latest online shopping packages.

I stretched and got up to make myself some tea. My last two books — pulpy psychological thrillers, the kind you read on vacation — had been doing very well. The publisher wanted a third to create a sort of trilogy.

"A trio of jilted girlfriends. We could sell it as a box set, and with the Easter eggs you planted in the first two, it's as if they're all in the same world — it's so marketable."

His words echoed in my thoughts. It was more pressure than I'd had in the past. When you don't sell a lot of books, there isn't much demand when you deliver them. But when your books start gaining traction, that's a different story. I already had to dodge requests for interviews and tours, claiming that I wanted to remain as much of a mystery as my novels and that a third book in a trilogy — one the publishing company would surely market as "highly anticipated" — would make it harder to remain a mystery. The two years since moving to Pine Lake had been pretty peaceful, and I wasn't sure I wanted to invite any drama into the bubble I had created for myself. At the same time, as a writer, the thought of more people reading my words was intoxicating.

I took my tea to the large window that faced the lake and saw my neighbor Brandy walk out of her house to do the same thing. We both loved staring at the lake with our tea, not that we talked about it.

You could categorize Pine Lake's residents into one of three categories:

1. Artists and creatives who wanted zero distractions. They ran the gamut from painters to writers, each hoping to avoid the constant distractions of city life and dedicate more time to their craft.

2. Retirees, both old *and* very young. I knew there was at least one retired tech billionaire who lived in Pine Lake, because he ran one of the coffee shops that I occasionally frequented. I could never figure out what most of the leisure-seekers did with their day, but I supposed that was the point in the end.

3. People who don't want to talk to you, and don't want you to talk to them.

Brandy was definitely in category three. She was a nice woman, deep down. After two years, I'd finally convinced her that I wasn't "trouble" and managed to coax out more than one single-syllable word out of her. We'd even had dinner together a few times. But Brandy had definitely moved to Pine Lake to get away from young people like me.

I knew we were finally friends when she gave me a jar of homemade kimchi and a bag of her favorite green tea. The next time I saw her through the window, drinking tea and staring at the lake, she gave me a small "cheers" with her teacup. I was elated and resisted the urge to call Celene right away and tell her that I had finally cracked Brandy's tiny, stony exterior.

It was after that when she'd invited me to dinner, and it had become an occasional thing for us to dine together and enjoy the peaceful quiet of the lake from the same table. We didn't talk much, as I said she was pretty quiet, and I respected that about her. It was nice just enjoying the peace together sometimes.

At that moment, Brandy was looking quite grumpy, so I decided to leave her be. I didn't know what put her in that mood, perhaps news of the latest town "drama." I knew one of the mysteriously rich residents was having an argument with another mysteriously rich resident over some kind of lawn sabotage, but I was uninterested in who'd poisoned whose magnolia trees.

The doorbell rang, and I pulled myself away from the window and my distracting thoughts. I had to stop reminiscing and get back to the book. I padded over to the front door and found Brian Oliver standing at my doorstep. Brian was the community's de facto "mayor" and a local real-estate mogul. He owned at least half of the properties in Pine Lake, both business and residential. He'd sold me my house and sold me on the town itself.

"It's a quiet community, perfect for someone who wants to dedicate themselves to their craft and produce better work than they have in years," he'd said.

Sometimes I forgot that he was a somewhat famous horror artist as well because it seemed like Brian was always trying to sell something. He had planned to rent the property, but agreed to a sort of "rent to buy" model when I mentioned how in love with the place I was, but that no bank would give me a mortgage due to what they saw as an unstable income. I told him that in three years I would either move out or pay cash for the remainder, and surprisingly, he agreed to my terms.

"It's probably not the best business decision," I told him at the time. "You'd be losing out on interest, inflation—"

"Don't worry about my business decisions. I have more than enough money to support myself and my art. I can tell you'll be a great addition to our little Californian utopia, and I want to help a fellow artist. Especially one who is bouncing back from heartbreak."

Brian always seemed to know exactly what to say in any situation, a skill I had always been in awe of. I might be a talented writer, but I hadn't had the conversationalist gene passed down to me.

Brian beamed at me from my doorstep. Did he step back a little bit so I could admire him in full? Probably. He was a little vain.

"Laura!" he exclaimed, as if surprised to see me at my

own house. "I was just passing by on my way to the hardware store, and I wondered if you needed anything. You're still my tenant for the next year or so, and I wanted to make sure you're being taken care of." He flashed his pearly whites, which seemed to glisten in the sun.

If Brian got me anything, he'd insist on installing it. And that would lead to dinner, which could lead to... well, something more. I had just started thinking about dating again, and I knew Brian wanted a spot on my (very empty) calendar.

I smiled as politely as I could. "Thanks, Bri, but honestly, I'm all good for now. That robot vacuum you got for me is doing great, though, thanks for that. I just wish I could find a place to put it that's not in the way."

"The company behind that thing probably designed it so the only place you could have it was in the way." He laughed.

I felt a pang in my chest. His laugh was like a warm, secure hug, the kind of laugh you wanted to feel against your chest as you held each other. "Exactly. I should return the damn thing and stop being so lazy about *actually* vacuuming the house."

"Let me take a look at it before you give up. I feel responsible. I was the one who purchased it for you in the first place."

"That's sweet, but honestly, it's fine."

I didn't know why I didn't want Brian to come in and help me move the heavy charging dock to a more appropriate location. But inviting Brian in to help would be the same as inviting Brian in for dinner, and after a day of plotting my ex's murder via the characters in my book, I just wanted to be alone and watch a trashy reality TV show.

"I know you're busy writing the next great American novel," he said. "You won't even notice I'm here."

"Unless you throw out your back moving that charging station."

"True. Then I'll need someone to nurse me back to health." He smiled again.

I could feel myself blush. Why was I so against having a man in my house? Dr. Delgado was trying to help me break that down in our latest sessions. As I decided to dip my toe in the dating world, I also had to trust the people in that world. Brian was a caring man, someone who didn't have to help me with that stupid robot vac he'd very generously bought for me when I complained about how much I hated cleaning. He was a very good listener, and he had clearly gone at least fifteen minutes out of his way just to make conversation with me, which was very sweet.

At the rate I was going, I was going to be like Brandy when I got old. A curmudgeonly shut-in, with few friends to speak of.

"Brian, why don't you come in? I'll pour you some wine, and we can tackle the robot vac situation together. Unless there was something you were desperate for at the hardware store." I smirked at him, calling his bluff. We both knew it was a ruse to begin with.

"Was I that obvious?" he whispered.

I nodded, feeling oddly proud for catching the most charming man in town off guard. I decided that I deserved a little flirt after a day of writing doom and gloom, so I opened the door wide and turned, giving him a good look at me as I walked into the house.

3

———

Brian and I each had a glass of rosé that afternoon while we set up the robot vacuum's little home in one of my hall closets. After a lot of maneuvering — and maybe a few unnecessary drops of the screwdriver on my part — we managed to fit the thing in there with a thin extension cord running to a plug in the hallway.

"That's the closest you're going to get to keeping it out of sight," he said, slinging back his last sip of rosé.

"Thanks, I could never have done it without your help," I said, weighing the option of inviting Brian for dinner or finding an excuse to get him out of my house.

As it turned out, I didn't need to figure out either because when Brian put down his glass, he started heading toward the door.

"I'd love to stay and chat — that rosé did hit the spot — but I have to get going. I've still got work to do. I just..." Brian trailed off for a moment, looking sheepish.

I raised my hand, as if surrendering. "It's okay. I'm not offended that you don't like me as much now that you know

I can't tell the difference between a Phillips and a flathead," I joked. I was lying. I definitely knew the difference, but somewhere in the back of my mind, my mother's voice told me that men don't like to be shown up when it comes to tools.

Brian laughed. "That's not it at all. It's a little embarrassing to admit, but, um... well, I actually wasn't in the neighborhood. I skipped out of work early to come by. I was going to ask when you came to the door, but then I lost my nerve, and I just blurted out the first thing that came into my head—"

"Brian, the sun is going to start to go down. I'm gonna need you to spit it out."

"Would you like to have dinner with me?" he said.

My breath caught in my throat. Despite thinking about dating again, I hadn't expected him to ask me out. For a split second, I considered saying yes. Dr. Delgado and Celene had both been trying to get me back on the dating scene, and I kept shying away.

Brian seemed so approachable and warm. It might be nice to dip a toe back in with someone I knew decently well, but I just wasn't ready. "Thank you, but I need a bit more time."

Brian looked disappointed. "I understand. Maybe we can have dinner some other time?"

"Sure, that sounds good." I grabbed his jacket. "Thanks for coming over anyway. It was a nice way to break up the day."

Brian smiled. "I'll see you later, Laura."

I waved at him as I watched him walk down the path to the street.

He turned back and gave me a wave and watched as I closed the door.

I hated to admit it, but I almost regretted my decision. I went back into the kitchen and poured another glass of rosé. The interruption was just what I needed to go back and tackle the rest of Andrea Caldwell's night.

That night, I decided to go out onto my back deck, have some tea, and maybe do a little reading. It was a nice evening, just warm enough that I could be out there for a while under a blanket and still be comfortable. I brought my supplies — snacks, tea, the book I was reading, and my journal — and got comfortable.

A minute later, I heard... something. Voices, I thought, but it could have been a TV set turned up higher than normal. Unusual for me to hear, since my only neighbor was Brandy, and from what I could gather from the few short conversations we'd had over dinner, she believed that TV rotted your brain. It couldn't be the house on the other side of me, either. The Carters were vacationers, only around on weekends in the summer and the odd winter holiday. I got up and went around to the part of my deck nearest Brandy's house. It was definitely coming from hers, and the yelling got louder the closer I got.

My porch wrapped around just a little bit, enough to look into Brandy's kitchen window. I was never a snooper; I didn't want to see anything I would regret — especially because the last time that happened, my entire life fell apart. This time, however, I was curious. Who could Brandy be yelling at? I'd seen a daughter before, once or twice. They didn't seem very close. Maybe it was someone else? A sister perhaps? Either way, it was most likely just casual family drama, gossip that I could pass along to Celene, who was always curious about my quiet, lonely neighbor whom I sometimes shared a meal with.

My jaw dropped when I saw it was none other than Shelly Blaze, Brian's assistant, arguing with Brandy in her kitchen. Shelly was petite with long blonde hair and liked to wear three-inch heels to make herself seem taller. Compared to Shelly, Brandy was smaller and much older. She was also feistier. Brandy stood defiant as she stared at Shelly, a mutinous look on her face.

Brandy's back was against the sink, her arms crossed, and Shelly stood with her back toward the window I was looking through. I couldn't quite make out exactly what they were talking about, but it sounded like Shelly was saying that Brandy was being impossible; a moment later she slammed her fist down on the counter right next to Brandy.

Just watching Shelly acting like this made me flinch, but Brandy barely budged. Shelly's burst of anger reminded me of my father's temper when I was a kid. It made me feel sick to my stomach, and I had to turn away. That was a memory I didn't feel like revisiting that night.

I went back to my deck chair and tried to focus on my book, but I could still hear the sounds of Shelly and Brandy's argument carrying over to my back deck. Staring out at the lake didn't help, either. If anything, it made me focus on their argument and the memory of my mom and dad fighting late into the night.

I couldn't really make out any words from the two women now, but after another round of loud screeches, I heard at least one glass break and decided to call it a night. Brandy was pretty tough, and she looked like she could take care of herself — if anything, I was more worried about Shelly, because she was younger and sometimes a bit of a space cadet, and even though Brandy was frail looking, I was pretty sure she wasn't weak. Not that I thought Brandy would put her hands on Shelly, even if she was angry enough to do so. Shelly either, for that matter. I went upstairs to my bedroom and put on my noise-canceling headphones.

I fell asleep staring out at the lake and listening to the sounds of waves. For the first time in a while, I didn't have a nightmare about Tony and Mary.

Instead, I dreamed about Shelly morphing into a monstrous image from one of Brian's horror paintings. She was like a banshee, her blonde hair turning inky, flying out behind her as she shrieked and yelled obscenities at me. Her arms, which seemed miles long, stretched out toward me, her nails like daggers as she tried to grab me.

The next morning, I woke in a cold sweat, shivering over the disturbing dream. I was used to not getting a lot of sleep, but this dream had me feeling groggy and paranoid.

I fixed breakfast and sat down at my computer, but I just couldn't focus. After about four hours of rewriting the same sentence over and over and over again, I decided today wasn't a writing day. Today would be an errand day.

The biggest drawback of living in a secluded community like Pine Lake was that the comforts I was so used to in the city — online shopping arriving at my doorstep, takeout, and delivery at any time of night or day — just didn't exist in the same way it did in the city. Uber Eats didn't deliver in the Pine Lake area, and while I could shop online via big stores like Amazon, I couldn't order locally. Even ordering from those bigger stores that said they delivered everywhere, well, they don't exactly. Pine Lake's deliveries don't come right to your door. You had to pick it up from the town's community mailroom. On top of that, the town had an unofficial curfew of 9 p.m. when everything closed.

It wasn't only packages that wouldn't be delivered to my home, but all my mail as well. I had to go into the town proper to get it from the community mailroom. I still didn't understand this practice, and I had asked around as to why it was so beneficial to the community. The only conclusion I could come to was that the majority of the population of Pine Lake — the retirees — followed a strict "get off my lawn" policy for any and all strangers, and picking up the mail in town was their exercise for the day.

I set out with my grocery list, reusable bags, and my granny cart, determined to ignore my work and do my errands. I was relieved to find the community mailroom was empty, which meant I wouldn't be accosted by anyone asking how my book was going or telling me about the latest Pine Lake gossip. I could sort through my mail in peace.

I was skimming a homeware catalog when the door burst open, and Brandy stomped into the mailroom in a huff. She was carrying a box that looked bigger than she was — how that frail-looking old lady had the strength to carry that but still needed an oxygen machine to sleep at night, I'd never understand — that she dumped on the counter.

At that moment, I suddenly had to know what Brandy and Shelly had been arguing about the night before. I didn't know what came over me, maybe it was something they pumped through the air in that mailroom, but I walked right over and stood next to Brandy, pretending I also needed something from the mailroom attendant.

"Ms. — oh, how are you?" I asked. I knew Brandy liked a formal greeting when out in public.

"I'm well, Miss Laura, just trying to send my daughter some kimchi that I made for her. How are you?"

"I'm alright, a little sleepy. I saw you and Shelly arguing

last night; I wanted to make sure everything was okay." I had never been this sly and gossipy in my life; Celene would be proud.

Brandy turned directly to me and shook her head. "I apologize, I hate it when people are causing trouble. And that is just what I was talking with Ms. Blaze about."

She was clearly agitated by her argument, so I perched myself on a nearby ledge and settled in for the ride. I silently wished I had some popcorn.

"I was telling her about how Mr. Oliver's residents are out of control. They're always fighting with each other about property and throwing accusations around. I've put in a number of complaints to his office, but Ms. Blaze always deflects my calls."

"What did she say?" I asked, egging Brandy on.

"The brat ignored my complaints again. Instead, she had the nerve to try to persuade me to—"

Just then the mailroom attendant came up to the counter, and Brandy turned to send out her package. She glanced back at me and added, "You have a good rest of your day, Miss Laura."

Even though I was disappointed that I hadn't heard the whole story, I smiled and said goodbye. I left the mailroom feeling less energized from the gossip sesh than I'd expected. Brandy definitely fit the profile of Pine Lake's original residents — grumpy, retired, searching for privacy and quiet in a picturesque Californian mountain town — and her opinion of Shelly reflected that.

But I had to admit, Brandy did have a point — the juiciest town gossip was usually about the ones Brian rented to. And they were the loudest residents as well. They were the ones throwing around accusations of poisoning each other's gardens and getting into complicated love triangles with each other.

Still, I dismissed most of what Brandy said about the neighbors as idle gossip, combined with a retired woman's strict standards about peace and quiet. Brandy wanted to be able to hear a pin drop from the other side of the lake, and that would never happen if the town's median age dropped below sixty.

As I went about my errands, I let my mind wander, coming up with more and more ridiculous reasons of what Shelly had tried to persuade Brandy to do, which had me laughing at myself. At the end of the day, I couldn't have asked for a better writing exercise.

I guessed Celene was right — I should gossip more often.

4

The next morning, I woke up to an ambulance siren piercing the quiet mountain air. At first, I thought I was dreaming; then I thought I was back in the city; then I realized — the ambulance was coming for me.

I jumped out of bed, checking my body for marks, then ran around my home, searching for an intruder. That was when I finally realized that the ambulance was coming for my next-door neighbor.

While frantically searching my living room, I glanced up through the glass doors and saw a gurney being wheeled through Brandy's home. I couldn't believe what I was seeing. I had just talked to her the day before — the woman was healthier than I was. It had to have been some kind of mistake or a prank call.

I ran outside to my front yard just in time to catch the paramedics wheeling out a small body under a white sheet and loading the gurney into an ambulance.

Brian was there, along with every neighbor on the block. We all knew Brandy — it was impossible not to get to know your neighbors here — and by the looks on their faces, I could see we were all in equal states of shock. I could feel tears streaming down my face, and the next thing I knew, I was collapsed in Brian's arms, sobbing into his freshly pressed shirt.

"It's okay, Laura. You'll be okay. She was old; it was her time to go," he said, patting me on the back.

"She was only sixty-seven — she's so young," I cried. I just couldn't understand how the woman I saw yesterday carrying a box that was bigger than her, walking faster than I ever could, was now being wheeled out of her home under a white sheet.

I waved Brian off and went to sit down on a bench at the end of my walkway. He had to go speak to the fire department anyway — I think he muttered something about "town business" — but I was too wrapped up in shock to pay any attention to him. As I sat there, more neighbors came by to watch as the fire department conducted an investigation.

"Do you know who found her?" I heard someone ask.

"Shelly. She went over this morning, and when Brandy didn't answer the door, she broke in."

"Lucky that she came by."

"Oh, don't say that—"

"Well, Brandy never has anyone over. Who knows how long she would have been in that bed if Shelly hadn't stopped by."

I turned away from that conversation. We all knew Brandy was a grump, but thinking about her rotting away in her bed like that just made me cry even harder. I didn't know her well, but she was a nice lady. And I liked to think we were friends, in our own silent way.

My sobs drew more of a crowd, and a few neighbors

came over to console me, cooing that they didn't know Brandy and I were so close. I think they were hoping for gossip, or what exactly had happened in that house, but how was I to know? I'd found out the same way they had, with sirens waking me from sleep.

"It was her oxygen machine," I heard someone say.

Brian came by to see if I was okay. We talked for a few minutes, then hugged and parted ways. He went back to the fire department so he could lend support to Shelly as she gave her witness statement. There was a lot of formality involved with finding someone dead in their bed, apparently, and Brian wanted to be with her while she spoke to them. It was rather nice of him, I thought.

Later that day, after the initial shock had worn off, I went to the coffee shop to read and clear my head, but all around me, people were talking about Brandy and what might have happened to her.

"She seemed so healthy." The same conversation I'd heard before continued behind me.

I sat lower in my chair so they wouldn't notice I was there and clam up, as some of my neighbors had done. I buried my nose in my book and listened to their gossip.

"She did. But she had sleep apnea, so she slept with an oxygen machine to regulate her breathing."

"I had no idea. I had an uncle with sleep apnea; he nearly died in his sleep."

"And that's just what happened with Brandy. Apparently, her machine malfunctioned, first it pumped her with oxygen when she didn't need it, and then stopped working when she went into some kind of attack."

"That's not what I heard," someone else chimed in. "I

heard she'd been on oxygen for a while now. She never came into town anymore because she didn't want anyone knowing how frail she was. She was thinking of moving back in with her daughter."

"Catherine, we both know that's not true. Brandy's daughter barely ever came to visit her; she wouldn't move in with her unless she was on the brink of death and the daughter forced her out of that house."

"Well, she *did* die, didn't she?"

That invoked concerned murmurs from the other neighbors who had gathered around the gossipers.

"Either way," someone else said, "she basically suffocated in her sleep. Can you imagine—"

Suddenly, all the gossip stopped. I could feel multiple sets of eyes staring at the back of my head. The jig was up; the gossipers noticed it was me, her inconsolable neighbor who was also very private and lived alone.

I slowly turned around to face about eight concerned faces.

"Oh dear, we didn't realize it was you."

"We are so sorry for your loss."

Reading their faces, I could see how badly they wanted to ask for more.

"I wasn't that close to her," I said to the awkward silence. "It's just a shock."

"No one wants to feel alone when they're surrounded by death," the woman, who I thought was called Catherine, said.

Her friend gave her a swift kick under the table, and I had to stifle a laugh.

"Thank you for the condolences, ladies. I should get

going." I tried to smile as I got up, but I was pretty sure it was more of a grimace.

Their gazes followed me as I left the café. As soon as I crossed the street, I turned back to see them back at their gossip.

I decided to take the long way home, around the lake. The town had a lovely little boardwalk — whoever built it knew most of the people who lived here would be retirees and homebodies who loved staring philosophically out at the water. I contemplated what I'd heard and tried not to feel paranoid that all the neighbors were waiting for me to die alone in my home, like Brandy.

I tried focusing on what I liked about her. The kimchi she made me once that was spicier than anything I had ever tried. The days we would silently stare out at the lake and cheer each other with our tea. No matter what, I kept thinking back to what I had heard about her death. Something had happened to her oxygen machine — either it overloaded her or suddenly stopped working — and Brandy had suffocated, alone. There was no one to wake her up or take the respirator off so she could breathe. There wasn't even anyone to call 9-1-1; it was pure luck that Shelly had been in the neighborhood and had tried to go and see her.

I had seen a bouquet of flowers by Brandy's door that morning, too early for anyone to have called a florist for condolences. I wondered where they had come from or who they were actually for. Surely not Brandy, right? Had she had an admirer in town that I hadn't known about? I didn't think so. So it was odd seeing those flowers there.

I was almost home when I saw a strange man lurking near Brandy's house. There was a stairway that led up from the boardwalk to the end of my street and snaked around

Brandy's home. The man looked like he was leaning back on those stairs, trying to peek into Brandy's house. The house was empty now and dark, since the police and fire departments had finished their investigations into the call and determined they had no further business there.

I froze. Was this guy trying to break into Brandy's home?

5

"Hey!" I called out.

The man jumped and turned to me, suddenly casual. "Hi there."

"What do you think you're doing?" I demanded.

He just cleared his throat and muttered to himself.

I started walking fast toward him, but he jogged up the stairs and out of sight. By the time I caught up to him on the street, he was too far away for me to interrogate.

One of my neighbors, Carl — a semi-retired tech genius who spent his days birdwatching — saw me panting at the top of the stairs and came over. "Lauren, how are you doing? I hear you were pretty broken up about Brandy."

"It's Laura, and yes, it was a shock, but I'm doing okay. Did you see a guy run up the stairs just now?" I asked, trying to get the "condolences" over with.

"Who, Graham?"

"I don't know his name. Do you know him?"

"Yeah," said Carl. "He's kinda weird, mostly keeps to

himself. But he's always around when there's gossip or drama."

"How long has he lived in Pine Lake?"

"Oh, I don't know. Longer than both of us, that's for sure. He's some kind of warlock. I've seen him in the mail center a few times, but he never says more than a few words to me. Anyway, I have to go; there's an island scrub jay that somehow made it up here that I'm dying to see," Carl said, wincing when he realized what he'd said.

"It's okay. I didn't know Brandy that well, just don't love being woken up by sirens."

"Yeah. It's why I got out of the city." He waved as he jogged down the stairs with his binoculars.

I slowly trudged home, looking back to where I saw the stranger run. Why was he so interested in Brandy's home? And why did he run away when I tried to confront him?

When I got home, I made some tea and sat out on my deck. I looked at Brandy's house, still dark. For a moment, I forgot what had happened that day. I gave her empty home a little salute with my teacup and curled further into my blanket.

I COULDN'T SAY if it was the shock of Brandy's sudden death or what, but when my mother called the next day, I answered the phone rather than let it go to voicemail. To put it simply, my mother and I didn't get along. In recent years, I was trying to patch things up with her. Therapy was helping a lot. It helped me to unpack *why* I didn't trust my mother, and why I felt anxious whenever we were alone.

My father was abusive. It's probably strange to put it so bluntly, but there's no other way to say it. He physically and emotionally tortured my mom and me throughout my child-hood. I haven't spoken to him since I moved out at eighteen. At the time, I just needed to get as far away as I could. A few years later, my mother finally did the same and followed me to California. She never admitted that the reason she left my dad was his abuse.

Nowadays, we just avoided the subject of my father and his "temper problems" — her words, not mine — and I discussed the rest with my therapist. Our phone calls were check-ins, during which my mom told me what was going on in her life and asked me why I ever left Tony.

"He was always so good to you, Laura. I don't understand why you let him go so easily," she would say.

I bit my tongue every time and tried to change the subject. Repeating that I'd caught Tony cheating *on the day of our wedding* meant nothing to her, and getting angry about it just made the situation worse and usually left me in a funk after our phone call.

When I moved out to Pine Lake, she said, "You can't just run away from your problems. Not everything is solved by uprooting your life to a place where you have no community, no family, no friends, and no familiarity."

I knew then that she was talking about when I moved out, leaving her behind. My father had isolated her throughout my childhood, never letting her get close to anyone or have any friends, so when I left, my mom was truly alone with my father. As I got older, I felt quite guilty about that, and sometimes, I thought my mother used that guilt to her advantage. My psychiatrist told me that it was a trauma response — the belief that someone was more likely to lie about their emotions to manipulate you. I was trying to work on it, which was why even though my mom reminded me of the worst time of my life and didn't seem to have a filter regarding the second-worst time of my life, I still talked with her regularly and sent flowers on her birthday and Mother's Day.

On this particular call, my mom wanted to talk about her book club. It was a group of divorcees with no friends and shitty ex-husbands. Sometimes they read classic novels, but the current selection was a romantic-fantasy novel — one of many in the vampire-falls-in-love-with-a-mortal genre.

"It didn't seem like a romance at all. It was just a pulpy novel in highbrow window dressing," she said, puttering on. "Tanya suggested it — she always suggests the most risqué books."

"Well, maybe she just joined to have a good time, not to relive an AP English class," I said distractedly.

"Honey, is everything okay?"

My tone was a dead giveaway. I should have known better than to drop my guard around my mother.

"You sound tired."

"I'm fine. I just" — I paused for a second before I made a big mistake — "my neighbor died yesterday." I could have said a million things, yet that day, I chose to tell my mother the truth.

"You mean that poor old woman who lived alone, without a husband?"

I hung my head and got ready for the upcoming battle between my mother and my singlehood. "She wasn't much older than you are," I pointed out.

"Still, she was so alone, poor thing. Do you know what happened?"

"I guess some machine she uses to help her breathe when she's asleep malfunctioned, and she suffocated."

My mother gasped on the other end of the line. "How long was it until they found her?"

I tried not to get annoyed with her desire for the gory details; I would probably do the same in that situation.

"The next day. A neighbor came by and called the fire department when she didn't answer the door." I guessed that was what had happened, even though I didn't know for sure. Hell, I didn't even know if her oxygen tank had failed; Pine Lake's grapevine had no way of confirming its information.

"Did it scare you?" my mother asked.

"Why would it scare me?"

"Because you are also alone, and you don't have anyone to check on you. Ever since you left Tony, it seems like you've sworn off men altogether."

"Mother, I have not *sworn off* men, and also I left Tony because he was unfaithful." I could feel my blood starting to boil. "And I'll have you know, I'm only thirty-four and don't need an oxygen machine just yet, thank you very much."

"Tony apologized. He's always been very apologetic, and you refuse to give him the time of day. He still apologizes whenever the subject of you comes up."

I froze. "What do you mean by that?"

"Tony always apologizes and wishes you would forgive him already. It's been three years. You should be over it by now and ready to make amends."

I tried a breathing visualization to calm myself down. I grabbed the nearest cushion and used it as a temporary stress ball. I did whatever I could not to explode. "Mom, why are you talking about Tony in the present tense?"

"How else would I talk about him?" she asked.

"When was the last time you spoke to Tony?"

"Last week. I stopped by that cute café near your old

apartment, and Tony was there, so we had a cup of coffee. We hadn't spoken in almost a month, and I wanted to know how he's doing. Apparently, Mary is a piece of work. You could easily have gotten him back from her if you had just forgiven him and *tried* to fix your relationship before throwing it all away to run off to the mountains, where you're in danger of dying alone."

My mother was oblivious to it, but I had opened my mouth and let out a silent scream. I wanted to murder her, but I also wanted to murder Tony — he had no business keeping in touch with my mom. If he saw her at a coffee shop, he should turn on a dime and run off with his tail between his legs. But Tony had many of the same qualities as my father; he could charm anyone into doing anything — especially women.

"Mom — are you — how long—" I kept starting and cutting myself off while my mother sat silently on the other end of the line.

"I knew you'd be unreasonable about this," she muttered.

"*Of course* I would be. Tony broke my heart, he ruined my life, he lied to me and to my friends, he made my life miserable, and you just casually get a cup of coffee with him? Like it's nothing?"

"I don't casually get cups of coffee with him; that happened once. I do wish him a happy birthday every once in a while, because he isn't the devil. He made a mistake, and he's remorseful, whether you believe it or not. You can't let your trust issues cloud your vision, Laura."

"And you can't let your horrible taste in men cloud yours. Just because I'm not married doesn't mean I'm unhappy. I'd rather be alone than with a man who isolates me, or tries to steal my money, or manipulates and gaslights me."

After my father, my mom dated a man who almost ran off with her entire life savings — which was not very much at that point, having spent twenty years as a stay-at-home mom. After that guy, she ended up with a man who turned out to be the leader of a cult; and after that was a man who almost convinced her she was having auditory hallucinations when in actuality he was calling his other girlfriend while my mother was trying to sleep in their shared bedroom.

Melba Whitmore had a long history of dating scum, and I had a long history of giving her futile warnings. She just wanted someone to protect her and refused to believe that she could protect herself. If anything, it made me even angrier with my father. He'd taken an intelligent and beautiful woman and turned her into a selfish gossiper who willfully ignored every red flag in her path.

"Laura Whitmore, that was a low blow," she said gravely.

I could hear her raspy breathing and immediately felt horrible for making my mom cry. "I'm sorry, Mom. It's just that I don't want to get back together with Tony. I want to get together with a man who treats me like I'm the greatest thing that's ever happened to him." I tried to make her understand, but I was pretty sure that I had crossed the line.

An awkward silence fell on our call. I didn't have anything else to say, and my mom was still sniffling.

"I think I hear someone at the door," I lied, searching for a way to get out of this absolute disaster of a phone call.

"Yes, I also have a lot to get to today. I'll call you later this week," she said. "Bye, Laura."

"Talk to you soon," I said, as I heard a click from the other end of the line.

I wished for the millionth time that there was an easier

way to talk to my mom, one that wouldn't have me yelling at the end of a phone call and throwing her romantic failures in her face. I wasn't exactly the picture of success on that front, so who was I to judge?

I hated to admit that she was right. I'd been completely unable to forgive Tony, and running away didn't solve your problems, it just delayed them because they always came back to bite you on the butt.

6

Brandy's funeral was held at the local Presbyterian church, and her wake was held at the Pine Lake Yacht Club — both beautiful venues surrounded by the nature that she loved. The Yacht Club was small by city standards but offered the best view of the lake and was probably the classiest event space in Pine Lake. Everyone commented on how much Brandy would have liked it, and walking around, I wasn't sure I even believed them.

What they said was true, Brandy *did* love the lake. I knew that from our few interactions over the years, and from how much time she spent on her back deck just staring out at it. Our neighbors, however, just said it because it was the nicest thing to say about someone. They had no idea of Brandy's likes or dislikes, but it was a pretty safe assumption that anyone who lived here loved the damn lake.

To be honest, talking with the other residents about Brandy made me feel sick to my stomach. It felt disingenuous, as if behind all their kind comments and caring smiles, they were just waiting to get home and gossip about the flowers and the venue and the fact that Brandy's daughter was almost late — she wasn't — she just hadn't shown up a few days early, as all the residents had expected her to.

To top it all off, whenever I turned my back, I swore I could hear them whispering about my public meltdown on the day Brandy was found. The whispers only emphasized my feelings that I would be the next Brandy — a grumpy old loner who was lucky to be found before she decomposed in her bed.

I really should reach out more. There was a Pine Lake book club, and I could easily do my work from one of the coffee shops in town. It might give me an opportunity to actually get to know some other people, maybe make friends, so I wasn't pestering Celene whenever I needed advice or someone to vent to. Dr. Delgado was wonderful to talk to, but he wasn't a friend; I paid him to listen to my problems. I supposed there was Brian. Even if we didn't fall in love, we could still be friends, and it might be nice to hear all the latest gossip from the man who heard it all first.

Walking around the wake, I kept trying to make eye contact with Brian, hoping we could chat, or that he could wrap me up in his arms. Not romantically, the man just gave good hugs, and I could use one right now. Every time I tried to get his attention, I found him deep in conversation with Annie, Brandy's daughter. Annie was the only member of Brandy's immediate family to come to the funeral — Brandy was a widow, and I guessed Annie was her only daughter. From what I overheard, Annie was also quite reserved and didn't seem to have a partner to accompany her to the funeral.

I talked to Annie for a second to convey my condolences and tell her how her mom was a great neighbor. "I'll miss her tea and her spicy kimchi," I said, hoping to reach across the void of strangeness to find my old neighbor deep in Annie's personality.

"Yes, my mother was a very good cook. I'll miss that about her as well," Annie said before turning away to the next mourner, who happened to be Shelly.

I had reached across the void, but it seemed Annie didn't want to reach back. That was fair, I didn't know her, and I barely knew her mother. I didn't know why I thought that comment would suddenly make us the best of friends.

I listened as Shelly explained, "I'm so sorry about your mom. I was the one who found her." She sniffled and looked even paler than normal. "I've never seen a dead body before."

Annie's lips tightened in a flat line, and her eye twitched. "Thank you, I'm sorry you had to be the one to discover her. I'm sure that was disturbing."

"It really was," Shelly said with a nod. "Oh, is that wine? Would you excuse me?" Without another look at Annie, she moved on.

Then Brian stepped in to speak to Annie. He seemed to know exactly what to say to her.

I almost felt jealous of how much attention Brian doled on Annie that day. At one point, I saw that he was alone, but as I approached him, he ignored me, making a beeline for Annie as she exited the women's restroom.

Was there something else going on? Was it possible that Brian knew Annie? Were they friends? Or something more? Of all the people at the funeral, Brian seemed to know Annie the best, judging by their close conversations.

Maybe he was never serious about me at all. Funny how that worked. A day ago, I was gearing up to tell Brian that I wasn't interested in having dinner with him, and I just wasn't ready to date again. But now, seeing him ignore me in favor of Annie Oh, I felt jealous and angry that Brian wasn't even giving me a chance.

I had to get out of there. My grief and jealousy were swirling into a dangerous combination. I said goodbye to some people I didn't really know, but were nice enough to chat with me about Brandy, and started walking home.

On the way back, I spontaneously bought some flowers at a convenience store — nothing special, just some bright chrysanthemums in a premade bouquet. I wandered back to the church and the graveyard behind it. Brandy had apparently requested a spot atop a hill overlooking the lake. Prime real estate, but she'd gotten in early and made a good investment in her afterlife.

I wandered up to where she was buried. The ground was still fresh, and the headstone hadn't been installed yet. There was a temporary marker that was covered in flowers from the funeral service. I went up and laid my flowers, plus a teabag that I had kept in my pocket.

"Enjoy your tea, Brandy," I whispered and started walking off.

I didn't get far before I crossed paths with the man I had seen trying to peek into Brandy's house the day she died.

He nodded at me, and I tried to remember his name — Jason, was it? I kept walking, but then ducked behind a tree to see where he was going and what he might do.

Turned out he did just what I did. Got to Brandy's grave and laid a small bouquet of peonies, ones that looked similar to what Brandy was growing in her garden. He smiled and laid a small bag of tea next to mine.

I turned and started walking home before he could see the tears welling in my eyes.

7

After the funeral, life quickly returned to normal.

I didn't think much about the man at Brandy's grave. I still couldn't remember his name, so I guessed it was a good thing I ran and hid from him because it would have been an extremely awkward conversation.

"Hello, Jason, why were you stalking my neighbor, and why are you now putting tea on her grave?"

"Hello, stranger, my name isn't Jason, it's Johnny, and Brandy was a friend of mine, a fellow recluse if you will. That's why I killed her in the middle of the night, and no one will ever suspect a thing, and if you tell anyone? Well, you don't even remember my name, so how do you expect anyone to believe you?"

Okay, I had no idea if he had been involved in Brandy's death — which absolutely no one, except my overactive imagination, believed was a homicide. My nightmares about Tony and Mary had come back, but this time, at the very end, I saw Jason/Johnny's eyes poking above a window, a witness to their crime of passion. That was probably influencing my mental picture of him.

Since Brandy's house was empty, it became very easy for me to go a whole day without seeing another human being. To keep from going completely insane, I started writing at a nearby coffee shop, the Rise N' Grind.

The owner, Tod, was a retired tech billionaire who had moved to Pine Lake after selling off some kind of app. He opened Rise N' Grind when he realized there was no place to get free trade beans, which he was so used to in Silicon Valley. This made the Rise N' Grind the top coffee shop for those of us under forty in Pine Lake, while the Morning Dew was where all the retirees and elder vacationers hung out.

Thanks to Tod's connections to the tech world, Rise N' Grind had the fastest, most reliable internet connection in town, which made it very helpful for the occasional video meeting I had with my editor at *Goosh*, Lindsay. I was determined to get myself out of the house and into Pine Lake, to be more than a source of gossip and a strange loner at the end of the street. Rise N' Grind was my first stop.

About a week into my new social lifestyle, I was leaving my house when I saw a pickup truck drive up to Brandy's house, and Brian hopped out with a man I had never seen before. We hadn't talked since Brandy's funeral. I assumed he was busy consoling Annie Oh, Brandy's daughter, and didn't feel like experiencing rejection on top of grief. But Brian saw me and, waving, jogged over to say hi.

I quickly checked my breath to make sure I didn't smell like eggs and shook my hair out as I met him on the street between my house and Brandy's.

"My, don't we look lovely today?" he said, grinning from ear to ear.

"You're not so bad yourself. I like this rugged look on you." I smiled, trying to keep up a flirtatious tone. "I almost didn't recognize you. Then again, that could be because I haven't heard from you since... all this happened."

Brian looked down at the ground. "I'm sorry, Laura. My behavior has been less than stellar. But soon, we'll be seeing a lot more of each other." He smiled, gesturing toward Brandy's house. "I'm your new neighbor."

I stared at him in shock. Behind Brian, another van pulled up, and a few construction workers came out. They all went into the house, laughing, not a single one removing his shoes as per Brandy's preference, which I knew from the handful of times she'd invited me for dinner. What was going on?

"Well," Brian continued, "*I* won't be your neighbor, but soon you'll have someone in there. I'm going to renovate the house — you should see it, the place is practically ancient — and then rent it out. You wouldn't believe how easy it was once I talked to her daughter—"

I had seen the inside of Brandy's home, and it was nice, but that wasn't what caught my immediate attention. "Daughter?" I asked.

"Yeah. Anna, I think her name was—"

"Annie."

"Right. Well, her daughter practically begged me to take the house. I bought it for way less than it was worth, all cash. And since I got in before it was on the market, there wasn't even a bidding war. Can you believe it? I'm gonna have this place flipped, rent it out, and I'll probably have my investment back in a year, even including the renovation costs."

"Didn't Annie want to keep the house? Wouldn't she need the money?"

"Are you kidding? She's a doctor, and her mom was a recluse. They've got plenty of money."

I winced at the comment. "So that's why you ignored me at Brandy's funeral?" I tried to be flirtatious, but I could feel a bubble of anger rising in my throat.

Brian threw his head back and laughed. "Is that what you think? I'm sorry. I definitely had my head in the deal and couldn't think of anything else. Believe me, I wasn't ignoring you. I thought you looked lovely in your dress."

One of the construction guys called out to Brian.

"I have to go. My contractor is a needy guy. I'll talk to you soon." Brian jogged back over to what used to be Brandy's home.

I stared after him for a moment and then turned and started walking to Rise N' Grind. It hit me who Brian reminded me of, and why I was always second-guessing myself in his presence. Brian Oliver was exactly like William Whitmore.

William Whitmore was my father; born into New England high society, turned big-city financial genius, someone with absolutely zero remorse for his actions and who was equal parts manipulative, selfish, and immoral. All this, and he thought he was an absolute superhero. To him, "goodness" was measured by how much money you had — not what you did with it, or how you acquired it. Don't get me wrong, he was a nice enough guy, until you got on his bad side.

Then again, I could be wrong. My daddy issues ran deep. It was something that therapy could never cure. I just had to go on living with them, trying to manage my mistrust of the world. Brian didn't seem abusive — but neither did my father. As of now, Brian was just an overly flirtatious real-estate magnate in a tiny town in California, who rented to people who were too young and got restless living in the middle of nowhere. The way he treated Brandy's property felt harsh, but Brandy's death had obviously affected me more than I thought it would, more than I anticipated when it came to a grumpy neighbor.

"It's just a house, Laura," I said to myself as I turned the corner. "Houses don't have feelings." I turned to look back at the vans arriving to renovate Brandy's home.

Houses might not have feelings, but I certainly did.

8

Brandy's house transformed before my eyes. What was once a simple little cottage became a modernist utopia. To me, it looked like two storage containers stacked on top of each other, painted in a dark matte gray. I was sure it would look incredible on the cover of an architectural magazine, surrounded by the pine trees and distant peaks.

However, I'd thought the house looked great before.

To Brian and his contractor's credit, the house was finished in about a month, and it was only slightly disruptive to me and the others around me. The only person who got angry was Carl, because apparently the sound of drilling scared away a rare yellow-throated something-or-other that he was watching.

The renovation brought Brian and I closer together. Whether I wanted it to or not, having him next door overseeing things inevitably meant we spent time together and found more to talk about than just Pine Lake drama. I still kept him at arm's length — he just reminded me so much of my father — and flirted less often than I had in the past. Brian was still generous enough to help me out around the house. He changed the handles on my kitchen cabinets to ones he removed from Brandy's kitchen — as a memento of hers. I felt a little bad for taking advantage of his kindness; it was sure to end once he realized I wasn't into exploring this relationship any further.

My life had taken on a new form of routine, one where I finally left home and started enjoying the town for what it was. There were a lot of young people around, and we formed a small army against the old fogeys who once dominated the town. But I couldn't relate to everyone. There were former tech entrepreneurs and cryptocurrency investors who, I thought, had too much time on their hands. I tried to join a book club, but then realized they only chose self-help or motivational books written by famous entrepreneurs. At one point, I made a joke about the fact that most of those books were ghostwritten by other writers, and I wasn't asked back. Who knew tech bros were so touchy?

I also saw the man who'd left tea at Brandy's grave more often in town. I would occasionally take a thermos of tea to Brandy's grave, mostly when the noise from her house — I still thought of it as hers — got too loud, and sat alone drinking. The man sometimes jogged into the cemetery, and we always nodded. Well, *I* would nod, and he would take the moment to sprint past me. He was very odd.

We finally spoke about a month after Brandy's death, when the house was almost finished. I was hovering outside the community mailroom, waiting for someone to go in. I hated to admit it, but I didn't want to be in there alone because every time I went to get my mail, I remembered the last conversation I had with Brandy and started to cry. I found if someone else was there, the mailroom felt less haunted.

As I hovered outside, I pretended to read an email on my phone. When I saw out of the corner of my eye that someone entered, I followed them as casually as I could. They stopped in their tracks, and I slammed into the back of them, my phone crushing itself against my face.

So much for smooth and subtle.

"Are you okay?" a voice said.

I adjusted my sunglasses and said, "I'm fine. Glasses and body are unscathed, haha!"

I looked up and saw the last person I wanted to see. The town weirdo, and the man who did everything he could to avoid a conversation with me — Jason, or was it Johnny? I still didn't know.

"Oh! Hello," he said, not moving a single inch, which meant we were stuck half in the door and half out.

"Um, hi. Can I—"

"Oh! Right, yes, sorry about—"

"No, no! It was my fault. I was staring at my phone."

We both chuckled and shuffled inside. I went to my mailbox; he went to his. I loitered at my mailbox; he also loitered at his. We kept sneaking glances at each other like we were preteens at a school dance.

"I'm Graham, by the way," he said and held out his hand.

I smiled. I'd been way off with Jason and Johnny. "I'm Laura. Nice to meet you." I shook his hand.

"I noticed you sitting by Brandy Oh's grave. Did you know her?" he asked. He was talking to his mail, but there was no one else around, so I assumed — I hoped — he was talking to me.

"Me? Well, yeah. She was my neighbor. Haven't you heard about the next-door neighbor who had a breakdown?" I tried to laugh off what I knew the whole town was saying about me.

"I did. I thought it was quite nice, actually. I know how Brandy liked her space, so if you had an emotional reaction like that, it must have been because you managed to break through her hard shell and see the warm woman beneath all that."

I must have looked taken aback because he blushed. I was shocked, because this wasn't the conversation that I had expected to have with the town weirdo who was apparently some kind of warlock.

"We used to drink tea together. Well, not together, exactly. We usually stood on our back deck or at the window facing the lake at the same time and drank tea. We always toasted each other with our teacups," I admitted sheepishly. "I guess it was a kind of bonding thing."

"You must miss that a lot."

"I do. I really do." I could feel my eyes starting to get hot, and I knew tears were close behind.

Without saying a word, Graham closed my mailbox and swept me out of the community mailroom. We walked quickly down the street, Graham guiding me the whole way until he sat me down on a bench.

Graham sat next to me and pulled out a handkerchief with a flourish. "Magic!" he said, smiling.

I couldn't help but laugh while a few tears rolled down my cheeks. "Where did that come from?" I stammered.

"Right here." He pulled another handkerchief from behind my ear.

I let out a yelp and then started laughing. "How did you do that? Are you a dad from the fifties?" I asked, my laughs turning into hiccups.

"No, but I do a little magic. Just as a hobby — not professionally or anything, those guys are weird."

"I don't know, I think sleight of hand is kind of weird." I laughed and slowly realized that Graham wasn't kidding. "Sorry, I don't mean to make fun."

"No, it's okay. I understand that my interests are a bit odd." Graham looked down at his hands and stuffed his handkerchief back in a pocket. "The occult often gets confused with what people think is satanic, so I guess I learned a few harmless tricks to make people feel more comfortable. I don't have to do this if you feel uncomfortable."

"I'm sorry — the occult?"

Graham looked at me with surprise. "I assumed you were avoiding me because of what the other residents have said."

"No, I've been avoiding you because I saw you staring into Brandy's house after she died. Besides, I thought you were avoiding me."

"I guess it was a little weird for me to do, but I missed her, and I just wanted to be around her things while I said goodbye, even though I couldn't go inside." He frowned. "You think I'm avoiding you?"

"Why else do you sprint past me every time I see you at the cemetery?"

He smiled, and his eyes twinkled. "That's because I thought *you* thought I was weird for jogging in the cemetery."

"Why *do* you jog in the cemetery?"

"I like running in nature, but the gravel paths on the trail aren't good for my back anymore. Besides, I like the sense of peace; it makes me forget that I'm even exercising."

It made a lot of sense, I supposed.

"Also, I like to think the spirits are cheering me on from the beyond."

Okay, that last bit was weird.

"Well, you don't have to sprint past. That's a perfectly reasonable explanation for jogging in the cemetery — I don't think you're the only one. My ex used to do the same thing in a cemetery near our old apartment. He said it was nice not having to dodge people on the walkways when he was trying to run."

Graham chuckled. "Thanks for that."

Then we just sat in silence on the bench.

I wanted to ask more about him and the occult, but it didn't seem like the right thing to do. I ought to just go home, wipe my eyes and redo my makeup before going on with my day. But Graham's presence was so calming and warm that all I wanted to do was sit with him in silence.

"Are you feeling any better? Would you like me to walk you home?" he asked.

I nodded, and we got up and started walking down main street in the direction of my house.

"So if you weren't trying to avoid me, why were you pretending to look at something on your phone when you first came into the mailroom?" Graham smiled as I blushed at him catching me in the lie.

"The last time I spoke to Brandy was in the community mailroom. Ever since she died, I hate being in there alone."

"Do you think her spirit haunts the mailroom?" Graham asked.

"Maybe. Not for everyone, but for me it does. I think it's because the last thing we talked about was petty gossip. I was pressing her for details about an argument I saw her have with Shelly. Our relationship was somewhat distant, with a few interactions here and there, but fairly whole-some, until that moment. I guess I feel guilty for ruining it and not being able to make it up afterward." It was the first time I admitted to myself why I felt so horrible being in the mailroom.

"Everyone has an unexpected reaction to death. It's normal to get hung up on the last moment someone was alive, how you would change things about it. But you have to know that your relationship with someone, and their memory of you, is made up of a collection of a million moments, not just one. Her spirit remembers you in the whole of your experience together in Pine Lake. Not one frustrating morning at the community mailroom."

Graham espoused wisdom like it was a natural thing. I wished I had him around when I was writing my column.

"That was beautiful; you ought to be a writer," I joked.

"I *am* a writer, actually. I write about the occult and cere-monial magic. In a former life, I was an anthropologist, and now I mostly do research and write academic papers." He blushed. "I'm working on a fantasy novel about the twenti-eth-century magician Aleister Crowley."

"Oh, wow. That's so... wait, you mean, like, actual magic? Abracadabra and all that?" I asked, completely fascinated.

"Um, well, yes. Yes, that is essentially what ceremonial magic is. Aleister Crowley was a real figure, and I want to introduce people to his ideas while also indulging in my love of fantasy novels." Graham was turning tomato red at this point. "I have to admit, fictional writing is not my forte."

"Everyone feels that way, even fiction writers. Every time I write something, I think it's the worst piece of rotting garbage, but then I tweak it. Change something here; add something else there; with a good editor, soon it will be just a small pile of garbage," I joked, hoping Graham would indulge in my self-deprecating humor.

He threw his head back and laughed, a deep guffaw. "Yes, that's so true. That's how I feel about every paper I've ever written; it always seems like complete nonsense until someone else clarifies what you were trying to say. It's such a satisfying feeling in the end."

"That's always been my favorite part of writing. Having a canvas for a story to tell," I said, smiling.

"What a beautiful thought," Graham said, and we continued our walk in silence.

I found myself daydreaming of writing with Graham — me on one end of a long desk, writing about murder and revenge, and him on the other end, writing about the battle between good and evil, or magical and mortal.

Graham broke me out of my reverie when we turned the corner on my street. He reached out and gently touched my arm, wordlessly asking me to stop.

"Is everything okay?" I asked him.

Graham had suddenly turned awkward and kept looking over his shoulder. "Yes, I just wanted to ask you something, um... before we arrive at your door."

"I'd love to have a drink with you," I said, anticipating him asking.

But Graham said, "Do you know why they were fighting?"

"What?" we both asked.

"You mentioned that Brandy and Shelly had been fighting, and I was just curious if you knew the reason. Not out of gossip, I hate how much people in this town gossip."

"Oh! Um... well, Brandy was annoyed at how many of Brian's tenants were disturbing the peace in Pine Lake." I didn't know why, but I left out the part about the mailroom attendant interrupting Brandy before she could tell me the whole story. It seemed like a moot point.

Graham looked a little disappointed at my revelation. "Ah, I see. Yes, Brandy also hated the gossip and petty dramas that plague this town. It's something we lonely grumps had in common."

"Why did you want to know?"

Graham shifted from side to side and ran his hand over his short dark hair. He didn't want to answer, I could tell.

"Just curiosity, I guess." He sighed. "Seems like everything happened so fast, with the death and the renovation." He stared at me for another moment before grinning from ear to ear. "Now, what is it you said about a drink?"

I winced. I kind of hoped he hadn't heard me.

"I thought you were going to ask me out." I bit my lip, trying to think of something I could say that would make me sound less like a stuck-up princess. "It's okay if you're not interested. Really, it is. I don't know what I was thinking." I started to turn away, but Graham gently touched my elbow, encouraging me to turn back around.

"I actually *did* want to keep talking. Perhaps we could have a coffee sometime? Maybe on the weekend?"

"That would be lovely. Yes."

"Of course. Thank you for accidentally asking me out."

Graham smiled, and I felt warm all over. He was the

absolute opposite of Brian; I didn't feel nervous or overly flirtatious. I just felt like I could be myself, with no expectations.

After we exchanged numbers, Graham waved and walked back toward town.

I watched him walk away, basking in the glow of a natural connection with a stranger and a moment of quiet in a town that was getting louder and louder by the day.

9

"I've already rented the cottage, so you won't be all alone anymore," Brian called to me.

I had decided to work on my back deck for the afternoon, and he was putting some finishing touches on Brandy's house.

"What was that?" I called back.

Brian came over to the rail, closer to my house. "I rented the house. Found a nice young couple who are looking to escape the city, and they're moving in right away. Didn't even want to wait until the end of the month. I told them I'd waive the first couple of weeks as a little welcome package to the town. Isn't that great? You'll have more welcoming neighbors this time around."

I tried to hide my disappointment — I enjoyed having no one around me, especially no one my age. I didn't want to feel obligated to become friends right away with some happy couple who no doubt would spend their nights loved up on their back deck in plain view of my still-broken heart.

"That's great," I called back, grinning to hide my true

feelings about the change. I immediately had the urge to text Graham and complain about my soon-to-be-broken silence. I felt like he would understand that as much as I was trying to be less of a hermit, I also wanted the *option* to be a hermit whenever I wanted to.

I was thinking about Graham a lot these days. He *was* a bit of a weirdo — I think if we were in the city, I never would have given him the time of day. But in the context of Pine Lake, of wanting simplicity in my life, Graham seemed like the perfect man. A fellow writer who just wanted a place to escape where he could write for hours with zero distractions and not have to deal with nosy neighbors gossiping about his every move.

The occult thing was... weird. But not much weirder than a guy who plays fantasy role-playing games or is obsessed with brewing his own beer. I lived in a town where a thirty-year-old spends his days watching and cataloging birds; an occultist wasn't much further along on the scale of "weird nerdy hobbies wealthy men develop in their thirties." As long as he didn't ask me to participate in pagan rituals on Halloween, I was okay with an eccentric hobby or two.

I realized Brian was still talking to me and shook my head, hoping he hadn't noticed me drifting off.

"... so hopefully before we transfer ownership, I can get those things done for you, and you won't have to worry about them." Brian beamed.

I smiled and nodded. "Well, now that the renovation is done, you'll have so much more time on your hands."

"Yeah," Brian said, staring at me like I had just disembarked from a UFO, "that's what I just said. Were you—"

"Oh shoot! I'm so sorry, I just realized I'm late for a —

um, a meeting. I'm sorry Brian, can we catch up later? I just have to—"

"Say no more. I can tell you have a lot on your mind right now." He waved and went back inside just as a moving truck pulled up to the front of the house.

It was perfect timing, I had a video appointment with my therapist, which would keep me safely inside and away from the view of a happy young couple in love moving into their Pine Lake love nest and rubbing their happiness in my heartbroken face.

"Now, that doesn't sound like a positive attitude at all."

I had relayed to Dr. Delgado my feelings about the new couple who were moving in. He sat calmly through my rant and at the very end delivered his patient cutting blow.

"No, it's the opposite of a positive attitude, and I know it," I responded.

"Perhaps we need to break this down using an automatic thought record. So, what happened?"

I sighed, partially because all I wanted was for someone to commiserate and tell me my new neighbors were horrible people for being in love. I wanted my audience to be on my side and to encourage my completely irrational thought, not to make me feel better about it or see the judgment for what it was.

"Listen, Dr. D, I know where this thought is coming from. I know there is no evidence to support the thought that I will be wildly heartbroken and unhappy while my new neighbors flaunt their love in my face. And I know it stems from my core belief that I will never find a trustworthy partner. I just wanted to complain about my neighbors and how much I miss Brandy."

"Do you miss her? I rarely heard you talk about her."

"I suppose I never did. But her presence was peaceful, and it makes me think of the sense of relief I had when I first moved to Pine Lake. Almost as if she was a stabilizing force, reminding me that this was the right thing to do. And now, after two years, that was suddenly taken from me and replaced with the *reason* I left the city in the first place. So, yeah, I miss Brandy and what she represented in my life here, *and* I resent the fact that I have to be reminded of the problems that I ran away from."

"Finally, an honest thought. I will say, you have mentioned your fears about becoming a hermit a lot lately. Perhaps this couple will provide an opportunity for socialization?" Dr. Delgado posited.

It wasn't the commiseration I wanted, but it would do.

"How?"

"Well, either you'll befriend the couple and be taken under their wing," he said, weighing the thought with his hands, "or their nauseating happiness will drive you out of the house, and you'll interact more with your community in Pine Lake. Either way, it will likely drive you toward socialization, whereas living next to a peaceful old woman who didn't socialize very often might have encouraged you to do the same."

I was silent. Sometimes I wished I could write this stuff down; it would be perfect as an intro to my advice column on *Goosh* — or even as a soothing monologue a morally ambiguous hitman would say in one of my novels.

"Can you say that again?" I asked, my pen poised over my notebook.

Dr. Delgado laughed. "If you want to use me, I need to be credited. And I'll want a cut of the royalties. Besides, we're all out of time today. Shall we meet again? Same time, same place?"

I nodded and clicked "accept" on the calendar link he sent me. We said our goodbyes, and I closed my laptop.

Behind the screen was the large glass of wine I had poured for myself before the appointment as a reward for continuing to work on my mental health even after I had successfully navigated my crisis. I took it and walked to my living room, contemplating whether to welcome my new neighbors today, or avoid the deed until tomorrow.

Just then, I saw two figures exit the French doors of Brandy's old house. I could only see them from behind, but it was enough to make my blood run cold.

I would recognize that blonde blowout anywhere. She walked out the back door and stood on the deck with her back to me. A second figure followed, carrying a bottle of Brian's favorite champagne and two flutes. It was a man, about my height, with long, dark, wavy hair. He approached the blonde from behind, shocking her with the cold champagne bottle, and she shrieked — her voice was high-pitched and whiny.

The figures turned to each other and shared a deep, passionate kiss, and my worst fears were confirmed.

It was Tony and Mary.

10

Tony *Ellison* and Mary *Casden* were my new neighbors.

The same Tony Ellison and Mary Casden who ruined my life three years ago. They cheated on me and then gaslit me and then turned my friends against me, and they were now the newest residents of Pine Lake.

Tony and Mary had moved from whatever hole they were living in and planted themselves in my utopia.

I must have stood in the same spot for an hour. Or maybe it was five minutes. I didn't know. All I knew was that, at some point, my glass of wine fell from my hand, crashing onto the hardwood floor. I looked down. *That's going to come out of my deposit, I guess.*

I was sitting in the far corner of my kitchen with the lights off, hoping Tony and Mary couldn't see me. I felt like an evil witch in a fairy tale, but I didn't know what else to do. It was too early to go to bed, but the back half of the house — the part that looked out onto the lake — was too open.

There were too many windows, and I was afraid they'd see me and try to talk to me.

I had heard from both Tony and Mary since the wedding. It had definitely peaked about two months after the ordeal and slowed down as the years went by, but it never completely went away. Every few months, I'd get an email from Tony or Mary — sometimes both — either asking me to forgive them or demanding that I "get over myself." No matter how many social media accounts I blocked, they would create new ones and try to follow me with them.

I sent them letters specifically stating that I didn't want either to contact me, but those requests went ignored. I even consulted with a lawyer to see if I could get a restraining order, but apparently neither had done *enough* damage for a judge to grant me one. Tony also knew to get to me through my mother, who demanded on his behalf that I forgive the pair. Mary tried to get to Celene, but thankfully, she proved to be a loyal friend. Celene would get the dirtiest gossip from Mary and pass it along to me over a bottle of wine and the fanciest possible cheeseboard.

Every time I saw an email from them, I had a panic attack. It would cause me to have insomnia because I'd stay up trying to avoid the inevitable nightmares. For a while, I was convinced that they knew and were watching me, laughing at my panic attacks and the anxiety that their presence caused in my life. Whenever the pair resurfaced, I ended up going to my therapist more often and retreated into myself even more.

What was I going to do now that they lived next door? I could never look out my window at the beautiful lake again, or sit on my back deck, or even exit my front door. The only option was to live the rest of my life in the darkest corner of my kitchen. At least I'd be close to the fridge.

I ordered takeout and snuck out of my kitchen to get it. That was the only day I ever wished I had one of those video doorbell things, just so I could make sure Tony and Mary weren't still moving their things into Brandy's house. I threw cash at the deliveryman, probably overtipped him, grabbed my food, and slammed the door shut behind me.

I was literally tiptoeing around my own house. It was ridiculous, I'd be the first to admit it, but I just didn't know how to handle the fact that Tony and Mary — the people who inspired my move to Pine Lake in the first place — now lived right next door.

How could that have happened? Had my mother told them where I was living? Even if she had, what would prompt them to pick up their lives and move next door? Who else was coming, my sixth-grade science teacher, who refused to let me do a project about Charles Darwin because she was a Creationist?

Was it Tony or Mary who had orchestrated the move? Was this Mary's ploy to get back in my good graces after she'd driven away all of her other friends? Why would Tony agree to it? Or maybe Tony wanted me back — as my mother often told me, he complained that he regretted how things went down. Was it possible that he was telling the truth, and this was his Hail Mary to win back my love? If *that* were true, why on earth would Mary agree to it?

It was also possible that whichever one orchestrated this didn't tell the other who would be their next-door neighbor. Even so, it would have been impossible to plan, since Brandy had only died a month ago. That was barely enough time to even give notice that they were moving out.

That was when I had a thought that almost made me choke on my pad Thai.

What if—

No, Laura, that's not possible; you're spiraling.

Brandy's death was so sudden —

And two people who lived hours away couldn't have had anything to do with it—

Without that death and Brandy's house, there was no way they could have moved in—

Laura, you may hate them, and they did ruin your life, but these people aren't killers. Pathologically selfish, yes, but not homicidal.

I shook my head and turned on some reality television to drown out my increasingly paranoid thoughts.

That night, I had the same nightmare that had plagued me for three years — the one where I am forced to be Mary's maid of honor — but this time, a blue-faced and suffocated Brandy was the one giving Mary away at the altar.

I WOKE up the next morning hoping it was all a bad dream. That I had fallen into a coma for the past month and dreamt about Brandy's death and Brian's renovation.

No such luck.

I walked downstairs and saw Mary on Brandy's — Mary's — back deck, eating a croissant and looking out onto the lake. She looked quite peaceful. I bet that was how I looked before she moved in next door.

I crept downstairs, trying to stay away from the windows as much as I could. That feat proved to be nearly impossible since the back of my house was basically one giant window from which I could see everything — as could my neighbors.

I slinked into the kitchen and ate my breakfast of cold cereal with the lights turned off. I thought maybe if they thought the house next door was abandoned, Tony and Mary would realize they'd made a big mistake and go back to the city where they belonged.

How long could it take? A week? I could do this for a week.

No, I could barely keep it up for a day. After thoroughly cleaning my kitchen and convincing myself it would make a great little office space, I tried to write standing up at the counter. I soon gave up. The angle was wrong, it hurt my neck, and I desperately wanted to stare out at the lake for inspiration. Not only that, but Andrea Caldwell, the protagonist of my novel, was turning into a homicidal maniac rather than a desperate housewife out for revenge. At this rate, no one would want to read my book. I didn't even open my *Goosh* column inbox because I knew it would be useless to try to give advice in the state that I was in.

There was no way I could possibly live like this. I was living like an intruder in my own home, and I was going to get vitamin D deficiency if I kept creeping around in the shadows. Also, I had finally been making progress socially in town. I couldn't let Tony and Mary take that away from me. It wasn't fair. They had already taken one life away; I wasn't going to let them have Pine Lake — not without a fight.

I glanced over at their house — the lights were off, and it looked like no one was home. I took the opportunity to stretch and actually *live* in the rooms I paid for. What could I do to make sure Tony and Mary wouldn't stomp all over my little Garden of Eden? I didn't have enough clout in town to spread malicious gossip — I found that icky anyway — but I *did* have a little sway with their landlord. I made a few notes about what I should say and called Brian.

It went straight to voicemail, and I left the most concise message I could. "Hi! Brian, it's me. It's Laura... um, Laura Whitmore? I'm actually not sure if this *is* a business matter, but it is urgent, so I'll definitely make sure to contact Shelly. Anyway, it's Laura — did I already say that? Of course I did. Anyway, this is about my neighbors. Not the Carters, they're not back yet, it's about the other ones. The Ellisons. Or the Ellison-Casden house. It's not too important, but please do call me back. Obviously, it is important, or I would ca—"

The voicemail cut me off. So much for an eloquent and cool voicemail.

I called his business line.

"Can I help you?"

"Hi, Shelly, it's Laura. Um, I'm trying to reach Brian; is he there?"

"No. Obviously he's not. He's busy. Call later." She sounded almost snide.

"Wait!" I nearly shouted, trying to get her to stay on the line. "Can you please have him call me? It's important."

"Then call his cell phone. Duh." She snapped her gum.

My fingers clenched. "I did. He didn't answer. Can you *please* ask him to call me?"

"Fine. Whatever." The line clicked dead a moment later, and I wasn't sure if she was going to tell him I called or not.

Once I put down my phone, I started twiddling my thumbs — literally. As if I had nothing else to do during this golden moment where I could be relaxed in my own home and not glancing over my shoulder at my neighbors'.

I decided I'd take a long midday bath and go to the Rise N' Grind to finish my writing for the day. I remembered that

Mary refused to drink caffeinated beverages after 11 a.m. in the interest of a "holistic lifestyle," whatever that meant, so there was no chance I'd run into either of them there. Besides, they must be busy unpacking and setting up their house.

I checked my phone to see if Brian had texted me, but my notifications were blank. I took a deep breath and set about my plan to avoid Tony and Mary and escape from my kitchen prison.

The journey to the Rise N' Grind was arduous for my paranoid brain. Everywhere I turned, I thought I saw Tony and Mary walking down the street toward me. The walk took twice as long because I kept ducking behind hedges and into driveways — it was enough erratic behavior for me to take the "town weirdo" crown from Graham for good.

On the bright side, I took advantage of the time I had away from home and got further along in my book and in my column than I ever had at home. I always did work better on a deadline — maybe the move would prove to be productive for me after all. I had coffee after coffee, and before I knew it, the Rise N' Grind had brewed its last pot.

"You're cut off. First — it's 6 p.m., and we have to close; second, I think if I serve you one more cup, you'll have a heart attack," the barista told me as I tried to order another cortado.

I looked around and saw that I was the only person left in the coffee shop, and one of the other staff members had started sweeping up around me. I apologized and left, checking my phone as I started back toward my house.

Brian still hadn't answered my message. I checked my voicemail, but there was nothing from him. No emails, no DMs on social media. I thought to call Shelly again, but it was long past office closing time. Had I thoroughly embarrassed myself with that voicemail?

Not possible. No one was good at leaving voicemails; awkward messages were de rigueur. I could just call again, this time leaving a slightly *less* awkward message. There was less to say, after all, just a simple, *"Hey! Call me back."* So I dialed Brian's cell again, and as expected, the call went straight to his voicemail.

"Hi, Brian. It's Laura. Again. Laura Whitmore. Though if you knew another Laura, it might be less embarrassing that I've left you two messages today. I could pretend one of them wasn't me, haha! Anyway, can you call me back as soon as you get this? I'd like to talk. Thanks. Bye."

Slightly less awkward, but awkward, nonetheless.

I took the long way home, by the water, so I could clear my head and stop overanalyzing the voicemails I had left for Brian. I had forgotten that I'd texted him a few times that day as well; all of them just said, "Hi!"

I could see they had been read, but not a single one got a response. Maybe this was why Brian was such a hot commodity; he manufactured obsession by not answering when you called and making you absolutely desperate for his attention — any attention.

I was spiraling for no reason. I wasn't even sure that I *liked* Brian. Not long ago I was repulsed by how much he reminded me of my dad; now I was taking my worth from whether or not he'd answer my call. It wasn't even a social call. I needed to speak to him on a landlord-tenant basis. I sat down on a bench and stared out at the lake, breathing slowly and counting to ten, just as my therapist taught me to do whenever I felt a panic attack coming on. It was the best method I had ever tried for clearing my head and climbing out of a spiral.

Just as I was getting ready to go home, Brian finally called back. I let it ring for a bit, in a moment of pettiness, before I answered.

"Hello, Laura, Laura Whitmore. It's Brian, Brian Oliver here," he joked.

"Hi, Brian. Sorry for all the calls. And messages. And texts," I answered, hoping I could somehow come off as flirtatious rather than desperate.

"No need to apologize; what man doesn't love looking down at his phone to see that Laura Whitmore is trying to get ahold of him? Sorry I couldn't answer. I was out of town at an art show. What do you need?"

I stared out at the water, taking deep breaths as I did. Was I being too paranoid? Probably, but also, Tony and Mary had managed to cause me panic at every turn for three years. It wasn't unreasonable for me to do everything I could to regain my sense of peace.

"It's about the neighbors," I said.

"A complaint already?"

"Yes, but it's not about their behavior, exactly. At least, not their *current* behavior. You see... this is kind of awkward."

"Well, I'll tell you what," Brian said. "Why don't you come over to my house, and we can discuss it over dinner?"

"I don't think—"

"Nonsense, you won't be putting me out. You're more than a tenant to me, Laura. I want to make sure you're feeling ok—"

"I'm actually feeling fine; I got a lot of work done today. I just wanted to talk—"

"—about Tony and Mary, right. I totally get that. How's

Thursday for you? I'll come pick you up at 7 p.m. Chat soon, Laura Whitmore." And just like that, Brian hung up.

I had been gearing myself up for a long talk over the phone, and somehow, I'd gotten a date out of it instead. I should have known; it was exactly the sort of thing my father would do when a business dealing wasn't going his way — railroad the person and get them to talk in person. Then he'd turn on the charm, confuse them with bizarre details and long-winded stories. Before they knew it, the other person was signing on the dotted line, and my father ended up with an even better deal than he started out with.

Not this time. I was determined to do everything I could to stand up for myself, like I hadn't been able to in the past. And luckily, I had enough experience with my father that I was confident Brian wouldn't be able to railroad me in person.

... On our impromptu date.

11

I sat on my stoop, mentally rehearsing what I was going to say to Brian while trying to hide myself as much as possible from my new neighbors. I could feel a bubble of anger rising. The more I thought about it, the more annoyed I felt. Was the dollar really worth more than a friendship to him? If he expected me to date him, why would he install a reminder of why I hate relationships right next door?

His luxury SUV turned down the road and roared toward me, disrupting the early-evening peace. I took a deep breath and got ready for an awkward date.

"You've barely touched your pasta; is everything okay?"

I glanced up and met Brian's concerned gaze. "I have a lot on my mind tonight."

Brian put down his fork and took my hand. His penetrative gaze was hard to turn away from.

"Tell me about it."

Brian, I'm coming to you as a tenant, not as a friend. It may sound facetious to you, but I need you to understand that having Tony and Mary next door to me could be damaging to my mental health, and it's a huge problem for me having them as neighbors. Obviously, you can do whatever you want as a landlord, but it hurts me that you would so casually rent to my former fiancé and not even consult with me first.

It was so easy to say in my head. I had crafted it perfectly. So why couldn't I just spit it out?

"It's about the neighbors. The couple who moved into Brandy's house."

"*My* house, you mean?" Brian winked. "Are my new tenants unbearable already?"

"In a way, yes they are. You rented the house to my former fiancé and his girlfriend. You know, the people who ruined my life? I told you about this, so you know exactly how I feel about them. You know this was the reason why I moved to Pine Lake, this is why I don't talk to people from my past, why I blocked them on social media, and you callously inserted them back into my world!"

I hadn't realized I'd raised my voice until I finished. Brian looked shocked, and I was out of breath and on the brink of tears.

"Is that so?" he asked.

"Yes. It's... it's a very real problem for me. Obviously, you can do what you want as a landlord, but I *do* wish that you had come and talked to me first." *Nice save, Laura.*

Brian laughed. "Well, at least you realize who is the landlord and who is the tenant in this situation."

I was taken aback. Wasn't he the one who'd railroaded me into this date? Or was it not a date any more now that I had something critical to say?

"Brian—"

"No, no. You need to let me defend myself. Laura, you may have told me a little about your past, but you never gave me their last names. What was I supposed to say, 'I'm sorry, sir, there's no way I could rent to you because you happen to have the same first name as my other tenant's ex-fiancé'?"

Brian sounded upset. I mean, fair, I had basically accused him of being a traitor with zero evidence, except my own deeply rooted anger.

"Why wouldn't I rent to them? Tony didn't fight me on the rent, paid a deposit for three months rather than two, and passed a credit check."

"How long is their lease? Can you break it?"

"They signed a lease for a year. No, I can't. I don't have any *legal* reason to kick them out. What do you want me to do? Build a hedge around your house?"

I thought about it for a second. A hedge might be nice, if a little over the top. "Maybe I'll move. I had hoped I could make this decision at the end of the three years living in the house, but maybe I just have to cut my losses and go to some other California mountain town."

"You're just going to run away from your problems?" Brian asked. "What if they find you again?"

"What do you mean?"

"Well, obviously Tony or Mary found out where you were living and jumped on the opportunity to live next door, to torture you and force you to watch their love from up close, after you blocked them from all social media. Maybe Tony got the information from your mother; that's a valid and easy way of getting it."

It was true, my mother wouldn't think twice about

telling Tony where I lived, with the hope that I would forgive and forget all the pain that he had caused me in the past.

"Laura, do you think Tony or Mary is going to hurt you? Are you afraid for your safety?"

What difference does that make? I thought. Obviously, money meant more to Brian. "I don't know. I'm so confused. I can't think straight when it comes to Tony and Mary. It all gets lost in the haze of heartbreak."

"So you're the first to admit it's more about you than them. Perhaps we need to find you a suitable distraction," Brian said, slithering his hand up my arm in a way that was supposed to be comforting, but felt predatory.

Now was not the time for Brian to hit on me, after he'd just told me he won't even consider telling my ex to move from the house he's barely lived in. Brian could just return the deposit or find Tony another house in Pine Lake — everyone knew he owned half the town.

"I didn't even have a way to find out what he looked like. You don't have him on social media. I couldn't creep him when you mentioned his first name, even if I wanted to. Believe me, I wanted to. I wanted to put a face to the name of the guy who broke your heart and threw away a chance at a woman as incredible as you." Brian was practically nuzzling my neck at this point.

I stood up so abruptly I almost flipped the table. "I need some air," I said as I walked away from him to the deck.

I was so angry, but now I had nowhere to direct my anger. Brian was right, he couldn't have known that Tony Ellison was the same Tony from my heartbreak, and I knew that, as a tenant, I wouldn't react very well to getting evicted because my next-door neighbor was mad. Everything Brian had said was perfectly reasonable, and deep down, I knew I had no reason to be angry with him.

But still.

"I have to go," I said, just as Brian was coming out with a bottle of champagne.

His eyebrows shot up, and he smirked. "Was it something I said?"

"No. It's not you. I just need some time to myself. To think about my options." I walked past Brian before he could envelop me in a passionate embrace.

He followed and caught up to me in the front hall. "Let me drive you home. You shouldn't be walking in the state you're in," he said, pulling on his coat.

I stopped him by putting my hand on his arm. "It's fine. It can't be more than a half-hour walk to my house, and I need the time alone with my thoughts." I squeezed his arm to show him that there were no hard feelings and walked out.

He tried to grab me, pull me in for a kiss, but I dodged him and let the door swing shut behind me.

I didn't need a kiss from Brian to confuse me. I was mad at him even though I didn't have a reason to be. He couldn't even tell me why Tony and Mary wanted to move to Pine Lake — he *always* asked. He was obsessed with "young blood" coming to the town and would sell every feature he thought they'd be interested in. I knew — I still remembered his sales pitch to me two years ago. He must know something more, some reason Tony or Mary gave for moving, because obviously they didn't tell him they wanted to move here to torture me.

The only thing left was to find out the real reason they'd moved here of all places. And did they know who their next-door neighbor would be?

_____

12

I spent a day trying to come up with a solution to my dilemma, to no avail. The only thing I could think of was to move. But I didn't want to. I liked Pine Lake. I liked the routine I had created for myself over the past month, I enjoyed working at the Rise N' Grind, and I especially loved my lakeside home. If I left now, I wouldn't have anything. I'd have paid Brian rent for two years with nothing to show for it.

I was running through my list of possible ideas for the hundredth time when I got a text message from Graham.

Hey! Are we still on for coffee today?

Shit! I looked at my watch and realized I was supposed to have met Graham an hour ago. I ran up the stairs to change, texting him on the way.

Absolutely. Was on a roll and lost track of time. Sorry about that. I'll be over soon.

No worries. See you soon.

I threw on the first clean dress I found and pulled my hair back into a bun. I didn't think Graham would care much about makeup, but still I swept on some lipstick, using it as a blush as well. Very casual, still very cute. I ran out the door and made my way to Graham's cottage.

When I arrived, Graham welcomed me inside to the aroma of freshly baked apple turnovers. What I thought was a very realistic candle scent was actually the real thing, along with Italian paninis made with Graham's homemade olive focaccia.

"There's coffee too, I promise."

It was incredibly sweet. I had expected instant coffee poured into half-boiled water —maybe because Graham had the air of a well-meaning, but bumbling nerd — and instead got the kind of star treatment I secretly dreamed of. Forget the fancy champagne and oyster appetizers — I wanted bread and pies baked especially for me.

Graham seemed nervous, and it was cute to see him buzzing around his kitchen as he made me coffee, asking about every specification I could think of. "I have oat, almond, soy, and macadamia milk; do you have a preference?"

"I actually take a little bit of cream."

"Oh! I have that too," he said, running back to the fridge.

"Do you usually keep your fridge this well stocked?" I joked.

"Well, no, but I didn't know how you took your coffee, and I felt awkward asking, so I just bought what was available. Always be prepared, as they say." He beamed, handing me a perfectly brewed cup with a dash of cream, just as I liked it. "I, um... it's been a while since I've dated anyone."

I smiled. It might have been a while, but Graham still remembered how to treat a woman. I couldn't help but compare him to Brian — probably because I had seen Brian the night before and still felt angry about our conversation. Where Brian felt pushy and overconfident, Graham was patient and humbly impressive. He truly was a man of many talents.

His decor left a lot to be desired, though. "What is that?" I asked, pointing at an elaborate wardrobe.

"That's a replica of one of Houdini's disappearing booths, one he used to practice his disappearing magic. I was obsessed with Houdini as a kid, I had all these books about him, and I even contacted a local magician to be his apprentice when I was thirteen. It's what got me interested in anthropology and the paranormal." He blushed. "It's very nerdy, I know."

"I love that. Nerds are just passionate people with unpopular hobbies. I don't mean unpopular in a bad way; I just mean it as in..." I searched for the right word to dig myself out of this hole, "as in their hobbies aren't trendy?"

Graham laughed — even his laugh was warm — and patted my arm. "It's okay. You don't need to apologize for your opinion. I'm not offended. And you're right, nerds are very passionate people with very unpopular hobbies. Is there anything you're nerdy about?"

"Pulp thrillers. The kind you get at the drugstore. My father hated them when I was a kid, he thought they were absolute trash and a complete waste of money, so I started reading them just to piss him off. But then I got deeply invested in them. I'd read every new one I saw. A good psychological thriller can suck you in, even make you start looking over your shoulder in the bright light of day. I remember thinking that it must take so much talent to get someone to lose themselves in a book, and that it's such a disappointment that we dismiss these novels because they weren't written by some Nobel or Pulitzer Prize winner."

Graham looked thoughtful as I spoke. Brian always seemed like he was waiting for his chance to tell his own vaguely related story.

"I never thought of it that way. To be honest, I'm one of those pretentious people who dismiss thrillers because they aren't written by someone who has won a literary prize."

"That's probably your nerdy contrarianism coming out."

"True, I should really check that. Maybe return to the world of popular hobbies every once in a while."

I laughed. We spent the whole day like that, just talking, eating apple turnovers, and drinking. Coffee turned to decaf, which turned to herbal tea.

When the sun started to go down, Graham invited me outside to watch the sunset. "Unless you need to be getting home. I have a nice bottle of Gamay that I opened last night; I'd hate for it to go to waste."

Any other person — Brian in particular — would have made that invitation somehow sleazy, but I knew that Graham just wanted to keep chatting. We were similar in that way, socially introverted people. Loved chatting, but knew where to draw the line and spend time with ourselves. As much as I didn't want this day to end, I had to admit part of my motivation to stay was because I didn't want to run into Tony and Mary on my way home.

"I'd love to share the rest of your bottle."

"Are you sure? It seemed like you had to think about it for a while."

I sighed. "It's a long story. But I guess I could tell you over wine and a sunset."

Graham smiled. "I'll go grab some glasses. Is this the kind of story that would benefit from comfort food? I can throw a pizza in the oven. I make my own and freeze them."

Homemade frozen pizza? I was on the verge of getting down on one knee and asking this man to marry me.

"That sounds heavenly. I'll be outside."

We ate our pizza as I told him the story of my heartbreak. At some points, it seemed like Graham wanted to ask me something, but he would always close his mouth and let me carry on.

When I was finished, we sat in silence, just chewing our pizzas and watching the sunset. I could see from the corner of my eye that Graham kept turning to me, opening his mouth to say something, and then snapping his mouth shut, whipping his head back to the lake.

Finally, I'd had enough. "Okay. Spit it out," I said.

Graham turned to me with an innocent look on his face. "What? Oh, I didn't say anything," he said, looking down at his empty plate.

"You've been wanting to — I can tell. I can see you open your mouth and chickening out over and over again. What did you want to ask me?"

Graham bit his lip and moved some crumbs around his plate.

I waited him out, folding my arms as I watched him quietly, hoping he'd finally answer me.

After another moment, he did. "You said you have no

idea how your ex ended up moving into the house next door?"

"No. I didn't know he knew I lived here. It could be a total coincidence. I called my mother yesterday and grilled her, but she has apparently not said anything. I also asked my friend Celene, but she didn't even know they had moved."

"Hmm. Interesting," he mused, turning his gaze out to the lake.

"Is it?"

"Yes. You might be surprised to hear, but you're not the first Pine Laker to suddenly find themselves living next door or across the street from an old ex or mortal enemy."

"I'm not? How is that even possible?"

"I'm not entirely sure. But this whole drama has happened over and over again. A mysterious death followed by the unlikeliest of residents, and then eventually someone — usually the Pine Laker who has been here longer — leaves."

"Someone keeps breaking mirrors, giving Pine Lake streaks of bad luck."

Graham smiled.

Note to self: luck is a great topic when flirting with an occultist.

"I wish I could laugh, but... well, yes. It's a streak of bad luck, but one that has been consistent these past fifteen years. I used to think the source must be paranormal. Perhaps the town was accidentally developed in the shape of a pentagram, calling up negative and mischievous spirits at all times of year. But I've walked this whole town a million times over, always taking different routes, and there's no way that could be it."

"Maybe the ground is cursed."

"I thought of that, too." Graham's eyes lit up. "So I contacted former residents who'd moved out of Pine Lake exactly fifteen years ago and asked them about their social lives. Not a single one left because of an enemy or an ex-partner. And not a single one admitted to cursing the town as they moved away."

"Did you really ask them if they'd cursed the town?"

Graham smiled. "I've been the town weirdo for a long time. I can get away with it."

I laughed at that; it was quite the achievement to get to the point where no one bats an eye if you call them out of the blue, asking about curses. "If it isn't a curse, what could it be?"

"In recent years, I've become a bit of a conspiracy theorist about it all. But I think the cause is closer to earth than I previously believed."

I leaned in closer, as conspiratorially as I could. "So? Who do you think it is? Is it Tod, at the Rise N' Grind? I think if I wanted to mess with the town's social brain, I'd open a coffee shop. Best place to hear all the latest gossip."

"No, I don't think so. Tod didn't come to this town until about five years ago. It couldn't have been him — though that is a good idea. No, I think it's someone more... more diabolical..." Graham blinked, turning away to the lake again. "I think I've said too much," he said, and started to clean up the small table where we were eating.

"Wait a minute!" I exclaimed, putting my hand over the food so he would stop clearing it. "You can't tease me like that and not drop the bomb. That's not fair. I'm invested in this conspiracy now. Maybe it'll help me understand why Tony and Mary suddenly up and moved to a small nothing town."

Graham looked me deeply in the eyes and leaned down. I got excited that he would kiss me, but he just gently moved my hand back to the chair and grabbed the plates.

"Maybe next time." He winked and carried the dishes back inside.

I blushed, in spite of myself.

Graham dropped me off at home and gave me a sweet goodnight peck on the cheek. He was exciting and kind. He listened — how pathetic was it that I was excited about the fact that a guy just sat and *listened* to me. That was a topic that would keep me going to Dr. Delgado for years to come.

I thought about Graham's conspiracy as I went to bed. If someone was pulling dramatic strings in Pine Lake, who could it be?

He was right that the residents of Pine Lake always seemed to have some kind of petty drama going on. I thought back to the mysterious lawn poisonings that had happened a few months ago, and to Brandy's complaints about the neighbors causing drama.

A lot of the town's new residents were young and wealthy, and with that crowd, there were bound to be exes and enemies, all deciding to find a quiet California mountain town to relax in.

It could just be coincidence.

But coincidences usually didn't go on for fifteen years.

13

I was still riding high from my date with Graham the next day. I hadn't had a date where we sat and talked for hours in years. It definitely had never happened when Tony and I started dating; maybe it had never happened.

Graham was odd, but he was a fascinating man. He told me about his adventures as an anthropologist and his decision to turn to writing full time. We talked about having writer's block, and the difficulty in sitting down to write when you lived in a place as beautiful as Pine Lake. It felt good to talk to someone who wasn't going to ask when my next book was going to hit the shelves, or who was judgmental about what I wrote.

My guard was down, so when my doorbell rang, I didn't even think to check the window to see who it was.

"Hi there, neighbor!" Tony was standing on my doorstep, grinning like a maniac, holding a large bouquet of flowers.

I almost slammed the door on him, but I found myself frozen to the spot in shock. "Tony. Hi."

"I just noticed we're neighbors. I hadn't seen you until now; I almost thought there might be a ghost in here turning the lights on and off. You nearly scared Mary."

I cringed when he said her name, but Tony didn't seem to notice. "Yeah, I guess we've just been missing each other."

"Funny how that can happen, huh? Well, I guess we've been busy setting up our home, and you're probably busy with your social life in town. I brought you these, by the way." Tony handed me the large bouquet.

I just stood there, holding it and staring at him. Wasn't he going to apologize? Or explain what he was doing in Pine Lake? At the very least have the audacity to *seem* guilty?

"What are you doing here, Tony?" I asked.

"I was giving you flowers. You know, start fresh with some fresh flowers."

"Start fresh? What does that even mean?"

"It means we're neighbors. Come on, I want to see your new place, and you should put those flowers in water."

He tried dodging past me, but I blocked him. Sure, we were neighbors, but we didn't need to be friends. We didn't need to get along; maybe we didn't even need to see each other.

"Laura, is everything okay?" Tony asked.

Did Tony have amnesia or something? Had he conveniently forgotten what had happened three years ago — or what he and his girlfriend had done since? I just stood there with my mouth hanging open, wheels spinning, as I tried to decide what to do or say.

"Everything's fine, Tony. I guess I'm still a little surprised. I didn't think I'd ever see you up here. It doesn't seem like lakeside living would be your style."

"Yeah, it isn't, but Mary and I have been looking for a

new spot, one that is a little more low-key. Besides, the city was getting cramped. It felt like everyone knew everyone and just gossiped about each other all the time, you know?"

"That's what people do in small towns."

"Right. But I guess we didn't know anyone in *this* small town, so it seemed like a clean slate. And now *you're* here, and it's like it was meant to be. The cleanest of slates." Tony held his arms out wide, like he was waiting for me to jump into them.

That wasn't going to happen. He eventually got the hint and crossed his arms, leaning against my doorframe for balance.

"You can't come in," I said, backing away.

"Aw, why not? It could be like old times. A quick coffee between friends? I want to hear about your new life, new beaus, it's all new."

Tony was starting to weird me out. This wasn't the Tony I knew; this person was more like Stepford Tony — the perfect man who brought the lonely neighbor flowers and could joke over coffee for hours. It was bizarre — did he really want a clean slate? If that was the case, why had he and Mary driven all of our friends away? Maybe they realized they had no friends left in the city, and that was why they had to move to Pine Lake.

My thoughts were starting to go off the rails. I had to find a way to end this interaction before I spun myself into a panic attack.

"Tony... I'm glad you want a clean slate, but that isn't going to be as easy for me. I came to Pine Lake to get away from you and Mary and the whole life I could have lived. Now that you're here — and you're my next-door neighbors

— I need some time," I said as politely as I could while a storm raged inside me.

"You've had three years to get over this. What do you mean you need more time?"

There was the Tony I knew. The man who never in his life experienced a single consequence to his actions.

"Yes, it has been three years, but it's only been a few days since you moved in, disrupting a lot of work I've done on myself in the process."

"We broke up. That's what happened. You're telling me that you've spent three years mourning a breakup? Laura, that's silly. We can be friends. We always got along, you and me — and Mary, too. She also should be in this little friend group."

Was I losing it? Did Tony just call our wedding day a "breakup"? As if he had taken me to dinner and let me down easy?

"Tony, what happened was more than a breakup. If anything, it was the most expensive breakup either of us ever had. The fallout lasted months — I almost had to sue you for some of the wedding expenses."

"Oh, that?" He shrugged. "It's all water under the bridge now."

I knew I wasn't going to get anywhere with reason. Talking to Tony was like talking to a toddler. He said "no" just because he knew he could and refused to make the most basic concessions "just because."

Rather than scream and cry into my bouquet, I took a deep, cleansing breath, looked Tony in the eyes, and said, "You need to go home and stop being weird. Then *maybe* I can consider allowing your ruining my life to be 'water under the bridge,' as you say."

Tony sighed. I knew he was disappointed that a single bouquet of flowers wasn't enough to undo the years of gaslighting and lying he had done. Tony never wanted to put in more than the bare minimum in our relationship — a fact that I was blind to until it was too late. But I had worked on myself for too long to undo it for a cheap premade bouquet from the convenience store in town.

I stared at the flowers as I closed the door on Tony's retreating frame.

He didn't even bother going to the actual florist, I thought. Still, it was a waste to throw away a bouquet. I found a vase and put it on my little dining table, just in view of the house next door. There. A nice, meaningless bouquet and in plain view of Tony and Mary's house so they could see that there were no hard feelings, and that I was also committed to a clean slate.

I just wanted to know why they'd decided to move, and why here? Who had initiated the move, and how did they find out that I was living here? Also, what did they do that they had to escape the city and hide out in a small town?

If a game was what Tony wanted, then a game was what he was going to get. Sure, I'd pretend that we had a clean slate and were just neighbors. But behind that, I'd press Brian and whomever else I could until I knew exactly what Tony and Mary were doing in Pine Lake.

14

I'm not cut out for espionage.

I learned this while trying to find out why Tony and Mary moved here and pretending that I didn't hate them with every fiber of my being.

I wanted Tony to see how unbelievably okay I was, sitting in the same room as his shitty bouquet, while he lived his life next door. I wondered what kind of work the two of them were doing. Tony's office wasn't modern enough to allow people to work from home, so he must have found something new.

And that was how I found myself working at my old desk, facing Pine Lake's eponymous lake, acutely aware of the fact that Tony had decided to work from the deck that day. It felt like he waved and beamed at me every time I raised my head. Was he watching me? Was that how Tony was spending his whole day?

Also, where was Mary? I hadn't seen her once since the couple had moved in, except the back of her head on that first day. Were they even still together? I never thought the relationship would last, but from what my mother said, Tony hadn't broken up with her. Maybe she was the one working while Tony played games on his computer all day. He would love that.

To top it all off, it turned out to be very difficult to write my book when I knew that Tony was watching me do it. It was easy to murder your ex in effigy when they were safe in another town; it was a little harder to do when you could accidentally look straight into his eyes after writing a paragraph describing his mutilated body.

It wasn't that hard. I mean, Tony was still the devil, and Mary was still his demon sidekick. But the fact that I could see him was distracting for my book, so I moved on to the column. I could answer casual advice about friendship drama and difficult relationships for a few hours, maybe even get ahead so I could dedicate a few extra days to writing my book.

When I tried to do that, I found it just as hard as staring into Tony's eyes while killing a version of him on paper. I couldn't give good advice, either; everything seemed to end in an elaborate plan for revenge. I forced myself to stop when I realized I wasn't being productive. Anything I wrote when I was in a mood like this would just have to be scrapped and rewritten anyway, so why waste my time?

Maybe I ought to take a walk into town. But what if Tony saw that I was leaving and tried to walk with me? I couldn't handle that. A passive life was almost bearable, but having to interact with Tony for a walk without strangling him was impossible.

I made some lunch. Maybe I'd call Graham and see if he wanted to have a drink later on. That way, if I ran into Tony, I could tell him I was going on a date. He wouldn't offer to walk me to the date — would he? No, he wouldn't; that would be truly insane. If that happened, I might start believing that I was dreaming.

I almost jumped out of my skin when I looked out my kitchen window and was almost eye to eye with Tony. He had to have seen me hit the roof. I reacted so dramatically to seeing him that there was no passing it off as a subtle twitch.

But Tony just smiled and waved, giving me a finger-gun salute for some reason.

That settled it. If this was going to continue, I'd end up having to move not by choice, but because I couldn't work and pay rent. I hated doing it, but I put the blinds down on that whole side of the house. It helped a lot. Out of sight, out of mind.

I went back to the *Goosh* column, hoping I could get some advice pieces written and submitted to Lindsay. I was contemplating what a girl should do about her boyfriend's betrayal when my email notification pinged.

It was from Tony. How did he have my new email? I supposed it hadn't changed in a few years, but the audacity to send me an email after everything that had happened?

My curiosity got the better of me, and it did not disappoint.

to: lau.whitmore
from: tontonton
subj: drapes?

why the long drapes? I feel like you've been avoiding me all day, don't u want to be friends? I know flowers are not enuf, but I hope u understand that it is a kind gesture to get us back on the right track.

plus, I really enjoyed our finger salutes as we worked. Like co-working spaces — fun!!

-tony

I could not believe that a man Tony's age was still using the letter *u* in place of the word *you* in an email. It was a casual email, but how hard was it to write two more letters? And the atrocious spelling and lack of capital letters on names had me cringing.

I hit reply and started typing out my response.

to: tontonton
from: lau.whitmore
subj: reply: drapes?

Go to hell Tony, go to hell Tony, go to hell Tony, go to hell Tony, go to hell Tony, go to hell Tony, go to hell Tony, go to hell Tony, go to hell Tony, go to hell Tony!

I looked over my work. It was ineffective. I don't think repeating, "Go to hell Tony," conveyed the message I wanted it to. I wanted Tony to understand that the only thing that would make me happy was if he went to hell and never came back. The email came off as a joke, a funny *"Haha, ex-fiancé, what a funny joke that you live here."* It was a joke that he lived here, but not the funny kind.

I started to compose another email, one that said, "Go to hell, Tony," in a somewhat professional manner, but I started to second-guess myself. I still didn't know who'd initiated the move, but either way, one of them had reached out the only way they could. Also, Tony didn't *have* to come over with flowers, extending an olive branch over the awkward chasm of our history. Was it petty of me to tell him to go to hell when all he did was try to connect?

Usually when I wasn't sure if I was making the right decision, I would send an anonymous letter to my *Goosh* column. The letter would appear in my inbox a few days later, after I had forgotten about it — thank you, "schedule send" function — and I could approach my problem from a subjective point of view. But I couldn't imagine how to remove myself from the situation enough to give my fake-self advice.

I don't know. Move?

If I moved, what would stop Tony and Mary from doing the same and following me to the next small town I found? Was this how my life would be from now on, running away from Tony and Mary at any suggestion of their presence? I would never tell one of my column's readers to do that. I was such a champion for confronting your fears and anxieties, so why was I holding myself back from doing the same in my own life?

The more I thought about it, the more it felt as though sending Tony an email politely requesting that he go to hell seemed irrational and immature. I could just forgive them and move on. I didn't even have to forgive them; I could decide to forget that they mattered and move on with my life. It would make dramatic days like these, and the constant panic attacks, fade into memory. Was I a big enough person to do that?

I'd run away from the city so I could cut out the toxic people in my life — my former partner, my former best friend, and the group of people who'd abandoned me in my time of need. That didn't stop them from reappearing. And when they did, I went into panic mode and literally hid in a corner of my kitchen to avoid them. It didn't even work. Tony still saw me even though I'd tiptoed around my house for days to make sure he wouldn't. Running away from my problems only caused me more problems down the line. I didn't regret my move, but I did regret not giving myself closure before I did it.

Years later and here I was, sitting at my computer, trying to decide if I was mature enough to resist sending my ex-fiancé an email that just said, "Go to hell."

That couldn't possibly be healthy.

15

D r. Delgado rarely did emergency appointments, but thankfully, he made an exception after I called him, crying because I couldn't decide whether to send my ex-fiancé an email telling him to go to hell.

On our video call, I updated him on the situation — that Brandy's house had been rented out to the very same people who'd made me run to Pine Lake in the first place, and that Tony had come over asking me to put the past behind us and start over with a clean slate.

"He asked you to do *what*?" Dr. Delgado roared.

Judging by his reaction, I was right to want Tony to go to hell. I didn't think I'd ever seen Dr. Delgado angry. Scratch that — I had never seen him emotional at all. I was so stunned I could barely repeat myself. "He asked to start over, from a clean slate."

"How did they find out you were living in Pine Lake?"

"I don't know; Tony didn't say. I confronted Brian, who is also their landlord, and told him I was disappointed he would rent to the two people who'd ruined my life, but he said I'd never told him Tony's last name, and he didn't know who they were. So it had to be either Tony or Mary who'd decided to move here."

"Well, that is obvious." Dr. Delgado huffed and sat back in his chair. "This is... ridiculous. That he would believe you could shake off your past so easily..."

"That's what I was thinking!" I exclaimed. "He called it our 'breakup,' like he had done it over dinner or in some other reasonable way. No acknowledgment that he and his girlfriend waged a campaign of gaslighting me and our friends for months afterward."

I hoped I wasn't tainting my therapist's view. That was what had happened, but I didn't want to seem overdramatic about the whole ordeal.

"Maybe I'm overreacting," I continued. "Maybe I should have moved on by now."

"Why do you think that?" he asked.

"Well, it has been three years. Clearly, *they* have worked out in some way, so maybe they're happy together. I can only assume they are. Meanwhile, I still have nightmares and panic attacks at the mention of their names, and I'm considering running away for the second time in three years just because they've reappeared. Isn't that immature? It feels like something a teenager would do."

I could see that Dr. Delgado was thinking deeply about what I had just said. "Why is it bad to do something a teenager would do?"

"It's not mature. It's not the adult way of coping with breakups."

"Ahh, but this wasn't a breakup, was it? You were confronted with the image of the two closest people in your life betraying your trust on a day you had spent your whole life building in your head. What followed was a very rapid breakdown of the life that you'd known and understood and built for yourself — after having left an abusive situation early in your life. Tony and Mary's actions repeated a pattern of behavior that you thought you'd escaped — the kind of negativity and duplicity introduced to you by your father."

I sat back in my chair. He said it in a much more intellectual way, but he was right. Tony was the first man I'd dated whom I felt I could trust, after years of feeling like I was building a castle on shifting sands when living with my dad. Since then, I just couldn't trust anyone new. I expected the worst of them. Finally, when I was starting to open up, here was a reminder of why I didn't trust people.

"So... it's not immature for me to not want to forgive them?"

"I don't believe so. I am, however, concerned about the fact that they've moved into the house next door. It can't have been on the market for long, can it?"

I shrugged. "Brandy died a little over a month ago, and Brian bought the place pretty soon afterward. He started renovations right away, but I don't know when he listed the place. Why?"

"It's strange that they were so adamant about getting the place next door. You said they paid a deposit for three months instead of two?"

"That's what Brian told me. They also signed a year-long lease, which I guess is pretty typical."

"And from what you've seen, it doesn't look like they are working?"

"I'm not sure. I know that Tony's old job would never

have let him work remotely. I haven't actually seen Mary at all except for a glimpse of her when they first moved in."

"What concerns me is that they may have spontaneously uprooted their lives to move next door to you. For them to have known about this opportunity independently, they would have to have been monitoring the rental properties available in Pine Lake."

I gulped. Dr. Delgado had just said out loud what I had been worrying about for days. I was hoping he'd just tell me I was crazy for thinking these things and cancel our call. I stared at the glass of wine behind my laptop. It didn't seem possible to wait until the end of my session to drink that glass.

"Laura," Dr. Delgado continued, "from what you have told me, I don't believe you are in any actual danger. However, I am concerned, since you don't have a strong community of support in Pine Lake. Do you feel safe in your home?"

"Yes, I feel safe. I don't think either of them is interested in harming me." *Just torturing me with their continued existence.*

"Good. In all honesty, the only way you can truly escape them is to move again and not provide a forwarding address, and pursue a restraining order against Tony and Mary. I know you've tried before and had it dismissed, but the fact that they followed you to a small town, where neither had any previous connections, and both would have to have given up work to do so, might be grounds to grant you a restraining order this time."

I thought about what he said while reaching for my glass of wine. I took a sip and a deep breath. "I don't think that moving is the right thing to do. I think I need to hold out, make Pine Lake my own personal stronghold, and show Tony and Mary that they can't antagonize me into forgiving them."

Dr. Delgado nodded. "I'm glad that you are taking this chance to stand your ground. I would like to mention one thing, though — you don't have to be the hero. You don't have to confront them or force understanding on their part — do you understand me?"

"I think so. Basically, you're saying don't start a fight when I don't need to."

"Yes. Take this time to work on your boundaries. Try to make it clear to them — Tony especially, since he seems to be the driver in your interactions — that despite your proximity, you are not interested in any kind of relationship. I wouldn't recommend inviting them back into your life, Laura. You have a penchant for second-guessing your own instincts when it comes to matters relating to Tony and Mary, in a way that makes me concerned for your mental health. Whenever you feel like you are going back on a decision, I would like you to make a pros and cons list, focusing on your original thought. Perhaps this will help you analyze your own emotions rather than your reaction to the emotions of people around you."

I nodded while bringing my glass to my lips. This was one of those moments when I knew I wasn't going to follow my therapist's instructions to a T. Unfortunately, I didn't have time to make a pros/cons list every time I second-guessed myself — it happened too many times each day.

"I would like you to also practice some grounding exercises every day — for example, the 5, 4, 3, 2, 1 exercise. Do you remember it?"

Of course I remembered it: I did that exercise all the

time. Name five things around you that you can see, four that you can hear, three that you can touch, two that you can smell, and one that you can taste — to ground you in the moment and distract your brain from the panic attack.

"Why grounding exercises?"

"Tony and Mary have a history of gaslighting you, and I would like you to find ways to remind yourself of the elements of your own reality. Grounding exercises are one way to center yourself in your own present reality."

I wished I could hug Dr. Delgado. I'd never thought to reinforce my reality when Tony was calling the wedding day a "breakup," or when my friends said I should have given Mary and Tony their space, or when my mother said I should forgive them.

"I'll make sure to do that. I think there are some people in town I can rely on, who will be on my side, so to speak. People who will remind me of what I like about Pine Lake." I blushed a little, thinking about my date with Graham from the previous day. I knew Graham would understand that I needed a grounding reminder every now and then.

"Laura, do you think you are still in crisis?"

"No, I think this call helped a lot. Thank you, Dr. Delgado. Thank you for doing these, by the way. I don't know if I would be able to find a psychologist as good as you are up here."

He laughed. "Well, if I ever retire, I know exactly where *not* to go. Don't want to be the old man giving out advice at the coffee shop."

I laughed awkwardly at that, thinking about how many times I wrote my advice column at the Rise N' Grind. He waved and ended our call, and I closed my computer and leaned back into my chair. I slowly did the 5, 4, 3, 2, 1 exercise.

Five things I could see: my laptop, closed, on top of my dining room table, a silly cat clock I'd found at an antique market last year, my fridge full of postcards that Celene had sent me over the past few years, the couch I'd splurged on when I first moved to Pine Lake, and outside the window, the lake, calm in the early-evening light.

Four things I could hear: the birds squawking on the lake, my dishwasher rumbling in my kitchen, the hum of my laptop still recovering from the RAM-draining video call, and my stomach grumbling from lack of dinner.

Three things I could touch: my luxury-rib cotton lounge pants, my smooth crystal wineglass, and my hair, greasy from a day without a wash.

Two things I could smell: the faint, but ever-present smell of lake water, crisp and musty at the same time, and the deep, oaky scent of red wine.

One thing I could taste: the bitter realization that I was going to have to learn to live next door to my ex-fiancé and former best friend, or risk losing relationships that could bloom and overshadow all the anxious horrors of the past three years.

16

5, 4, 3, 2, 1.

That was how I started my day. It was the first thing I did the next morning before going into the bathroom and looking at myself in the mirror. I touched my cheek and repeated to myself, "I am here. My name is Laura Whitmore, and I am here."

It was a little hokey, the kind of vaguely spiritual wellness dribble that *Goosh* was well-known for. But it worked. For the first time in days, I didn't feel like I was waking up from a nightmare into a dream. My reality was valid, as were my concerns about Tony and Mary.

My phone call with Dr. Delgado had validated my concerns and relaxed me at the same time. It made no sense. I ought to be more afraid or more convinced that I had to move from Pine Lake. Instead, I felt calm, like I had avenues to go down if Tony and Mary's behavior turned erratic, but until then, I could focus on myself and not allow them to interrupt my peace.

5, 4, 3, 2, 1.

I checked my email, and the first thing I saw was an email from Dr. Delgado with a series of breathing techniques and apps to introduce people to meditation.

I looked through the list slowly. I recognized a lot of the exercises — box breathing, and body scans had been introduced to me years ago when my panic attacks and nightmares about the wedding had been at their absolute worst. I printed out the email and left it on my fridge as a reminder for the next time I was hiding from the duo of exes, to take a moment for myself and move on.

The fact was that they lived their lives selfishly. It was evident in their behavior before and after the wedding fiasco, and moving next door to me was just another example in a sea of examples of self-centered behavior. And you know what? They were perfectly happy moving through the world not second-guessing what people thought of them or trying to please someone else, or any other thoughts I had that brought me nothing but panic. Perhaps I needed to take a page out of the duo's book and live life for myself — hold my head high and walk through the streets of Pine Lake thinking of no one but yours truly.

That was what I did that day. The Rise N' Grind was open, so I headed over to work. I had never been more chatty than that day. I unabashedly went over to the gossipy tech wives to ask them what the new juice was. Unsurprisingly, the new juicy topic was me and my exes living in apparent harmony. I asked how they had heard about it — so far, the only people I had told were Graham, Brian, Dr. Delgado, and Celene — but they just smiled and giggled at each other. No matter. I went up to the counter and ordered another coffee, allowing them to stare at the back of my head and wonder if I was in on the spread of the Tony-Mary-Laura gossip.

After what had to be a record-breaking productive day, I went to the organic market on the young retiree side of town to get fresh pasta, a bottle of wine, and a bouquet of hand-cut flowers. The florist, Katie, was a former child star who had appeared in an insanely successful series of movies. She'd moved to Pine Lake a year ago, living mostly off royalties and investments, to start a wildflower-arranging business. Her floral designs were otherworldly, and she talked about the practice like it was art.

"Brian mentioned you'd been having a hard time lately; perhaps some yarrow would be nice? Birds use it to repel bugs from their nests," she said with a wink. "Could be useful right now."

I smiled. "Thanks, the yarrow is lovely. Glad it can do double duty."

So it was Brian all along — figured. There was no way Dr. Delgado or Celene could have said anything. Even if they wanted to, neither had any connections to Pine Lake. Graham was the town weirdo. Even if he had some juicy gossip to spread, no one would take him seriously or stick around him long enough to hear it. Why was Brian spreading my business all over town? He knew that this was a sensitive subject; if my words hadn't made that clear, my paranoid actions certainly had. What could he possibly gain by airing out my dirty laundry? Was he mad that I didn't want to date him?

I brushed it off for now. There was no use working myself up when I had a gorgeous bouquet and fresh pasta waiting to be transformed into a decadent evening alone. I took my usual long route home by the lake, breathing the air deeply as I went.

When I got home, I put the yarrow-filled bouquet on the

deck and waved it around a bit. Maybe what Katie said was true, and I would be able to repel Tony and Mary and their negative energy. Maybe, with enough yarrow, *they* would be the ones to leave Pine Lake.

I was in the middle of a dish of cauliflower and herb agnolotti, sipping a glass of extraordinary organic sauvignon blanc, when something began attacking my front door. It sounded like the world's largest woodpecker, and it would not stop.

For a split second, I considered ignoring it, thinking it would tire itself out before it ruined my night. But that wasn't today's Laura — today's Laura confronted interruptions to her peace and quiet head-on; she didn't bury her head in the sand and wait for the trouble to go away.

That being said, I took a spatula with me, just in case.

"I'm coming!" I yelled as the battering of my door went on. I opened the door and found out that the some*thing* was actually a some*one*.

Mary stood in front of me, a little more haggard than I remembered. Her hair was usually styled meticulously, with not a single ironed curl out of place. Today, her blonde locks were a little more "bummy" than "beachy," her clear blue eyes were bloodshot, and there was a hint of visible makeup covering deep dark circles under her eyes.

"Mary, hi," I said.

Mary didn't say a single word. She just took a step back and stared me down.

I didn't know whether to run, slam the door in her face, or pinch my arm to check if I was dreaming. Her body language wasn't aggressive; it was almost like she was a ghost. A spirit of her former self who broke through from the spirit realm to—

"What the fuck do you think you're doing?"

Never mind, I thought. "What do y—"

"You think I don't know? You think I can't see right through you? Well, Laura Shit-more, I know exactly how you work. You always thought you were *so* much smarter than me. Well, guess what, you're just like the rest of us. Tell me the truth."

"Truth about what?" I was trying to encourage Mary to speak more softly. I could already see people appearing on porches and near windows.

"The truth about you and Tony!" she screeched, getting even louder.

"Mary, can you please stop shout—"

"I know that he was over here. He brought flowers. I know what flowers *mean*. So tell me, did you plan this? Were you just waiting for the moment to steal him back? You couldn't leave us alone. Always making a point about how upset you were, and you saw a chance to force him back into your arms."

From the corner of my eye, I saw a hall light go on at Mary and Tony's house.

"I think that now isn't the time to have this conversation," I said, trying to get control of my rising heart rate.

"Now is not the *time*? That's all you have to say to me?" She was completely unraveled and carrying on like a maniac.

I could see more neighbors gathering for the scene of the century. "Seriously, Mary. You're making a scene."

"Don't you tell me I'm making a scene! You're the queen of making scenes over nothing. Now why won't you just tell me: are you two having an affair? How dare you do this to me and force me to watch. How did you dig your stubby little claws back into him? Tony's mine, and there's nothing you can do about it."

"That's it!" I screamed. I couldn't handle being yelled at on my own property and being told that *I* was the bad guy once again. "Mary, get out! Get off my lawn!"

She blinked, probably shocked that I'd actually stood up to her. "What gives you the right? This isn't even *your* lawn—"

That was when I saw him. Tony was bounding over the lawns toward Mary, who was still screaming conspiracy theories about me luring Tony to Pine Lake, where she was going to end up destitute and alone. Between curses, Tony scooped Mary up in a fireman's carry and started stomping across the lawn.

"What the hell are you doing? Tony, let me go!" Mary was kicking and screaming, pummeling Tony from behind as he carried her down my driveway and over to their house.

"Mary, you're being paranoid. I told you I haven't talked to Laura in years," Tony said, steadily trying to be heard over Mary's shrieks.

The door of their house slammed, and it muffled Tony and Mary's continuing argument.

I waved at the "casual" jogger and at those neighbors who were now standing at windows with wine and tea. I fixed a small flowerpot that Mary had knocked over — the one where I keep my spare key — *Glad she didn't find that*, I thought — and went back inside.

My agnolotti wasn't as decadent and my wine not as luxurious now that I could hear the muffled shrieks from the house next door. This was just what Brandy had said — all this drama and noise from Brian's tenants. Too many young people invading a quiet town.

I put on my noise-canceling headphones as I cleaned up, listening to a podcast about meditation that Dr. Delgado had suggested in his email. I sat down in my living room, staring out at the lake.

The podcast ended, and I heard banging at my door. Was it Mary again, back for round two? Well, this time I was ready for her. I put on my game face and walked to the door, head held high.

But it wasn't Mary. It was Tony, swaying slightly and smelling like whiskey.

"Hey, Loo," he said, as if using my old pet name would help.

"What do you want? Did Mary send you out to fight her battle?"

"No! No, no, no, no, no." He went on, shaking his head. "Mary is just confused. She's... she's been confused, y'know?"

I softened — after all, Mary had been my best friend once — and nodded at him to go on.

"She's messed up now... she thinks a bit like... paranoia."

How drunk was he? I had had my headphones on, so I didn't know how long the fight had lasted. Enough time must have passed for Tony to have knocked back at least two glasses.

"Tony, you're drunk. You should go home."

He hung his head. "Yeah, I know. You probably don't believe me. I just wanted you to know. Mary's a little out of it right now. For a while she's been out of it, thinking... the wrong thing."

I nodded, mostly to get him out of there. "Tony, I have to go to bed."

"You understand though, right? She was always angry, but now it's like, more," he said.

I turned him around and gave him a push. Tony waved back at me and stumbled back home, and I closed the door on this whole evening.

What was Tony trying to say? It sounded to me like he was implying that Mary was somehow... ill. That her mental health was unstable, or maybe she was experiencing reality a little differently from the rest of us. It would explain her paranoid comments earlier.

In bed, I started thinking about moving again. If that scene was just the beginning, I didn't want to see what Mary would be up to next.

17

T hat night, and for the next few, I slept horribly. I was starting to look like Mary had when she showed up at my door.

That isn't very nice, Laura, I thought. I was never one to just believe it when a boyfriend called his girlfriend crazy, but with Mary, I could honestly believe it was true. She didn't seem like herself; even her hair was messy in a way that it never would have been before. She also seemed to think, for some reason, that I was behind the move. It was possible he'd gotten the information from my mother, and somehow that got misconstrued as me. It also made me think that maybe Tony had continued to stray while in a relationship with Mary.

Whatever it was, my only business was keeping myself safe. I began to reconsider moving away from Pine Lake. What seemed like a bit of a facetious decision now was a question of whether I would be safe in my home. Combined with the fact that the neighbors had set up chairs on their porches every night, waiting for round two of Mary vs. Laura. I was ready to cut my losses and get out of here.

I was also getting mystery flowers again. This had happened a few months prior when Brian revealed that he wanted to take our relationship a step further. I assumed these came from him as well. After the third bouquet, I decided to give him a call.

"Brian Oliver speaking."

"Hi. It's me."

"Lovely Laura, why on *earth* could you be calling? This is such a *wild* surprise. I never was expecting it."

I tried to laugh, but I thought all that came out was a puff of air. "Listen, Brian—"

"I know it was a little much, but I suppose it was the least I could do. I heard about that fight; it sounded like an absolute doozy. I'm only sorry I wasn't there to help. Are you okay?"

"You heard? I'm surprised you weren't the one telling people," I said, not in the mood to entertain his hot air.

The line went so quiet I thought that we had been cut off, until I heard Brian's booming voice coming over the line. "Why don't we talk over dinner?"

"I don't know if a romantic dinner is what I need right now," I said, trying to dismiss Brian and get off the phone.

"It's the least I can do, and I feel bad that I wasn't there to rescue you from Mary."

"I didn't need rescuing. Mary used to be my best friend. I know how to deal with her pretty well. Tony came and got Mary before she did any damage. Anyway, I just wanted to say thank you for the flowers. They're beautiful, but unnecessary, and I really hope we can be just friends. I'm not interested in anything more right now."

The line was quiet again. I wanted to think Brian was sad and trying to console himself over the phone.

"What do you mean, *right now*?"

"I'm very stressed. I have a lot on my mind, and it's not as if the demands on me in the real world have stopped. In the meantime, I'm working on a new book and trying to keep up with my advice column. I don't want to be lavished upon; I just want to deal with my life." I didn't mean to go into detail like that. I would have preferred to just say, *"Well, Brian, I'm just not that romantically into you. I would rather be just friends."* Or something else vague. It could have led to fewer questions.

"Dating isn't stressful. Besides, what could be less stressful than having dinner and perhaps a lovely bath prepared for you?"

That was it. We had reached my line. I wasn't interested in forced intimacy or being with someone who was just waiting to get me into bed. What would happen when that was through? Would I be tossed out in favor of the next new resident of Pine Lake?

"Laura," Brian's voice came over the phone.

I realized I was quietly seething and probably breathing heavily into the phone.

"Is there another reason that you don't want to see me?" Brian suddenly sounded meek, making me even more suspicious. "Is there someone else in the picture?"

I thought about Graham. It had been a few days since we last saw each other, but if I was being honest, I was more interested in the town weirdo than the town hero. Graham made me much more comfortable than Brian, and I didn't feel as if I was a piece of arm candy. When we talked, Graham asked questions that revealed how much he loved to dive into hobbies and other interests. When I talked with Brian, I often felt he was waiting for me to ask the right question, one that would lead to a story that he had been itching to tell.

I knew that telling Brian I had seen Graham, after he'd spent days sending me flowers and was already lamenting that he couldn't be my hero when Mary attacked me, wasn't going to get the reaction I wanted. If anything, it would make him feel more competitive and would lead to more phone calls and more flowers.

"No, there's no one else."

"Great. Because I saw you out with Graham Silverton—"

"We have a mailbox at the same community mailroom."

"Right. Well, that must have been it. I would recommend you be careful around him, Laura. Graham seems innocent, but he always seems to show up when something weird happens. He's always at the latest crime scene, often goes around asking questions about the victims. And he lives basically alone in the woods, just far enough away from any neighbors."

I struggled to swallow my rage. "Brian, I'm not juggling a bunch of guys right now. The thing is, your new tenants are possibly the worst people for me to be around. Not possibly — *definitely* the worst people to reappear from my former life. Not only that, but it seems their animosity toward me, especially Mary's, hasn't faded in the years since. They're still ready to gaslight me into apologizing for breaking up with Tony when I found out he was cheating on me with Mary. I don't know who it was, but clearly one of them arranged to move up here and live right next door to me, and if I'm being honest, I don't think I'm going to stick around Pine Lake to find out who."

"What do you mean by that?" Brian asked, clearly panicking that we would soon be in a long-distance relationship.

"I don't feel safe here. I am always on the verge of having a panic attack, and Mary was ready to physically attack me the other night. I can't stay here; it isn't good for my mental health."

"Laura, be serious," Brian replied. "I gave you a deal on the down payment, allowing you to pay it like rent. You're telling me you're going to take the loss on the house? You can't afford that."

"I know, but I'm willing to go back to living in a studio apartment in the city if it means I can be far, far away from Tony Ellison and Mary Casden." There, I'd said it. I was being selfish and prioritizing myself. I didn't care what the neighbors might say when they saw me leave. Being perpetually miserable and afraid wasn't worth it, even if I *did* love this house.

Brian was quiet again for a moment. Was it possible that I had finally forced Brian to think about someone other than himself?

"I didn't realize you would actually consider leaving. I guess I thought it seemed too unreasonable for you, given your financial situation and how much you love this town."

"I don't want to, but I spent too many years sacrificing my happiness for the comfort of others. I'm going to take my own advice for once and leave a situation that isn't serving me." I regretted sounding so harsh. His forwardness about dating aside, Brian hadn't done anything to make me hate him. "Brian, this isn't your fault. I'll be sure to keep in touch wherever I go."

"I'll see what I can do about Tony and Mary. Luckily for

you, Tony is working from home, so if you continue to leave early and go to the Rise N' Grind, as you've been doing, you will probably miss him."

"How did you know I've been going there?"

"Oh, I've seen you from the window. You seem to be there pretty regularly."

Right. Just because a coffee shop has become your safe haven doesn't mean it erases you from the rest of the world. It was still easy for other Pine Lakers to walk past the shop, monitoring my mood, waiting for the next morsel of juicy gossip.

"If you could just please, please reconsider breaking their lease?" I begged Brian once again, knowing what his answer was going to be.

"You've been a renter; imagine you just moved into a house in a brand-new town, and your landlord says you have to leave because his friend next door doesn't like you. As a landlord — one who hopes not to go to court and also to continue to rent to others — I can't do that. But I'll see what I can do about hedges around the property; maybe I can come by and install a video doorbell for you so you can at least know who is coming up the drive and alert the authorities if need be. Does that sound fair?"

I thought about it for a minute. It seemed the fairest that the situation could get.

We hung up. I wasn't sure if the phone call was successful. At the end of the day, Tony and Mary were still going to be my neighbors, Brian was going to keep asking me out, and the town was still going to talk about the strange love triangle that I was unwillingly involved in.

What could I even do about it?

Sure, Brian's hedges and video doorbell would remind

Tony and Mary that I wanted them to keep their distance, but there was no way of knowing what would happen if they broke that unspoken social pact.

What advice would I give in this situation if a reader needed help like this?

Dear Jane Doe,

I wouldn't want you becoming yet another Jane Doe in a morgue. Another victim of violence. Please seek out an order of protection and communicate to your friends and loved ones that you do not wish to be contacted by these people. I don't know if that advice is enough. If you have a real stalker on your hands, there's not much I can do or say as an anonymous advice-giver in an online magazine. But if you feel uncomfortable, you should trust your instincts.

Please be safe.

18

Maybe I was being overly cautious and there wasn't any reason to be as paranoid as I was, but I *was* dealing with two stalkers.

I still didn't know whose idea it was to follow me to Pine Lake — I suspected it was Tony's, but from what he was saying about Mary's condition, she could have manipulated him into living here, right next door to her perceived enemy and the woman she seemed to believe Tony was having an affair with.

I opened my computer and started searching what I could do to prepare for a protection order. I had been unsuccessful in the past, but that was back when Tony and Mary's actions had been comparatively innocent. Blocking me on social media and spreading malicious gossip was not directly harmful to my day-to-day life, nor did it put me in physical danger.

It just casually eroded my psyche, starting with my self-confidence and ending with my sense of trust in other people, but of course, that wasn't dangerous at all.

I remembered the feeling of sitting with my lawyer as he told me there wasn't enough to put together. A few text messages, DMs and social media that had been deleted, so there was no way to prove I wasn't photoshopping them together for revenge. This time, years had passed with no incident. That must warrant an investigation, at the very least.

Who would enforce an investigation? I rarely saw police in Pine Lake. Since the town was so small, we were under the jurisdiction of the locally based state police force. The sheriff lived one town over, and getting him out to Pine Lake was apparently impossible. Neighbors would call in the middle of a fight, and the police would show up a few hours after the fight was resolved. What was the point of a protection order if there was no one to serve and protect?

Stop second-guessing yourself. There was nothing wrong with putting it on paper that I was worried about what could happen with Tony and Mary. There was nothing wrong with guarding my life against Mary's apparently increasingly erratic behavior.

I picked up the phone and dialed the number for the local division of the state police.

California State Police: 0; Laura Whitmore: 10! It's a miracle, the underdog who never played basketball in her life has managed to defeat the defending state champions with her third 3-pointer in a row! Can you believe it? The crowd is going wild! Hear them roar!

I was entertaining myself in a way that the state police department's hold music could not. I had already choreographed two dances to the gentle hum and made up a little song to go along with them. I had checked out, checked back in, and checked out again, and now I had created the ulti-mate sporting event.

Garbage Can Basketball State Championship, winner takes all: Laura Whitmore vs. the California State Police.

I was winning in my game, but nothing could defeat the hold music that just droned on and on and on.

I must have been on hold for an hour. I was transferred three times before I was put on hold indefinitely. I was convinced that they were going to leave me on hold until I gave up or their workday ended. Twice I considered hanging up and calling again, but I couldn't bear the thought of having to start the whole process again.

I heard a click from my phone and rushed over, but soon, the hold music started again.

So there was definitely someone there, and whoever it was really didn't want to talk to me.

"Thank you for holding," a faint voice said, coming from somewhere under a pillow. I had fallen asleep waiting for them to answer; at first, I thought it must be a dream.

"Hello?" the voice asked.

I jumped and scrambled to pick up the phone. "Hello? Um, hi, I'm here."

"You were on hold asking about a protection order, right?" the voice asked.

"Yes, that was me."

"Okay, hold while I transfer you." The line clicked once again, and I whined loudly.

"Are you okay?" asked another voice, male this time.

"Oh! Um, sorry, I thought I was being put on hold again."

"Nope. Sergeant Applewood here; you were inquiring about a protection order, is that correct?"

"Yes! I am having some trouble with my neighbors. I've tried to settle this dispute privately, but I believe I can't. I think I'm in personal danger and would like to ensure I have some protections in place. Just in case."

"Can you explain the details of the situation?"

I took a deep breath and told him the whole story. From the very beginning, pausing at the wedding day for dramatic effect and ending with Mary's outburst from the other night.

The sergeant listened passively, occasionally whistling at a particularly dramatic segment of my recent life story.

"That's quite a doozy, but there's not much we can do."

"Pardon? What do you mean?"

"Well, you have insufficient evidence that they purposefully moved to live next to you and — as you call it — 'torture you and your placid utopia.' Unless you can prove that these individuals have followed you for an extended period of time and that this isn't just an unfortunate coincidence, you don't have enough to categorize them as stalking you."

I sighed. He was right; there was no way I could prove that the move was intentionally made to target me.

"Furthermore, when a person known to you gives you flowers, it is not considered to be a violent act. I agree, it is pretty concerning that she went over to your house. If anything happens with her, you can give us a call, and we'll send someone right away. But at this time, neither has done anything worthy of an arrest. There's no point in issuing a protection order because there's no judge who will uphold it. I understand that your situation can be frustrating. I'm sorry, ma'am." At that, the phone clicked, and the line went dead.

Did he just hang up on me?

He had. Sergeant Applewood had calmly hung up on me

once he had decided that this was nothing more than two friends fighting over a man.

What else was I supposed to do? Who was going to protect me from experiencing another breakdown, courtesy of Tony and Mary? I felt helpless, stupid, and small.

There was only one person who could help me now.

19

C elene arrived the next morning. She timed her arrival to be hidden under the cover of darkness. "So that the happy couple doesn't try to say hello." That meant I was actually still in bed when she arrived.

"Good morning, sunshine!" she called to me as she opened my blinds and wafted the scent of fresh coffee toward my half-asleep body.

"Why are you doing this? What time is it?"

"It's 7 a.m. The sun is rising over the lake, and it is absolutely exquisite. If you don't catch it, you'll miss the most beautiful sunrise I have ever freakin' seen. I've rummaged around in your kitchen and found a couple of eggs and made you a French omelet—"

"Celene!" I cut her off.

"What? Is everything okay?"

I slowly sat up in bed and opened my arms, inviting my best friend into a long hug. "Hi, Celene. You forgot to say hi."

We held each other for a long time as I quietly cried on her shoulder. The past week had become a rolling elastic ball of stress, growing steadily day by day. To be able to sit and hold my friend was a relief like nothing else. Celene felt safe. She was the friend who found me when I ran away from everyone on my wedding day, and she was the one friend who stuck by me when Tony and Mary were slowly destroying my reputation to anyone who would listen. If the police wouldn't give me a protection order, that was okay. I still had Celene, the ultimate protector.

Celene slowly extracted herself from my embrace. I wiped my eyes, and we both laughed.

"I'll let you sleep a little longer if you want," she said.

"That's okay. I wanna see this sunrise you're making such a big deal about," I said, getting up.

Celene squealed and bolted down my stairs, stopping before going onto the back deck. She checked to see if there was anyone outside, but the coast was clear.

"Your utopia is undisturbed," she said as she stepped out onto my deck.

It felt so good to see my best friend again.

Celene had been up to visit me before, so we took the time to walk around town and visit her favorite artisanal shops that she remembered. As we walked through town, I felt relaxed because I knew Celene was on the watch for me. I didn't have to look over my shoulder; Celene did that for me.

We ended up at the ice-cream shop, splitting the biggest sundae we could order, as we got down to business.

"I've said it before, and I'll say it again, Tony Ellison is pure trash."

"Wish I had known that before I—"

"Stop right there. It isn't your fault. He had us all fooled. A guy as charming as he is can't be trusted, and now you know. On the bright side, romantically, he isn't your problem anymore. He's Mary's, and frankly, they deserve each other. If they want to swim in that toxic relationship forever, you need to let them."

"I'd love it if I could just ignore the fact that they live next door and move on with my life, but I just can't. Honestly, I think I might move."

"Why? You love this place; you love your house. Also, I love visiting you in this town."

"I know I love the house, and the financial hit would suck, but I could get over it. I could take a couple of extra jobs or maybe pitch the *Goosh* columns to a publisher and make them into a book. That would help me recover. I still don't know if this town is worth the psychological stress."

"Laura, have you ever thought that maybe Mary is coming from a good place?"

I stared at her over the banana-and-whipped-cream-ice-cream mountain. "Did I just hear you say that?"

Celene smiled. "I know you hate thinking about the possibly optimistic side of the situation, but please hear me out. Mary came to you in a panic and said a lot of things she probably shouldn't have said. However, she's had to deal with *Tony Ellison* for the past three years. You can forgive a girl for going a little crazy, right?"

"I suppose," I said, through a mouthful of ice cream.

"Maybe she wants to offer an olive branch, but doesn't know how to go about it. Or *she* wants to make peace, but Tony is getting in *her* way."

"Then why was she accusing me of having an affair with him? That doesn't seem like a very peaceful offering to me."

"True," Celene said, thoughtfully toying with the cherry stem from the sundae. "Well, you're the queen of overthinking. How long would you say it takes for you to go from a rational perspective on a situation to the wildly paranoid perspective of the same situation?"

"Less than a minute."

"And how long does it take to walk from Mary's house to yours?"

"About thirty seconds." I thought about it. In that thirty seconds, it was easy to come up with a million horrifying scenarios, each more paranoid than the next. "But why go straight to that? Why immediately accuse me? She had to know it would push me away."

Celene shrugged. "You'd have to ask your hot therapist that."

I rolled my eyes at Celene's obvious crush on Dr. Delgado.

We continued to eat our ice cream in silence for a while before I asked, "Why would Mary even want peace with me after all these years?"

"You two were friends for longer than you have been enemies. Maybe she realizes she threw away a friendship for Tony, and she is hoping to have some semblance of it back. But of course, living under the umbrella of Tony means even the most positive thought can be twisted into blame. Her nerves about asking you to reconcile turned into the worst possible thought—"

"That I had reconciled with Tony and not with her."

Celene nodded. "You wouldn't take that very well either if you were in her place."

I turned back to the ice cream. What Celene said made sense and also helped me feel less afraid of Mary and what she was capable of. I realized that I had only been talking to men about what was happening to my former friend, and that maybe what I needed all along was a feminine perspective. Men always wanted to tell you that women were crazy, in part because they could never understand the many emotions coursing through our veins.

"Can you imagine if you were a man and could just forget about your emotions and the feelings of others?" I asked Celene.

She shuddered and made a face like she was puking.

We both laughed and joked about how emotionless men were, especially when it came to relationships. That turned to gossip about Celene's love life and her horrible luck when it came to using dating apps. Soon, the ice cream was long gone, and the day was almost done.

Celene stayed for one more day, making a little weekend trip out of my emergency need for my friend. We went on a hike and on the way back said hello to Graham, who made us a banana loaf and coffee.

Celene repeatedly whispered, "What a catch," whenever Graham would leave — sometimes when he was nearby. It was embarrassing in the way only your best friend could be.

That night, I made Celene dinner and uncorked a fancy bottle of wine to celebrate her impromptu journey.

"Have you given any more thought to what I said yesterday?" she asked.

"Are we talking about dating apps, or how I should be a morning person to enjoy more Pine Lake sunrises?"

"Neither. I was talking about Mary."

I stared down at my plate and pushed the food around. "A little, I guess. I can't be friends with her again, but it would be nice to at least bury the hatchet and feel like I had some closure. I've thought about forgiving her, but every time I do, I feel sick to my stomach."

"Why do you think that is?"

"It's hard to imagine your life one way, to think it's perfect, and have that illusion shatter. It's even harder to pick up the pieces afterward. Not only did that happen, but Mary and Tony also made my life so miserable that the only thing I could think to do was leave — and even that didn't completely help. I guess I've spent so much time picking myself up and putting myself back together again that the thought of help from the person who broke me in the first place was just..."

"It made you feel vulnerable?"

I nodded. I could feel hot tears behind my eyes, ready to spill and ruin my pasta. At the end of the day, I just couldn't trust that Mary wouldn't betray me again, and I couldn't help but be paranoid that this was some kind of ruse.

"Having a relationship with Mary is risky," Celene reminded me, reaching out to hold my hand. "I'm not saying it isn't. I just think that making peace with Tony and Mary is a risk worth taking. Pine Lake has been a great place for you. You seem calmer, more at peace with the world. I'm only making this suggestion because I think it would be a shame if you ran away from somewhere that was good for you just because of Tony and Mary. I want you to win this time, Laura."

I laughed. "I *do* hate letting them win."

"Then keep fighting. But maybe change tactics. If a protection order isn't going to happen, maybe protect yourself by neutralizing the negative force you're fighting."

I squinted at Celene.

"You know what I mean," she said, "even if I didn't make much sense."

We finished our dinner and cleaned up. Celene didn't

have a long drive back, but she wanted to get going so she could be up early the next morning. She said goodbye, but not before reminding me that becoming a morning person would improve my day-to-day life. I stood on the street, waving at her car until it turned the corner.

As I turned to go back into my house, I saw Mary standing at the window, watching me.

20

I had plans with Graham the next day. I was exhausted and standing in front of the mirror packing makeup onto my face in the hopes that it would make me look more awake. Unfortunately, the more makeup I put on, the more I looked like a porcelain doll.

Seeing Mary standing at the window had spooked away all of the positivity that Celene had provided. I had nightmares of her light blue eyes staring into my soul, judging everything I did, and slowly taking me prisoner. It wasn't a very vivid dream, but I woke up feeling panicky, nonetheless.

Celene had sneakily set my alarm for 7 a.m. so I could watch her precious sunrise, but with the little sleep I had, it made me feel nauseated. I tried, but I couldn't get back to sleep. I had to hope that Graham would be just as charmed by me when I was half asleep as he was when I was awake.

Our plan was to meet at the community mailroom and then go for a short hike. I knew he probably had some kind of picnic planned — by now I knew that whenever I met with Graham, he would go far beyond what I expected for a date — so I packed some tea in a thermos. I decided to leave the makeup at home and rely on the fresh mountain air to keep me looking young and spry. With that in mind, I washed it all off my face.

As I got ready, I saw Mary on the back deck, sitting in the chair nearest to my house. She kept glancing over in my direction, and the one time we made eye contact through the window, she immediately turned away and ran back into the house.

She's being creepy, but that doesn't mean she's dangerous. Celene told me to repeat that to myself so I could differentiate between violence and weirdness.

I headed out. Behind me, I heard a small amount of chaos. I turned and saw Mary's door open. Mary popped out onto the porch, staring at me. I smiled, waving awkwardly, but she continued to just stand there.

I walked away before anything could happen. Why did she keep staring at me like that? Was what Celene said true? If it was — why was Mary being so weird about it?

When I got to the mailroom, I tried to act casual as I checked my mail, but it was very hard when you were laden down with hiking gear and waiting for a date.

Graham burst in, smelling of sweat and pine. "I'm so sorry I'm late. Got a little sidetracked, but it's all good now. Are we ready to go?" he asked, barely hiding the huge grin on his face.

That was when I knew for sure that this hike was going to end in an elaborate picnic.

"I'm ready; let's go." I waved at my neighbors, who were blatantly watching us go off together. Let them stare. I was okay with their gossip now. I had bigger problems on my plate with Tony and Mary next door.

Speaking of that, guess who was sitting outside the community mailroom, holding a newspaper to hide her face as she watched Graham and me leave the building? Mary Casden. Possibly the world's worst stalker and most obvious spy.

This time, I smiled and waved directly at her so she knew I could see her and was very aware of her decision to follow me around Pine Lake.

"Who did you wave at?" Graham asked.

"Oh, just my stalker," I replied.

He wrapped his arm around me and looked behind us. "She doesn't seem to be following you, so you're safe for now. Why don't we take a different route? It'll be harder, but she definitely won't be able to follow us in those flimsy flip-flops."

I nodded and grinned. Mary could go ahead and follow us — it might be good for her — but she certainly wasn't going to have an easy time. *I won't allow you to ruin my utopia, Mary.*

For the first mile or so, we could hear Mary panting behind us, but that soon drifted away as the hike got harder. I was having a harder time than Graham, who had clearly hiked this path before and was generally more experienced with the woods and trails around Pine Lake. Thankfully, he recognized this and was there with a hand to help me every step of the way — until he found a very good walking stick for me. Our picnic was perfect, and he managed to time it so that the sun started to set just as we were ready to go back down the trail.

"Don't worry," he said as I glanced warily at the path that we'd taken to get up there. "We can go down the easy way. I don't think Mary was able to follow us the whole way."

Graham walked me home and politely declined a glass of wine. We gave each other a quick hug goodbye, and he strolled down my path and turned down the street toward his house.

In the house next door, the light in the front window flicked off, and the curtains snapped shut. I suspected Mary had watched the whole time.

The next day started in much the same way. I woke up from a dream where Mary's disembodied eyeballs followed me around the house as I went about my day. It seemed like an innocuous dream, but the sense of foreboding danger made it hard to get up and start my day fresh.

I walked downstairs, and, once again, there was Mary sitting on her back deck, "reading" the same newspaper as yesterday. I could tell by the picture on the page facing me. Tony drifted outside and stood by Mary. He waved when he saw me through the window, causing Mary to snap at him. Tony cringed, yelled something back, and stormed into the house.

Clearly, it wasn't supposed to be obvious that Mary was spending her day tracking my movements. But if Tony was at home, wasn't that proof that we weren't carrying on an affair behind her back?

Her cover blown, Mary went back into the house, sending a not-so-casual wave and strained smile my way.

I returned the gesture and retreated to the cover of my kitchen, not wanting to encourage her blatantly spying on me. If I recorded her actions, would that be enough for a judge to finally grant that restraining order?

No, I should at least give what Celene said a chance. Mary was never good at apologies, and clearly, her behavior had become more erratic since we'd last hung out.

I went to the Rise N' Grind to finish a chapter of my latest novel. The deadline was coming up, and I knew my editor wouldn't accept "my exes moved in next door, and I'm afraid of them" as a good excuse for missing it. I took my noise-canceling headphones with me and chose a seat away from the window, partly to minimize my distractions and partly to minimize the chance of Mary shadowing me.

Most people see a pair of large headphones as a conversational deterrent, but for Brian Oliver, they were an invitation.

"Whatcha workin' on?" he asked, tapping on my shoulder as his brilliantly white teeth blinded me.

"I have to finish this draft before my editor has my head. I didn't realize you came here often."

"Oh, I was just hoping to run into you. My little birdies tell me this is basically your new office."

As I looked up at Brian, I caught Mary pacing back and forth in front of the window, holding two iced coffees. Had she been inside the coffee shop, and I didn't even notice? How much time did she spend hovering behind me? I shuddered and whipped back around to my computer.

"Is everything okay?" Brian asked.

"Yep. Just worried about my deadline." I tried to smile and resisted bolting out of the coffee shop and screaming at Mary to leave me alone. It was beyond creepy now. How many iced coffees had she ordered while watching me type in my little corner?

"Totally understand, you're in the zone, and I distracted you. I just wanted you to know I got the video doorbell installed, but I know you're busy, and this could have waited. Need to make it up to you over dinner." He waved and jogged off before I could tell him I didn't want to be made up with over dinner.

I turned back, but Mary had disappeared again.

I finished out my day at the Rise N' Grind, and for once, I wasn't the last person there.

As I made my way home, my shadow rose from a bench and started following me, hiding behind bushes and her day-old newspaper along the way.

I wondered what had happened to those two iced coffees — had she drank them or just abandoned them on whatever bench she camped out at?

I couldn't lose her, even by taking the long route by the water, and decided I would just confront Mary once and for all. If she really did want peace, this was a creepy way of going about it, and it was annoying to feel like I was being watched by her all day long.

I waited until there was no one around and finally whipped around to confront her.

Mary jumped when we made eye contact and turned toward the water.

I slowly walked over. "Mary, I *can* see you," I said, as gently as I could.

She just turned her head farther away from me.

I counted to five, trying to rein in my anger. I didn't want to do this, but if I continued to ignore her, I would just have an annoying shadow following me around for the rest of my life. That seemed a lot worse than confronting her, so I tried again, a little more aggressively this time.

"Mary, I know you've been following me around, and I'm sick of it. You're not very good at it — subtlety was never your strong suit — so you might as well just tell me why you've been tracking my every move." I stood beside her, waiting, showing her that I wasn't going to budge an inch until I had a proper answer.

Eventually, after avoiding my gaze for a solid minute, she sighed and turned to face me. "Laura, you make it hard to approach you. Every time I build up the courage, you go off with that guy Graham, or the landlord, Brian, or Tod from the café, and by the time you are done, I'm nervous again. It's not fair. I'm just trying to tell you that I wish we could still be friends."

I ignored the mild deflection of blame and let her continue.

"I feel bad that I hurt you. I really do, and I feel bad that I was mean about it afterward, but I've gotten a lot of help since then, and I realize I'm stuck with Tony when I could have been thriving with a truly good friend."

"How are you stuck with Tony? You could get rid of him," I responded to the part of the speech I could believe. The rest would take some processing.

"I am stuck with him; he's the only one who... oh, never mind. You're not sleeping with him, are you?"

"No!"

"Are you sure?"

"Yes, Mary, I'm positive I haven't been having an affair with Tony." I resisted rolling my eyes, Celene's voice ringing in my ears, telling me to give the woman the benefit of the doubt. If you'd been cheated on as many times as she probably had been, you would be asking the same questions.

"Good. Still, he's probably going to try. I know he still loves you, and I think you being nearby just reminded him of that. You'd tell me if you were having an affair, right? Please?" Mary pleaded.

"I have absolutely zero interest in Tony, and I wouldn't

touch him with a forty-foot pole. Besides" — I took a deep breath before admitting out loud what I didn't want to jinx — "I'm dating someone."

"Brian?"

"Uh, no. I'm dating Graham."

"The weird guy who does magic?" Mary asked.

I couldn't tell if she was intrigued or judging my poor taste in men.

"Yes, the weird guy who does magic. And he doesn't 'do' magic, by the way. He studies the occult from an anthropological perspective and assists in ceremonial rites of evocation."

Mary raised an eyebrow.

"Okay, fine, whatever. Yes, he does magic," I said. "But the point is, I like him, he's nice to me, and I have absolutely no interest in going back to a guy who cheated on me with my best friend on my wedding day."

Mary winced at that one. "Well, good. That's good for you that you have someone."

We were silent for a while, each of us staring out at the lake.

"I'm sorry I've been following you around," Mary whispered.

I tried not to look shocked at her admission of guilt — something Mary tended to avoid doing. "Why didn't you just say something?"

"I thought you'd be mad. I didn't want you to yell at me the way I yelled at you. I didn't want to lose control again." She paused and took a deep breath. "I got diagnosed with manic depression a couple of years ago, and it's been pretty manageable since I've been taking medication. But my new bottle of medication hasn't arrived — I used this new online pharmacy, and they sent it to the wrong address, and then they sent it to the right address, but it somehow got lost. Without it, I start to slip into... well, being a crazy bitch."

"Thanks for telling me." I felt for her and was glad Celene had convinced me to hear Mary out. She'd been right. Mary didn't deserve to be painted as a crazy woman out to get me.

"I really hope we can be friends again," Mary said. "I know it won't be the same as before. But maybe we can start from a clean slate?"

I hesitated before answering, "Yeah, maybe. It's hard. You really hurt me."

"I know."

We both stared at the lake for a little while longer. Eventually, Mary went home.

I stayed and watched the sunset. When the light finally dipped below the horizon, I started back home.

I TRIED to write the next day, but I couldn't stop thinking about my conversation with Mary. I understood why she would be so paranoid that Tony would cheat on her with me. He did have a wandering eye, and, after all, we had been about to be married when their relationship had its explosive start.

I was glad she'd told me about her mental health problems, as it made me sympathize with her. An explosion like my failed wedding day had repercussions all around. I felt like I'd had a nervous breakdown, leading me to move to Pine Lake. It seemed that Mary had experienced something similar to trigger her manic depression that led to a diagnosis and real help. A move to a community like Pine Lake made sense for her, as it could help encourage a more stable mind. I hoped that she got the medication she needed soon — for her sake as well as my own.

Later that day, I had a video call with Dr. Delgado. I told him that I'd confronted Mary about stalking me around town.

"How do you feel?" he asked.

"It felt good to tell her that Tony was her problem now, not mine, because it solidified in me the feelings I have for Graham. Unexpected positive outcome, I think. Also, Mary opened up to me about her manic-depression diagnosis and admitted that part of the reason she's been so erratic lately is that her medication ran out, and the refill was lost in the mail."

"That's good. I'm proud of you. It seems that you really have outgrown both Mary and Tony. They may have toxic behaviors, as evidenced by her decision to stalk you rather than talk to you, but now you know what's what. I would caution you against getting your hopes up, friendship-wise."

"Why is that?"

"I doubt that they've changed much at all," Dr. Delgado said.

It was a blunt response to hear from your therapist, but it seemed right. Mary had yet to apologize for betraying me, and based on what she'd said, Tony was still the same cheater he always was.

"Do you think I should engage with them? Now that there's this bridge between us?" I asked.

"Honestly? No, I don't think you should. You still don't know the actual reason they moved next door. It could have been coincidence, but if Mary was anxious to reach out to you, it could be that she orchestrated this plan to rekindle your friendship on forced terms. I think it's best for you to focus on your safety and well-being above theirs. Mary's mental health and happiness are not your responsibility."

I nodded. We continued to talk — believe it or not, Tony and Mary were not the only reason I was in therapy. There was my estranged relationship with my mother, the trauma of my abusive father, and the general "what am I even doing with my life?" to discuss, and I wanted to turn the conversation away from the matter of my exes next door.

I thought a long time about my conversation with Dr. Delgado. I didn't like how dismissive he'd been over Mary's manic depression. Mental health was real; as a psychologist, he should know that best. I couldn't imagine how she must be feeling being off her medication and what side effects that could lead to. He'd barely taken that into consideration when I told him she had mentioned it as the reason for acting erratically.

His advice felt harsher than usual, with more of a line drawn in the sand of what I should be doing. Usually, he let me come to conclusions like this alone. Had I been overdramatic when I found out that Tony and Mary had moved in next door?

If I was "over" the whole situation, why couldn't I just let it go?

21

My mind spun in circles, going over and over and back and forth and back again, trying to decide whether I was ready to put the past behind me and forgive Mary for what she had done. Tony was out of the question; it was obvious that he was still pure trash. But Mary was just... another woman stuck with a man who treated her horribly.

I never forgave my mother for staying with my father for as long as she did. I thought doing so left her so vulnerable that the only behavior she now knew was toxicity. She couldn't help but defend horrible behavior because she had spent over twenty years of her life doing that. Mary was headed down the same path, and I was not sure I could consciously let her do so — even if we were no longer friends.

Part of me wanted to talk to Graham about it. His behavior on our date just reinforced the feeling of comfort and trust that I had around him. He listened to what I was saying and acted accordingly. He saw that I was uncomfortable and did something to change it; he hadn't forced a relationship on me or tried to get me into bed before I was ready.

But I didn't want to cling to this sudden new relationship. I needed to learn how to rely on myself. I also didn't want Graham to feel I was bombing him with my life and interrupting his peace. Besides, I still wasn't sure how I felt about his love of the occult — it *was* a little weird, no matter how you spun it. Did I want to be the woman defending her boyfriend's weird hobbies for the rest of her life?

Before I knew it, I was calling Celene. She was going to get sick of talking to me about the same problem over and over again.

"What did Tony and Mary do?" she said, answering the phone.

"I knew you'd ask that. I'm sorry. I feel like this is the only reason we talk anymore," I whined.

"It's fine, and it's not the only reason we talk. You have also diligently updated me on your personal life. So spill — what did the demonic duo do?"

I laughed at her nickname despite my gentler feelings toward Mary. "They didn't do anything, but I'm sure you'll be glad to hear you were right about Mary."

"She wants to be friends again?"

"Pretty much, yeah. After you left, she stalked me around town. I told her to stop following me, and she admitted she was just doing it because she didn't know how to approach me."

"See? There was an explanation all along." Celene squealed over the line. Her positivity was infectious.

"I know, and I've got to say that I'm relieved. She definitely thought I was having an affair with Tony, but I cleared that up for her. I told her she could keep that piece of trash for herself."

We both laughed at the idea that *anyone* would want to have an affair with Tony — his charm only went so far — and then theorized for a bit about whom he would target next.

"All jokes aside," Celene said, "do you think it was a good conversation? Do you feel better about them living next door?"

"Yeah, I think I do. I don't know if I want to be friends just yet—"

"Why?"

"I still feel hurt and vulnerable. I don't know if I can let that go just yet. I don't want to be carrying around residual anger with Mary, so I'm happy to work toward that, but I definitely wish they lived somewhere else in town, where I would at least have the option to not see them out my back window as I came downstairs every morning."

"That's fair, but maybe you need to use the opportunity in front of you rather than throw it all away."

"What do you mean?"

Celene paused, and I could hear her draw a deep breath. "I think you should have them over for dinner. Give them a chance to explain themselves and talk things out."

I could not believe my ears. "Celene, after all these years — are you going to tell me there's an *explanation* for what they did?"

"Not like that," she said, backtracking a bit for me to understand. "I mean an explanation for why they moved to Pine Lake. There must be a reason, and if this week has taught you anything, it's that you're not going to get a satisfactory answer through aggression. You need to use a bit of optimism to get the right answer. Haven't you ever heard that old adage — you catch more flies with honey than you do with vinegar?"

I sometimes wondered where Celene got her positivity from. First, she grew up in a fairly uneventful household. Her parents were still very much in love; they were high school sweethearts who talked through every argument to come to a mutually beneficial conclusion. It was the healthiest display of love I had ever seen, and I thought it made Celene somehow jaded in contrast to the way I was. Where I thought every relationship was doomed to fail, Celene had on rose-colored glasses and believed any relationship could be the one that lasts forever. Where I couldn't trust anyone to the point where it was a fault, Celene was overly trustworthy with almost everyone she met. I wondered what it would be like to see the world through Celene's eyes.

"Celene, I don't want to have them over for dinner," I said.

"Why not? You know you wouldn't take Tony back, which will calm Mary down, and it will give you a chance to lay down some peaceful ground between you two."

"But why does it have to be at dinner?"

I could practically see Celene rolling her eyes. "Don't you ever read anything other than those romantic thrillers you write? Like fantasy novels? Everyone knows you can't kill your host if they serve you dinner."

"You can't what?" I squeaked, my eyes widening as a new traumatic thought rolled through me. "Do you think Tony and Mary want to kill me?"

"No! I'm just saying that they won't do anything at a dinner. You'll feed them, maybe you guys will argue a bit, but then you can get your plates clean and clear for the rest of your lives. Start from fresh and be cordial, for real. Plus, if you make them dinner, they'll owe you, which will give you a little power over them, which I *know* you'd enjoy."

She was right. I would enjoy having a little power over Tony and Mary. "I'll think about it."

"That's all I ask. *Really* think about it though, don't just say that to get me off the phone," Celene cried.

"If I wanted to get you off the phone, I'd..." I tried to think of what I'd do, but to be honest, there wasn't any topic I could think of that would force Celene to hang up.

"You can't think of anything, can you?" she said, snickering. "That's because I listen no matter what it is. And you don't even have to pay me."

I rolled my eyes at that one. Celene was positive, but that didn't mean she was humble. We said our goodbyes, and I put down the phone.

I couldn't sit at my desk any longer. I got up and stretched, deciding to take a long walk around town to clear my head of Dr. Delgado's negativity and Celene's positivity. I needed to find a way to get back to neutral and decide what, if anything, I was going to do.

The ice-cream shop in town seemed to have a magnetic attraction. Ever since going there with Celene, I had a craving for their avoca-dough ice cream — a creamy avocado base with cookie dough mixed in. Without even realizing it, my feet led me there, and soon I sat outside, enjoying two scoops of extremely creamy, decadent goodness.

"Fancy seeing you here," a voice said.

I looked up excitedly, thinking it was Graham, but was surprised and slightly disappointed to see Brian. Somehow he'd pitched his voice lower, or maybe I was just hoping it was Graham who'd greeted me. "Hi."

"Hello, may I sit?" he asked as he sat.

Didn't give me much choice in the matter.

"I was asking my usual landscaper if he could add a hedge, but he said it wasn't possible right now. Something about the timing of the season..."

"Oh, it's fine."

"How are you feeling? I heard Mary's been bothering you — is everything okay?"

"I ran into Mary, actually. It was pretty okay."

"Oh?" Brian asked. He seemed taken aback, but I guessed I had called him multiple times, begging him to get rid of his latest tenants.

"Yes. She had been following me around town, but I confronted her about it, and we hashed it out. I think we're going to try to be friends."

"Friends? With your ex-best friend? How modern of you. I don't think I could be friends with an ex if you paid me," Brian said, laughing.

"Well, not *friends* friends. I think we'll be more like friendly acquaintances in the end. I invited them to dinner so we could test it all out." That was a lie; I hadn't even decided what I was going to do on that front yet, but saying it out loud made it feel more plausible. I also wanted to avoid Brian inviting himself over to "comfort" me or insisting that I go out with him again.

"I'm surprised. When you called, you seemed so... helpless. But it turns out you didn't need my help at all. You solved your own problem." Brian grinned his Cheshire cat grin.

I couldn't tell if he was annoyed or happy for me. He seemed annoyed that I'd managed to solve the problem myself — probably because that meant he wouldn't have many more excuses to invite me over for dinner.

"I was definitely in a panic when I called you, and I want to thank you for at least listening to my paranoia. I'm hoping this means I can truly find closure on the whole situation and just move forward with my life. Stop dragging around the weight of Tony, Mary, and the wedding that never happened."

"I hope that for you as well," Brian said, sounding more genuine than ever. "No one needs the baggage of an ex dragging them through life. Maybe this dinner is the first step on your new journey."

Brian and I smiled at each other, and, surprisingly, I let him talk to me about his art while I finished my ice cream.

I didn't stay long though — now that I'd told someone I had invited the exes over for dinner, it meant I actually had to *do* it. Our love triangle was still prime town gossip, so if dinner didn't happen, Brian would definitely hear about it.

I took flowers with me, just in case. The flowers would either smooth over the interaction or provide a small line of defense against Mary's wrath. I summoned the courage, waved to the one neighbor who seemed to sit outside all day waiting for another scene, like the one that had happened when Mary came over, and walked to their door.

I rang the doorbell and heard a small crash from inside.

A few minutes later, a frazzled Mary came to the door. "Laura! Hi. Sorry, the doorbell scared me, and I dropped a glass," she said, blinking nervously. "We don't get a lot of visitors."

"That's okay. Did you hurt yourself?"

"No, I'm totally fine. Just have a mess to get back to — are those for me?" she asked, smiling and reaching out for the flowers. Mary really hadn't changed; anything that seemed like it could be a gift was *always* for her.

"Um, yes, they are. I wanted to, um... well, I wanted to invite you and Tony over for dinner. If you do want to make amends—"

"I do," Mary interrupted. "Oh, thank you, Laura," she said as she enveloped me in a very tight hug. "You have no idea what this means to me."

I could feel Mary's wet tears soaking my shoulder. I wasn't sure why she was crying. I figured it must be that she still didn't have her medication, but I didn't want to seem judgmental about it, so I just silently patted her on the back until she let go.

"Well, why don't we do it tomorrow? I can get fresh pasta from the market and make us something tasty."

Mary stared into the flowers and wiped her eyes, nodding at my suggestion. She said a teary goodbye and closed the door. I heard a thump, and I assumed it was a relieved Mary slumping against the door. She didn't seem okay.

I hoped I wouldn't regret this dinner.

22

The dinner was either going to be a disaster, or it was going to be perfect; there was no other option. I didn't even know how I felt about it anymore. I had gone back and forth and back again about whether or not it was a good idea.

I didn't tell Dr. Delgado. I didn't know if it was a bad idea to blatantly ignore your therapist's advice and then not tell him you were doing so, but...

Well, it was too late now. I'd already bought the fresh pasta.

I was cleaning my house when I heard the doorbell ring. I freaked out, thinking that somehow time had sped forward, and I wasn't even close to being ready. The doorbell kept ringing, which convinced me it was Mary either canceling the dinner or coming in ready to start a storm. I shuffled over in my cleaning clothes, fluffing up my hair as much as I could so that I would at least look good when I greeted my guests with dust bunnies and uncooked pasta.

Brian stood at my door, holding a plastic bag. "Laura! Fancy seeing you here."

It was his flirting voice.

Had this been a couple of months ago, I would have puffed out my chest, dimpled my cheeks, and played along with his game. But it wasn't, it was after Brandy's death, after Tony and Mary and, most importantly, after meeting Graham. Besides, now was *so* not the time.

"Hi, Brian. Did we have plans today?" I asked as casually as I could.

"Absolutely not, sorry for catching you, um, in the middle of something?" He smirked at my outfit.

I was not cute in my cleaning outfit, it was a pair of old paint-splattered overalls, and I usually wore a sports bra beneath so that I wouldn't get it dirty or bleach-stained.

"It's fine. What is that?" I asked, pointing to his bag.

"I saw you in town this morning at Mangiare, buying fresh pasta, so I figured you were entertaining. I had these coat hooks lying around and thought I'd pass them along to help you spruce up the place before you had guests." He smiled his megawatt smile and handed me the bag of very heavy coat hooks.

"Thanks, I, um... I don't think I need them. Besides, these are heavy; I feel like they'll bring down the whole wall."

"Not at all. That just means they'll stand up to whatever you throw at them — literally," Brian said as he brushed past me into my entryway. He placed the hooks on the wall and stepped back as far as he could.

I had to admit, they looked much nicer than the cheap ones I'd bought. They probably wouldn't fall out of the wall when I put my parka on them, either. I closed the door and decided to entertain Brian — just this one last time.

"Let me change, and I can help you out," I said, scurrying past him.

"Don't worry about it. I love this look. You could be a painter — a younger Leonora Carrington or something," he said with a wink.

"This really wasn't necessary," I said, blushing in spite of myself.

"Even if things are going well with Tony and Mary, I still feel bad that I couldn't move them for you. Also, I feel like you've been so busy lately, there's no way I could see you unless I made up an excuse."

"You're lucky these are nice hooks, or else you would have wasted a trip." I winked — what was I doing? Something about Brian made it so easy to flirt with him. "Do you want a glass of rosé?" I asked as I padded into the kitchen.

"Sure, I'd love one."

"Great. Because I certainly don't have any tools for you."

"Don't worry — I thought of that, too."

I felt horrible admitting it, but it felt nice to just flirt with Brian for a while. Graham was wonderful, but conversations with him often felt too weighted, almost a little too significant. With Brian, I was just playing a strange game.

We installed the hooks quickly, but Brian fiddled for a while with their placement, muttering about the hooks being "seen" by my guests. I thought he was just trying to find reasons to stay longer and teased him about it.

"I suppose I am just trying to see a little more of you," he said.

After that, we finished our drinks, and I sent him away, making the excuse that I had to keep cleaning.

Brian finally left, after I dodged two kisses and countered with an awkward hug. I rushed to clean the entryway from the debris of our small reno project, then showered and dressed.

I tried drinking tea to calm down, but it didn't work, so I just gave in to my anxiety over the dinner and stared at the clock on the microwave until the moment I knew Tony and Mary would ring my doorbell.

At 8 p.m. on the dot, I heard the buzzer. *Ladies and gentlemen, I hope you're ready for a show.*

I went to the door, smoothing my dress and fluffing my hair in the process. From behind the closed door, I heard the sounds of bickering.

"I told you we should be a bit late," Mary said. "Now she's going to make us wait."

"You know that Laura hates it when people are late. Besides, who's gonna care? We're not going to some fashion party, Mary; it's just some awkward dinner you roped us into."

"Well, she's *your* ex—"

"She's *your* ex-best friend."

"Shhh! She can probably hear us."

The voices went quiet. This was going to be a very interesting night.

I waited a moment, so they wouldn't think I'd heard them, before opening the door with the biggest smile I could muster. "Hi, guys. Wow, you both look great."

They looked okay. Mary had made an effort; her hair was done up like a Texas beauty queen — as was her makeup. Tony's clothes could have used an iron, but at least he'd managed to tuck in his shirt and wear a belt — that was more than I could ever get him to do.

"Hi," Mary exclaimed. "This is for you. I'm assuming you're still a big wine drinker." She handed me a nice bottle of organic red Cabernet, the one I often drank. I wondered if she had spied me drinking it, or if she went to the wine shop in town and asked what I liked to buy.

"Thanks, you remembered Cabernet is one of my favorites. Don't just stand on the porch. Come on in." I ushered them in, glancing behind at the crowds that had started to gather on some of my neighbors' stoops. I smiled at them as I slammed the door in their faces. Unfortunately for them, tonight's show was going to be a private one.

I followed Mary and Tony down the hall as their eyes roved around my house. I had great decor, I must admit, but there was no need for them to gawk the way they did.

"This place is huge. How can you possibly afford it?" Mary blurted out.

"Mary, that's rude," Tony said, nudging her in the side.

"I was just commenting that this place is such a steal. I'm sure Laura understands, right, Laura?" Mary turned to me and bored her eyes through to my soul.

"Does this wine need to be chilled?" I asked, staring down at the bottle to avoid the couple's invading gaze. Each seemed to need me to be on their side.

"See, Mary?" Tony said through gritted teeth. "When you make people feel uncomfortable, they don't want to continue the topic of conversation. No one likes to be forced into doing anything against their will."

"No one's forcing you to be here, and if you want to talk about being rude, how about declining a lovely invitation to dinner?" Mary shot back. "Or fighting with your girlfriend when you arrive at a dinner party?"

The couple stared each other down, and I wasn't sure if they were going to start making out or tearing out each other's hair.

"Why don't I get our dinner on the table?" I offered, but they didn't seem to hear me.

Tony and Mary had graduated from using their words to fighting using sharp glances at each other. I was almost impressed at how much they could convey in those darting glances. Finally, there seemed to be a pause, and their gazes turned gentler.

"I'm going to wash up before we eat," Tony said, gently rubbing Mary's arm. "Laura, where's your bathroom?"

"If you pass the stairs and hang a left, you'll see the powder room that's down here."

"There's *two* bathrooms?" Mary exclaimed.

"Mary," Tony scolded.

"It's okay," I mediated. "I was excited too when I heard, but downstairs is just a powder room. It's a toilet and a sink that was fitted into a broom closet, nothing to be impressed about. It wasn't like the dumbwaiter you had in your old apartment, Mary. Remember that thing?"

"Oh yeah. That house must have been a million years old, and we could always hear the couple downstairs fighting—"

"— or making up after fighting."

Mary and I laughed. For a moment it was like old times, giggling over a glass of wine as we told each other about our horrible days. I'd tell Mary about all the confusing edits I'd get on the articles and books I was writing, while she'd tell me about the evil customers at her latest retail job. For a second, I was sad that I didn't know anything about Mary's life as it was now.

"So, Mary, what do you plan on doing here in Pine Lake?"

"Well, I've been talking to Katie at the flower shop. I

asked if she'd ever want part-time help. I haven't followed up yet."

"How come?" I asked. "I'm sure she'd love the time off."

"I've just been a little... frantic, I guess? Depression and anxiety meds aren't fun to go off cold turkey. I've felt nauseated and can feel a manic period coming on. I didn't want to give her a bad impression. Besides, she probably doesn't even remember."

I sympathized. It couldn't feel good to know the medication you were on that helped you get through your day was missing somewhere in the postal system, likely never to be returned.

"So, how did this diagnosis happen? What made you go out and get help?" I asked.

Mary bristled at my question. "The wedding, basically. I didn't see that situation the same way you did. I could only see it from a selfish perspective. To me, you ruined a moment that I had finally been able to have alone with someone, when my spontaneity took hold, and I could live outside of reality for a second. At some point, you just sent an email that said, 'Get help,' and I guess... well, I did. I found a therapist who helped me understand that my manic depression was probably why I had ruined so many relationships in the past — both romantic and personal. But I didn't go on medication right away."

I sat back, stunned. I wasn't expecting Mary to admit to getting help, or that I was the inspiration. And did she say that she was being selfish on that fateful day? I think I must have been staring at her with my mouth hanging open because Mary finally cleared her throat and got up from the table to walk to my back window.

"How did you find this place, anyway?" she asked.

"A friend at *Goosh* was writing a blog post about the most picturesque Californian mountain towns. I saw a picture of Pine Lake and immediately went online to see if there were any properties available." I saw my chance at finding out how they ended up next door. "How did you and Tony end up here? You guys seem much more city-bound."

Mary snorted. "We are. I hardly know what I'm doing here, but Tony found the place, and we needed a move so..." She trailed off.

So it was Tony's idea? I wondered where he even saw the listing. It couldn't have been up for more than a day before they saw it.

I was about to ask Mary for more info when Tony burst back into my living room, swaying a little on his feet. "Damn, Laura, that is one tiny bathroom."

"Tony, don't be rude. What were you doing in there? You were gone for, like, an hour." It was Mary's turn to be the decorum police, I guessed.

"I wasn't being rude. Laura's right, the bathroom looks like it was built into a closet."

The two continued to bicker over my powder room and whether it was rude to call it what it was — inconveniently tiny.

In the meantime, I silently went to the kitchen and started plating our meal and pouring some of the wine Mary had brought. I poured a little extra for myself, since the happy couple definitely wouldn't notice.

"Dinner's ready," I called out, hoping to be heard over the angry whispering.

Tony and Mary both went quiet and stared right at me, making me feel as if I had done something wrong by interrupting their strange toxic ritual. Neither was making a move toward the table, so I figured I would start the party.

"I don't know about you guys, but I'm hungry, and I'm excited about this pasta. I got it from Mangiare, that Italian market in town? It's a ricotta and spinach 'mezzaluna,' which I learned today is Italian for half-moon."

My enthusiasm was met with strained smiles and a badly rehearsed duet of *"Wow."*

The first part of our meal went by in silence. Tony drank a lot more than Mary. He practically chugged his first glass of wine, and if it hadn't been for one of Mary's "looks," he likely would have chugged the second as well.

The night was going about as well as a train wreck.

"Laura, we wanted to talk to you about something," Mary said, looking at Tony.

"Oh, yeah," he said, putting his glass down. "We know it's awkward, but we want to address what happened on that day. You know, the day we were supposed to   "

"I know which day you're talking about," I cut him off before he could say it. What was this? Had I walked into another trap?

"I just want you to understand that we both feel bad about what happened," Mary said.

I felt her nudge Tony under the table and saw him wince when her heel struck his shin.

"Yes. We want you to know that our happiness should never have come at your expense, and we didn't choose a very good moment to um... reveal our true feelings for one another."

At that, the couple looked at each other, and for a moment, they looked like they lived in bliss. After all, they had survived the past three years and were still together.

There must be something working underneath all that sniping at each other.

"Do you understand what we're saying?" Mary asked me, her left hand grasping Tony's and her right hand reaching for mine.

I wanted no part of this strange communion, so I just nodded and reached for my napkin. "Mmm-hmm, I absolutely do, but, Mary, it looks like you got some pasta sauce on your dress," I said, pointing. I thanked that little dollop of pasta sauce for helping me dodge this awkward situation.

Mary jumped up from the table and ran off to the powder room, holding the pasta stain out so it wouldn't spread to the rest of her dress. Tony and I watched as she rounded the corner into the powder room.

"Good call," he said, leaning his body to my end of the table.

"Well, it was good timing, I guess. I'm glad you guys are apologetic, but I don't need to say grace over it or anything." I tried to laugh it off, but Tony just stared at me, confused.

"Huh? Apologetic about what?" he asked. Tony was drunk, I could tell, not in his words, but in his eyes, which couldn't quite focus on me.

"About the wedding," I clarified, "about what happened on the day that was supposed to be our wedding?"

"Oh *that*," Tony said, rolling his eyes dramatically. "That's more Mary's thing, honestly. I know you're still into me though, and that's totally fine."

I froze. Apparently, only one of them had done any work on themselves in the past three years. "What?"

"I mean, it's okay. We can keep this up in front of Mary, y'know. Play the exes who hate each other. But Mary goes to bed so early these days, we could just meet out on the deck and y'know." Tony smirked at me and gently stroked my wrist.

I pulled it away and resisted the urge to slap him. "What are you even saying?"

He sighed. "I still have feelings for you. It's not like they went away. They just hibernated. When Mary said we had to move, I resisted it, but now…"

All I could do was sit there and stare at him. Tony was hitting on me, but he was also saying Mary had been the one to spur their move to Pine Lake. "Did Mary find this place?"

"I think so. She always had these real-estate brochures lying around. Never thought she'd find somewhere so perfect. I mean, think about it; she doesn't have to know. And now that you're friends again, it makes even more sense that I'd be working on our friendship." Tony winked.

I felt my stomach curl in on itself. It was the same feeling I'd get when we were together, and I knew he was lying. "Are you wasted or delusional?"

"Neither, baby. I'm just enamored by you."

He reached down to kiss my hand, but I slapped it away. Just in time, too, because Mary came out of the bathroom, beaming at her now-clean dress.

I felt sick to my stomach. Tony and Mary had each told me that the other was responsible for moving to Pine Lake, and each gave me a good reason why they'd wanted to move. Mary to patch things up and get away from the city, and Tony just wanted to cheat on Mary wherever he went. However, as to who it was who'd decided to come here of all places, I had a feeling it was Tony, and he was lying. The question was why, and did I really care to know? Not from him, I was sure of that. I'd get the information some other way.

"You guys have to go now," I said, standing up from my seat. I surprised them both, but I was having a hard time holding back the bile that was rising in the back of my throat.

Tony just shrugged.

Mary awkwardly moved toward me. She opened her mouth to say something.

But Tony cut her off. "You heard her, Mary. We have to leave now." He winked at me over the back of Mary's head.

Mary gently patted me on the arm, but I could see that her smile had venom behind it. "I guess we'll leave the wine and the rest of the food here for you to enjoy," she said, the saccharine words tainted with sarcasm. She walked away slowly, slinking her body toward Tony, who stared at her like she was some kind of meal. Mary wrapped her arms around Tony's waist. "Come on, honey. Let's see if they'll even deliver a pizza to this nothing town."

They made out the whole way down the hall.

Dinner was a disaster.

23

I was burned out. That was my excuse for taking an extra day off. As far as anyone knew, I was calmly typing away at my computer, with an idyllic view. They didn't need to know that I'd actually woken up late, taken a bath, and then decided to bake cookies all afternoon.

I didn't even want to review what had happened yesterday. It made my entire body cringe and gave me a pounding headache. It was like dealing with my mother, multiplied to the tenth power.

First, there was my sense of guilt over flirting with Brian, even though I clearly had stronger feelings for Graham. Brian had been perfectly nice yesterday, like old times when he would come by to help me fix things around the house or make a slight addition here or there, yet I knew that, in his mind, it was another step forward in our relationship. I wondered how long this would keep up once Brian realized that I didn't want to sleep with him.

Next were Tony and Mary. Their behavior was bizarre, to say the least. At times, it seemed like they resented each other, that they were somehow "stuck," even though there was nothing sticking them together — no legally binding marriage, no kids, no mortgage. They bickered any time they were in the same room, and at times their bickering wasn't even out loud. They had a strange connection that allowed them to argue telepathically. Maybe Graham might be able to explain the ability for toxic couples to transcend the plane of spoken communication. Their apology was typical of them — self-serving and weak — and their motivations were totally in conflict. Tony had drunkenly hit on me and then left my house passionately making out with Mary. It was disgusting.

To top it off, the one benefit that might have come out of that dinner was totally confusing. They each blamed the other for their move to Pine Lake. One of them had to have made the decision, which meant that one of them was lying.

Unless it was an outside influence. Maybe it was my mother dropping off all those real-estate pamphlets to persuade the move and get Tony to take me back. It seemed that was what he wanted — to bring me into their strange relationship and turn it into a toxic threesome. Mary's intentions might have been good, but considering her attitude when I put my foot down and kicked them out, I had a feeling that I would become her punching bag soon after we became friends again.

I ought to have listened to Dr. Delgado. For every step forward I had taken, Tony and Mary either took a step backward or stubbornly stayed in place. They only navigated within a toxic framework, and because they spent most of their time together and deflected all blame onto those around them, there was no one to pull them out of it.

But that was yesterday. Today was a cookie-baking, rest-of-pasta-eating day, a luxurious recovery from too many too-exhausting interactions. I wanted to spend my time quietly with someone who made me easily comfortable. I had to admit that what I really wanted to do was to spend time with Graham.

We hadn't spoken since we went on the hike. Mary's comments about my boyfriend who "did magic" had made me rethink whether or not I wanted to be *that* woman in town with the weirdo boyfriend. To add to that, Graham had continued to talk about his strange town conspiracies while on our hiking date. At the time, it didn't bother me because I was more concerned that Mary was stalking me through town. Now that I had some time to think about it, I had to wonder whether it could be true, or just the ramblings of a man who lived alone in the woods.

I knew that none of my reservations would be resolved if I continued to avoid Graham. Besides, even with his quirks, he was still the person I felt most comfortable around in Pine Lake. I figured he'd enjoy a cookie surprise — it was the least I could do considering he showered me with baking every time I went to see him. This time I would come bearing gifts.

My cookie recipe was a classic; everyone always asked what I did to make them taste so good. Joke's on them — I just follow the instructions on the back of my favorite chocolate chips. It had never failed me — the only difference was that I let the raw cookie dough sit, covered, at room temperature to make the flavors melt into each other. I saw it on a baking competition show once and never looked back.

I decided not to text Graham on my way over, and just surprise him with my baking, as he had done for me so many times before. Part of me worried that I would catch him at an inopportune time, but that was just my stressed-out brain talking, wishing for a small relief from the exhaustion of the days past. It was more than Tony and Mary and Brian — it was the fact that for the past two months, there hadn't been any relief from the emotional roller-coaster ride I'd been on.

It was starting to feel like Brandy's death was years ago because of how much had happened since. Come to think of it, the first day I saw Graham Silverton, peeking into Brandy's house, was on the day she died. If I believed in the occult the way he did, I'd have said that Graham was a bad omen, come to warn me what would be coming to that house.

Walking up to his door, my hands had started to burn a little bit from the heat of the cookies, I was suddenly nervous — what if Graham didn't like the cookies? What if he was angry that I hadn't called? What if—

"Oh, Laura! Hello," Graham said.

Somehow, without realizing it, I had already rung the doorbell and knocked.

"Graham, funny seeing you here." My brain could not think of anything else to say except for a lame dad joke.

Graham took it in his stride. "I know how it must look — me coming to the door of my own house in the middle of the day, but it's not what you might think. I'm working." He made a dramatic gesture like he was ashamed, putting his hands over his eyes like I was paparazzi, and we both laughed. It was the lamest joke, but Graham going along with it made it funny.

"I feel bad that you keep feeding me baked goods, and I've done nothing in return, so I baked you some of my famous cookies," I said, revealing the platter with a flourish.

"Well, they aren't famous. But everyone I've given them to has said that they're really good."

"They look amazing and very fresh," Graham said, taking one and delicately breaking it in half. "Ahh, just look at that chocolate pull. So much moisture packed into these." He smiled and popped half a cookie into his mouth.

"Do you watch the *Greatest Baker in Town*, too?" I asked, recognizing the jargon from my favorite baking competition show.

"Uh, yeah, obviously. It's the only baking show worth watching, in my opinion."

"*Mine too.*" I squealed like a teenager who'd just found out that her crush likes the same popular band she does. *Get it together, Laura; you're not fifteen.*

"I'm not a fan of much reality television, but I find that show extremely wholesome," he said, taking the platter. "I've really got to get back to work. The deadline, unfortunately, won't meet itself," Graham sang out and backed away from the door.

"Oh, well... great. Yes, those deadlines can be a horror show," I said awkwardly. I wasn't necessarily expecting a date in the middle of the day, but I also wasn't expecting to get the brush-off so early on.

"Goodbye, Laura. Thank you for the moist cookies. I'll let you know if you get the Best Baker's Medal for them," he said, waving as he closed the door in my face.

That could have gone worse, I thought. Then again, it could have gone better.

Later that night, I was sitting down to a dinner of leftover pasta when I heard my doorbell ring. I shuffled over in my slippers, wiping a hand on my sweatpants. Graham's reaction had put me into a funk. I had hoped that the visit would lift my spirits, but instead it had made me feel like I was someone's sixth toe — unwanted and an eyesore.

I didn't even bother checking my reflection, I was sure it was horrible, and besides, it was probably just Mary coming to yell at me about Tony, or one of my neighbors inventing a reason to snoop around my house for more morsels of Tony-Mary-Laura gossip.

Much to my surprise, Graham was at the door, carrying the plate I'd left with him in one hand and a fresh chocolate banana loaf in the other.

"Graham! What are you doing here?" I asked, trying to discreetly sniff my armpit while smoothing down my hair.

"I'm returning your platter and returning the gesture. Two birds with one stone, as they say," he said, glancing over his shoulder. "Do you mind if I come in? Your neighbors seemed curious as to—"

"Say no more. Come on in," I said, ushering him into the entryway. "They've been waiting for a show ever since Mary came to scream at me. So far there's no sign of a sequel, much to their disappointment."

"I understand that. I have never loved how people have become so hungry for a show around here." Graham cleared his throat.

We were standing so close to each other that I could faintly smell pine on his shirt. I wanted to reach my arms around his neck and kiss him deeply, breathing in the scent of the woods as I did.

Instead, I made a strange choking sound and felt my face get hot.

"That's my plate," I said.

"Yes, and this is a chocolate banana loaf," he said, gesturing to the loaf with my plate. "They're both for you."

"Thanks," I said, taking the two items. I felt like a kinder-gartener with a crush on Santa Claus. "These are great."

We stared at each other for a while. Neither of us could think of what to say next. Anything I could think to say sounded incredibly dorky.

"Maybe I could give my neighbors a piece as a consola-tion prize for not giving them more of a show," I said. *That sounded a lot less paranoid in my head.*

A serious look washed over Graham's face. "Laura, I have to apologize to you. I feel like I've tainted your view of Pine Lake with my strange theories. You have been incredibly polite to nod along as I talked about them, especially on our picnic. I was worried that you had reached your limit and I'd scared you off. I was so shocked to see you again today that I panicked and practically slammed the door in your face. I'm really sorry. You didn't deserve that."

My whole body melted, starting with my knees and ending with my heart. "Graham, you don't need to apologize. You didn't slam the door in my face, and even if you did, it's totally fair if you were in the middle of working and needed to kick me out."

"Not at all. I was being a hermit and should have communicated better with you. Also, no matter what I'm doing, you didn't deserve to get a door in the face when you made me freshly baked cookies. Clearly, you don't feel great about it — you don't strike me as the kind of woman who would let anyone see her in a sweatsuit."

He had a point. I was selling myself short if I was telling a man that it was okay to shut the door in my face.

"Well, thanks for your apology," I said, "but it's really okay. The sweatsuit is just because I'm feeling a little stressed out and oversensitive. I'm burned out dealing with Tony and

Mary and all of my emotions lately. I feel like I've spent the past month doing nothing but analyzing my emotions. I thought I'd put Tony and Mary behind me, but their move has made me realize that there's a lot that I've avoided dealing with when I ran away to Pine Lake, and I guess I didn't want to be reminded of it. At the same time, trying to face my past or find any closure has just created *more* problems in my fairly peaceful life, and—"

Graham interrupted me by pulling me in for a hug. He wasn't even hugging me, he just held me tight in a bear hug until he could feel my breath slow and see the tears stop streaming down my cheeks.

"As for your theories — I'd rather spend the whole day listening to your stories about bad luck and conspiracy in Pine Lake than have to listen to people gossiping about me."

We stood in silence in a bear hug for a little longer as Graham gently rubbed my back and I sobbed into his arms. It was like taking an aromatherapy bath — warm, sweet smelling, and comforting like nothing else.

"If I'm ever adding to your stress — or the cause of it — please tell me. I'd rather you say something than hide how you are feeling because it's the 'right' thing to do."

"Honestly? I feel better around you than anyone else in my life. I don't remember the last time I've felt this comfortable."

I stood on my tiptoes and kissed Graham, deeply, for a long time, bathing in his woodsy scent, comforted by the security of his arms.

24

I closed the door as Graham walked away, feeling like I was on cloud nine.

It was only a kiss, but it was a really *good* kiss. I hadn't been kissed like that in years. Not even Tony had kissed me like that.

There was no way I could have a nightmare after a kiss like that.

Turned out, I was wrong. I dreamed that the entire neighborhood was watching our kiss. Some of them cheered, others laughed, and some got violently angry that I had chosen the town weirdo over the town hero.

"How could you?" they shouted as they led a shocked Brian away from my house.

Graham and I had to run to save ourselves from the town mob.

Once again, I woke up in a pool of my own sweat. I was going to have to find a strong sleeping pill, one that would eliminate my dreams altogether.

My only goal that morning was to make myself an

incredibly strong cup of coffee, one that could electrocute me out of my daze so I could get some work done and maybe daydream a little about that kiss.

Barely a drop had fallen into the pot when someone started rapping at my front door. It started delicately enough, but didn't stop and got more and more aggressive the longer I went without answering it.

What could Mary possibly want at this hour?

I stumbled in my half-asleep haze to my front door. I opened the door to see —

"Brian?"

"Laura," Brian said as he brushed past me and stormed into my house.

"Come on in." I yawned as I closed the door and went after him.

"Where is he? Huh? Where is the bastard?" Brian said as he roved around my house, searching for someone who wasn't there.

"Who are you talking about? What are you talking about?" I asked, sleepily following him.

"Graham Silverton. Where is he?" Brian whipped around and headed for the stairs that led to my bedroom.

But I managed to leap ahead before he could go up there. "Graham isn't here."

"He didn't spend the night?"

"No! Why would you think he did?"

"Oh please, Laura. I know he was here and that you've been seeing each other behind my back."

I hadn't told Brian that I was seeing Graham — to be honest, I didn't think he cared. I'd heard from the gossip girls at the Rise N' Grind that he was seeing some other artist, stringing her along while he was dating a pianist in the next town over. I was definitely not the primary object of his affection... right?

"He was here last night, briefly. Why does it matter?" I asked him.

Brian stood in front of me, huffing and puffing and red as a lobster. "It matters because I thought we had something special. And now I find out you're cheating on me with *Graham Silverton*?"

"Brian, I could hardly call it cheating on you." I knew what it was like to be cheated on. I knew what kind of trust had to be built up between the two parties. Brian and I didn't have that. We barely knew each other. "We've had dinner once; we weren't exactly promised to each other." I tried to laugh it off and defuse the situation, but my laughter only seemed to egg Brian on.

"You think this is funny? That my emotions are some kind of game?"

"Well, no. I—"

"So why? Why did you do this, Laura? Why did you cheat on me with Graham Silverton?"

"Can you stop saying his name like that?"

"How am I saying his name?"

"Like he's some kind of pariah. You say his name like you're a duke and he's your stable boy."

"He might as well be."

That really got under my skin. No matter Brian's feelings, there was no reason for him to treat Graham with this amount of disdain. Not only that, I couldn't figure out how he would have known that Graham and I had been out, and especially how Brian would have known that Graham was at my house.

"How did you know he was here?" I asked.

"Don't change the subject. I'm deeply hurt and disgusted that you would betray me like this."

Brian picked the wrong exhausted woman to fight with. I wasn't about to stand around having insults thrown at me. "Betray you how? Need I remind you, *again*, that you and I have only been on one date? Not only that, but I know you've been seeing other people. This town has ears and eyes, especially for its golden boy. I hear about every date you go on from the gossip mill."

"That's different. Those women don't *mean* anything. Besides, it's different for men. We have needs."

"You have needs? What, are those needs somehow different from women's? Do women not crave sex and attention just as much as men?"

"No, they don't. Women shouldn't crave that stuff; it's disgusting."

Now it was my turn to fly into a rage. "Disgusting? What, you think I should be just sitting at home, waiting for you to finally slide your lecherous hands over my body for your own satisfaction, and that's it? Am I just some kind of trophy to you? What's going to happen when you 'have' me? Will I get thrown away into your pile of discards so you can tell the next woman I didn't mean anything to you, meanwhile accusing me of cheating the moment you find out I was with someone else?"

"It's not the—"

"Not the same? Of course it isn't, because if we were to start dating — which, by the way, we aren't — I would just be another possession to you. We all know your possessions mean nothing; just look at Brandy's house. Her body was barely cold before you took it over and renovated it completely, adding it to your little collection in Pine Lake."

"You're being unreasonable and overly emotional — it was just a house. Who cares about a house?"

"The people who live in it, that's who. And the neighbors." I was so angry that my head was spinning. This was too much excitement before my first cup of coffee. I took a deep breath, trying to gather myself and sound as calm as I could under the circumstances.

"Brian," I said, after a moment, "you need to get out of here, right now. We are very different people, and I don't think it's healthy for us to see each other like this. As soon as you step out that door, you will be nothing but my landlord. I'll gather what cash I need to pay off the house, and then you'll just be my real-estate broker. I can guarantee right now that you will not be my boyfriend."

Brian looked like he had steam coming out of his ears. He stared me down and then slowly turned and walked away. I heard the front door close quietly. Somehow, that was more unsettling than when he'd roared into my house at full speed.

I sat with my coffee on the back deck, trying to work through what had just happened. Brian's exit was far too calm for the state he was in, and I worried that there would somehow be repercussions to standing up to him. I didn't know what made me feel that way, but I remembered that I was the most afraid of my father when he was quiet, not when he yelled. And Brian often reminded me of my father.

I still couldn't understand how Brian knew that Graham had come over last night. Graham came by late, long after they could have encountered each other on the road. Maybe a neighbor said something, but there's no way they could have known that Graham's visit was romantic.

Was it possible that Brian was watching me?

25

L*aura, get it together. There's no way Brian is watching you.*
       I repeated that sentence to myself a couple of times, but for some reason, I just couldn't get myself to believe it. How could Brian know that I was dating Graham? Was it just that we lived in a small community? I supposed he could have talked to Mary, who spent enough of her time watching me, and I *had* told her I was dating Graham. Was it possible that Brian had sent Mary to spy on me, and the excuse about becoming friends again was just a cover-up?

Laura, you aren't living in a spy novel.

I thought I was most disturbed by Brian admitting that he thought women shouldn't want to pursue relationships, especially sexual ones. He really thought we were nothing but playthings for his ego, and that was the biggest turn-off for me. Until that moment, Brian had still been different enough from my father that flirting with him seemed ulti-mately harmless. But now I knew for sure that if anything were to get serious, I would be stepping into the same situation that my mother had been in for over twenty years. A trophy, a punching bag, someone who was seen but not heard, whose opinion meant nothing, nor did her feelings. Brian wanted to have his cake and eat it too, and he seemed to have no understanding of why that might not be okay.

If Brian's ego was this overblown in romantic relationships, I wondered how it was with the other townspeople and his tenants. Brian owned half of Pine Lake, and he was the town's mayor and frequently ran unopposed in an election — despite the number of ambitious personalities in the town. I had to get answers from someone who had known him for longer than a few years — someone whose opinion wasn't clouded by flirtation.

I had to catch up on work, but as soon as I felt that I had written enough for one day, I made the trek over to Graham's. My stomach was tumbling, in part because I was constantly looking over my shoulder for who might be following me.

Graham answered the door and ushered me in. I felt like we were having a clandestine meeting, even though we were still two single people who weren't even currently on a date. When had Pine Lake turned into a paranoid circus?

"Is everything all right?" Graham asked, taking my coat and handing me a coffee. "You sounded strange over the phone."

"Yeah, it's... well, no. I'm not all right. Can we sit down?"

Graham nodded and led me to the living room.

I sat back in an armchair and sipped my coffee, trying to decide where I would begin. "Graham," I finally said, "have you talked to Brian Oliver lately?"

"No. Frankly, I try to avoid talking to him as much as I can."

"Really? Why is that?"

Graham shrugged. "Call it a jocks vs. nerds kinda thing. I don't think we've ever gotten along."

"You've known him for a long time, right?"

"We've lived in Pine Lake for almost the same amount of time. I moved here maybe six months before he did. To be honest, I don't know; it's been at least fifteen years."

I nodded. So they weren't friends, I wasn't stepping between anything, and they didn't talk much. "Did you tell him we've been seeing each other?" I hadn't meant to be so blunt about it, but I needed answers, and I didn't want to beat around the bush to get them.

"Well, um... I didn't really know we were going out. I thought you might not be... I thought I'd scared you off and... I wouldn't say anything... don't want to jinx it, you know?" Graham smiled as he stumbled over his words.

"I see. I'm just confused because Brian came over. He was upset because... well, I don't know if I've told you, but I've gone out to dinner with him. Before we officially met. Anyway, he was angry because he found out you and I have been seeing each other. But I haven't even told anyone we'd gone out — in part because I have no one to tell, well, except Mary, who I was trying to get to back off, but also because I've been distracted by the whole Tony and Mary as neighbors thing and didn't want to bring you into that mix."

I was rambling. I felt bad telling Graham about my date with Brian, worried that it would spur a scene like the one with Brian.

Graham sat, nodding along and looking at me like he had something to say, but was hesitant to say it. If he didn't say something soon, I was going to start rambling again and might end up without a boyfriend at the end of it.

"Laura, can I trust you with something?" he finally asked.

I nodded enthusiastically — anything that would explain what was going on.

"You can't tell anyone about it, not yet anyway. I don't think it'll do you any favors in town if you do, especially when it comes to Brian Oliver."

"When it comes to Brian, I am done. He's shown his true colors, and I want nothing to do with him. I just want to know that I can trust the person I'm interested in — which is you. I'm sorry if this seems excessive, it's—"

Graham put up his hand to stop me. "You don't need to explain. I understand. You can trust me."

It was true. I knew that I could trust Graham. He was genuinely charming — not in the "wink and a nod" kind of way that Brian and Tony were so well versed in. Graham was charming in how passionate he was with his hobbies and how honest his gestures were. He didn't go out of his way to hire caterers and champagne for a date, for example. He made a simple apple turnover and then went into great detail about how the lack of humidity up in Pine Lake made it hard for the flour granules to naturally absorb moisture, so it was hard to get a truly flaky crust.

In other words — Graham was a nerd, Brian was a jock, and at the end of the day, the nerds were usually more trustworthy because they had nothing to lose.

"Graham, you can trust me, too."

Graham nodded and reached out his hand. I took it, and he led me into his office.

"It's a little messy in here, but hopefully, it makes sense."

Graham opened the door. His office wasn't much messier than my own, with loose pages of notes floating everywhere, spare pens, and abandoned pen caps all over. To the left was his desk, beneath a window that opened to a gorgeous view of the lake. To the right was a large chalkboard, the kind that was on wheels, so you could flip it and move it around the room. I bookmarked the idea for myself as a good way to keep track of notes and storyboards.

Graham flipped the chalkboard, and I saw why he'd brought me in here.

On the other side of the chalkboard was a corkboard with a tacked-up map of Pine Lake. Over and around the map were photographs, news clippings, letters, and printed-out emails, all tacked up and connected with multiple colors of strings. I knew that there was some kind of organizational system, but for now it looked like... well, it looked like a conspiracy theorist's map of unrealistic conclusions.

"What is this?" I asked cautiously. I was worried about what the answer would be.

"Well, basically, it's a map of how Brian has been manipulating the people of Pine Lake for the past fifteen years for his own personal entertainment."

That was what I was worried about.

"The green thumbtacks are where I think he's set up security cameras around town. I found one of them once, facing a house that he ended up purchasing a month later. Purple thumbtacks are his tenants, and if they're connected by a red string, it means they have some kind of bitter rivalry between them. Some of the rivalries happened over seemingly petty dramas, which escalated due to rumors in town — those have a yellow flag. Some of the rivalries happened *before* those people moved to Pine Lake — similar to you, former rivals or exes who found themselves living next door to each other — those have an orange flag."

I could only sit and stare with my jaw hanging open. What had I got myself involved in?

"I have a list going on the side of people who moved away from town because of those rivalries," Graham continued. "I tried to conduct interviews with each of them, but not everyone got back to me. For the most part, those who moved away wanted nothing to do with Pine Lake once they'd left. The green thumbtacks are mysterious deaths that have occurred, where Brian either bought the house right after they died or was closely involved with them prior to their deaths."

Graham went on, detailing the many ways in which he theorized that Brian had manipulated town members, creating a sort of living soap opera. He had a scrapbook of everyone who'd either moved away or died, and how they were somehow in competition with Brian. There was a slideshow detailing the various methods that Brian likely gathered and disseminated his information — the internet, secret cameras, a gossip network, and potential murders.

The only name I recognized on the list of potential murders was Brandy, and I had to admit that the fact she'd died shortly after having an explosive argument was suspicious. But she'd been fighting with Shelly, not Brian. It made me wonder why Graham wasn't investigating Shelly instead. Did he have a grudge against Brian that clouded his vision?

When Graham initially brought me in here, showed me the board, and told me his theories, I thought they were a little off the wall. How could it be possible? It wasn't like we were living in some spy drama. Then he began to go into detail with a tinge of paranoia, combined with his belief in the supernatural, which created a story in his mind to explain the coincidences in Pine Lake.

The problem was that petty drama and gossip existed in all small towns, and there typically wasn't only one mastermind creating them. It was just people who lived too close together and got annoyed, like families or roommates, but on a bigger scale. Brian might be charismatic, but that didn't make him a lunatic.

He was going so hard on this train of a sociopathic Brian Oliver that I started to think about whether this was maybe a ploy of his own to get me to distrust Brian further. It wouldn't take much, considering that Brian had ruined his chances with me already, but if I believed Graham's theories, it would definitely seal the deal and leave Graham to pick up the pieces.

"Laura? You've been pretty quiet. Are you okay?" Graham asked. He finished his presentation while I spiraled.

"I'm just a little overwhelmed," I said, forcing a smile. "This is a lot to take in."

"I understand that. Do you see what I'm theorizing though, about Brian's obsession with controlling the town and its residents?"

If I was being honest, I didn't. I thought Graham was more than likely making mountains out of molehills. Brian was a narcissistic, opportunistic asshole, but I doubted that he was some puppet master manipulating Pine Lake for his own gain. That was psychotic, and people in real life didn't behave that way. The more I stared at Graham's scrapbook and bulletin board, the more I felt this was just the lonely guy jealous of the outgoing guy's popularity.

However, Graham made some good points. It was strange how situations like my own had happened more than once in Pine Lake — old rivalries and exes coming out of the woodwork and causing problems, which spread throughout the town. I also noticed that there were fewer angry rivalries between the townspeople who weren't Brian's tenants, and whom he often bought up properties from after they were given up under mysterious circumstances.

"Graham, you've clearly been working on this for a while. I feel like I don't even know Pine Lake well enough to understand this map you've created. I don't know the people involved who lived here and left, or who died. I need to just... I need to think about this a little bit."

Graham's face fell. Clearly, he had been nervous to show me his working theory and had been hoping I'd hop aboard, no questions asked.

"I know that you don't, and you're right, I have been working on this for a long time. I was hoping that maybe you'd understand, but..." He trailed off and sighed, running his hand through his hair as he avoided my gaze. "I hope this doesn't make me seem like some crazy shut-in."

I reached out a hand to assure him, placing it on his arm, and waited for him to meet my gaze. "It doesn't, Graham."

His cheek quirked up slightly. Not quite a smile, but almost one for half a second. "It's not like I spend all day staring at it. I just occasionally make an extra point here and there, hoping it'll add up to something." His brow furrowed as he glanced back at the board.

"I believe you."

He turned back to me, and his eyes widened a little. "I'm not crazy, Laura. Please believe me."

"I don't think you're crazy; you're just shaking the foundations of my world a little bit. I came here hoping that you would say you accidentally let it slip while out on a run or something, and instead, you've just told me that I'm basically living in a forty-year-old man's dollhouse."

A genuine smile spread across his face. "Right. That's a good point," Graham said, with a chuckle. "Do you want me to walk you home?"

"No, that's okay. I think I need the time alone to go over everything."

Graham's smile faded as he nodded, but he didn't try to encourage me to let him walk me home.

I stood up, and we walked back to the hallway. Before he closed the door, I glanced back at the map and all the notes connected by string. Was it all coincidence, or could Graham be seeing a pattern where no one else could?

Graham stood awkwardly nearby as I put on my coat and shoes. He stared down at his feet the whole time.

"I guess this is goodbye?" he asked.

I smiled and pulled him in for a long kiss. Even if he was a conspiracy theorist, I still really liked him, and I knew he at least believed what he was telling me. "It's just a 'see you later,'" I whispered.

I walked slowly back to my house, my head spinning with theories and paranoias and second-guessing my every thought or move. I truly didn't know what to think, and even though I did trust Graham not to hurt me, I wasn't sure I could trust his judgment on this issue, so then whom could I trust? I hadn't the faintest idea.

All I really knew was that my rose-colored glasses where Pine Lake was concerned were broken beyond repair.

26

The stress of the past few months had me feeling more alone than ever, and after Graham's revelation, I didn't feel as comfortable going over there. Not that he was somehow dangerous, but I knew he would ask what I thought about his theories, and I still didn't have an answer. I honestly couldn't decide if they were paranoid, manipulative, or the truth, and I knew I couldn't ask for clarification without getting Graham's hopes up.

So I turned to Celene. I felt more comfortable telling her about my potentially paranoid boyfriend than I did telling my therapist. I convinced her to come, promising that we would do sunrise yoga on my back deck, and that I would watch every sunrise with her while she was here. It wouldn't be too hard, I hadn't been sleeping very well, so I was usually up for the sunrise anyway. Might as well enjoy it with a friend.

Celene and I wandered through town, going into the small boutiques to sniff candles and stare at the beautiful, handcrafted vases. True to her positive nature, Celene was very into crafting as a hobby.

"Making things with my hands relaxes me," she said as she turned a rustic clay mug over in her hands. "You ought to try it sometime; you definitely have the space."

I shook my head. "The smell of hot glue just doesn't do it for me."

"You could paint watercolors or gouache. You could mold air-dry clay, or you could even paint figurines. Your nerdy boyfriend might love that," she said, winking at me.

I elbowed her in the side and made a "zip it" motion with my fingers. I didn't want one of Brian's "little birdies" to hear and tell him I was going around calling Graham my boyfriend. Brian had started his usual cycle of apology — a bouquet of flowers each day, the occasional bottle of organic wine at night — and while I wasn't interested in dating him, I was hoping to stay on his good side by keeping my relationship with Graham as ambiguous as possible.

Celene dutifully zipped her mouth and glanced around to make sure no one heard. We quickly paid for the mug and got out of there before Celene said anything else. We giggled as we left the store, as if we were teenagers talking about high school crushes, and didn't even see Shelly Blaze, Brian's devoted, yet perpetually bored assistant, almost crashing into us.

"Oh my gosh! Michelle Blanchet, what are you doing up here?" Celene exclaimed, grabbing Shelly by the arm.

Michelle *Blanchet*? Did Celene and Shelly somehow know each other? Was Michelle her actual first name? I was completely confused.

"Oh, Celene! Hi." Shelly blinked at us. "I'm just, um... visiting."

"That's so funny; I'm visiting too. This is my friend Laura," she said, gesturing to me. "I think I've told you about her."

"Yeah, I think you have," Shelly muttered and stared at her feet. For some reason, she wouldn't look me in the eye.

"We've met, actually," I said, "but mostly we've just talked on the phone. How are you, Shelly?"

She just smiled at Celene, keeping her gaze on her, and ignored me altogether. "Sorry I haven't answered your messages about the group. It's been kinda crazy around here."

She could say that again. I stared at her, wondering why the hell she was acting like this was normal behavior. What was going on with her? Why was she treating me as if I were invisible?

"Oh, that's totally fine," Celene said as she looked from Shelly to me. "I didn't realize that you two had met. Michelle told me she just moved to a small town from the city after a breakup, and I told her that my friend had done the same thing and that she should look you up. I didn't realize you two had already crossed paths, let alone lived in the same small town." Celene laughed and glanced back to Shelly. "Michelle, do you want to join us? I think we're gonna grab some ice cream."

Shelly muttered something under her breath and ran away. It was very odd behavior, even from Shelly, who was often pretty spaced out.

Celene and I watched her scuttle away and looked at each other.

"That was weird," I said.

"Yeah. Very weird — I didn't know you knew Michelle."

"I didn't know *you* knew Shelly," I responded as I tried to process what just happened. "How do you know her?"

"We met online through this crafting community. She said she was getting into crafts as a therapeutic thing after a breakup, and I was saying how I've been *trying* to get you into the crafting game for years, but that you decided to run away to an idyllic mountain town instead."

"Did she introduce herself as Michelle Blanchet to you? How well do you know her?" I asked.

"Yeah, isn't that her name? And not very well, to be honest. We chat occasionally, and she's been in a few virtual knitting nights — that's how I recognized her. She usually pops her head up when she needs some advice about her ex, and you know how craft ladies get. Any time a chicklet needs help, us mother hens are there to pick her up."

It was such a bizarre coincidence. I knew absolutely nothing about Shelly, so who was to say some of that wasn't true? All I knew was that she had worked for Brian for years, first as a virtual assistant, and then she became a permanent fixture in his office.

"Well, first of all, I know her as Shelly Blaze. And she definitely didn't move to town recently because she's Brian's assistant," I corrected Celene. "Shelly's been here longer than I have. She was here when I was negotiating with Brian over the house, and that's been two years now."

"Really? Okay, that's very strange. Maybe she is thinking of moving again, or didn't want to say too much to a bunch of strangers on the internet?"

"Maybe, but the name thing... that's really odd. Why change her name?"

"Again, it's the internet; maybe she was trying to be anonymous?"

I supposed that was possible; still, it had me wondering. "What have you told her about me?"

Celene froze on the spot and stared at me. "I don't know. I guess I did tell her a lot of surface information."

I drew in a sharp breath. "Like what?"

Celene cringed. "I know I told her you moved to Pine Lake after you got cheated on. And I might have said that Tony was an asshole who deserved to live in a dumpster. I think I might have told her about your mom and how she still talks to Tony." She blew out a breath and sighed. "Look, it's not like I gave the girl your social security number or anything."

"Geez, Celene, you may as well have. Don't you see that she's probably feeding all of that information to Brian?"

"No, I don't. At least I didn't at the time. I had no idea she *knew* Brian until now. You know how those groups are, Laura. We just sit around knitting or painting or whatever and talk about our lives. I talked about myself, and obviously, I talked about my best friend. Especially to someone who, I thought, was going through something similar."

I realized I had grabbed Celene's arm. I stared into her eyes, searching for the truth. Celene looked genuinely afraid of me. It must have been how I looked after Graham showed me his manifesto. I knew Celene only had the best intentions, and she was right: I had never talked about Shelly. So how was she to know that the woman she knew as Michelle Blanchet was really Shelly Blaze, a fellow Pine Lake resident?

I let go of Celene's arm, and she rubbed it with her hand.

"Sorry, Celene."

"That's okay. It hurt a little, but I'm more concerned about you. Are you okay?"

I shook my head. I wasn't okay, and I wasn't sure that Celene could help.

I went over to Brian's office the following Monday. He had left a bag of tools at my house when he came by to install the coat hooks, and I had been avoiding returning it. I went in the middle of the day, hoping everyone would be out to lunch and I could just leave it by the door with a note because I really didn't like going into his office. He displayed his paintings on the walls, and it often creeped me out seeing them.

When I arrived, I saw Shelly sitting at her desk, staring out the window. I wanted to run off, but she saw me and waved cheerfully, so I felt duty-bound to go inside.

"Hi, Shelly," I said. "How was the rest of your weekend?"

"My weekend was fine; I bought a gorgeous new mug for Brian. His was getting so stained from coffee. How was your weekend?"

"It was great. So nice to see Celene — I had no idea you knew her," I said, dropping the tools on her desk as I avoided looking up at the images on the walls.

"Who?" she asked, staring blankly at the bag.

"Celene. Celene Shelby?"

"I don't know her. Are you confusing her name with my name? I'm Shelly." She smiled vacantly, it must be nice to have so little flowing through your brain, but I had to wonder if it was all an act.

"Celene said you know each other from a crafting forum, and that you've chatted."

Shelly's eyes twitched, and she started drumming her fingers on the desk. "I don't spend my days crafting online; that's very weird." She turned back to the bag, setting her hand on top of them like I might try to take them back. "These are Brian's tools."

The way she was acting was incredibly peculiar. "Yes, I know. He left them at my house, and I was just returning them."

A cloud passed over Shelly's face, and the room grew colder as her attitude toward me got icier. "Oh. Good that you brought them back, since they aren't yours. They're Brian's tools."

"Yes. That's why I brought them—" I cut myself off, not wanting this bizarre conversation to go any further. "Can you just apologize to him for me? I meant to bring them back sooner, but kept forgetting."

"Sure. Is there anything else?" Shelly asked, putting the bag away under her desk.

I hesitated for a moment, then said, "Do you really not remember running into me this weekend? With Celene?"

Shelly gazed up at me and pressed her lips together like she was about to explode into a rage. She breathed heavily through her nose and then tucked a strand of blonde hair behind her ear. "I don't remember running into you this weekend at all. My life is very busy, you know. I don't remember everyone I see. You and your friend must have run into someone else."

"But she called you Michelle." Which I knew was her proper name.

Her eyes flicked at the name, and I knew she was lying about having run into us. I just didn't know why. "I don't know what to tell you; that wasn't me you saw. I'll tell Brian his tools are here, thanks." She smiled in a way that made me feel very unwelcome.

Shelly acted like a space cadet, but something made me think she was much smarter than I had given her credit for.

The interaction with Shelly was just strange. *I don't think I've ever been so confused in my life, and somehow doubting my own reality.*

I called Celene on my way home and got her voicemail — probably better this way.

"Hi, Cece, it's me. I need to talk to you about Shelly again. It's just that... I had a really weird conversation with her. Can you call me back? Thanks. Love you. Bye."

I needed to get to the bottom of this. All of a sudden, it was getting too real — and too surreal at the same time.

27

I was fixing dinner when my phone rang. Thinking it was Celene, I leaped out of the kitchen to pick it up. "Celene?"

"Laura?" It was a man's voice at the other end of the line, so quiet I could barely hear him.

"Who is this?" I whispered.

"It's Graham. Are you busy?"

"No, I was just making dinner. Why are you whispering?"

There was silence on the other end of the line, some shuffling, and then I heard a door close. Graham cleared his throat. "Can you still hear me?" he asked, at normal volume this time.

"Yes, I can hear you just fine. Graham, what's going on?"

"Well, um... I'm not sure how to tell you this." He sighed, and I could almost see his brow furrowing through my cell phone.

"What is it? You have me worried."

"Mary's here. At my house."

"Doing what?" I demanded. What could Mary possibly be doing at Graham's? What would she want from him — unless... "Graham? Are you still there?"

"Yes, I am." Graham was very uncomfortable; it was clear in his voice. What wasn't clear was the reason why. "Mary's here, and she's, um... wearing a very sexy dress."

I'd never heard a man sound so guilty.

"Did you invite her over?" I asked.

"What? No!" Graham raised his voice, and he cut himself off. When he came back on the line, he was whispering again, "No, I would never do that to you. I've never spoken to her, that's why I was so confused when she appeared — I didn't even know that she knew me or where I lived."

"Graham, is she just sitting in your house right now?"

"Not anymore."

"Start from the beginning, please. I just don't understand what is going on."

"Neither do I," he said. "She showed up here about an hour ago, wearing a very short, revealing dress and high heels. When I opened the door, she tried to kiss me, saying stuff about how she's been thinking about my hands on her body since she saw us on the hike. I pushed her away and told her that this was inappropriate, and she needed to go home. She looked kind of confused and then giggled and said, 'No one says no to this dress,' and then tried to kiss me again. I told her she had to leave, that this wasn't right, so I took her by the arm and led her outside."

"But, Graham, that was an hour ago. Why are you whispering now?"

"She's out on my lawn. I'm hiding in my office."

I couldn't help but giggle at the thought of a man of

Graham's stature crouched in his office and hiding from Mary, who must have been less than half his height.

"I already threatened to call the police, but she ignored me. She's out there dancing."

"Is she playing any music?"

"I don't think so. I'm a little afraid of her, actually."

I was furious with Mary, but a little delighted with Graham. My heart swelled at the fact that he had called me to tell me Mary was trying to seduce him. Mary was gorgeous. She had a smile that would make any man or woman blush, so his nervousness was totally justified. The thought that he'd rejected her in favor of my feelings made me feel like I was on cloud nine. How strange that it made me feel special to *not* get cheated on.

"Graham, call the police. They might take a while, but they'll get her home safely, and then you won't have to deal with her."

I'll deal with her for you, I thought.

"Okay, that sounds like a good idea. I'm gonna wait in my office until I hear them come."

"You don't have to. You can just go about your business; she can't hurt you from outside."

"That's certainly true. I'll hang up and call the police, then. I just wanted to let you know because I—" Graham cut himself off again. I could hear him taking a deep breath. "I like you, Laura. I don't want to jeopardize what we have."

"Thank you, Graham."

We hung up. I went to my back deck and waited for Mary to come home.

It took almost two hours before I saw the police cruiser drive up to Mary's house and help her up the walkway. She was sipping from a bottle of water, carrying her heels in her hands. I saw her brush the officers away and pull a spare key out from under a rock — I guessed Tony was away for the night. The police made sure she made it inside, and then they returned to their cruiser and drove away.

I stormed out of my front door and made a beeline for Tony and Mary's. Two could play this game, Mary Casden. I strode up to the door and battered it with my fist.

"I'm coming, I'm coming, jeez," Mary said, her words slurring a little bit. She opened the door, and her eyes widened when she saw it was me. "Hi! Laura! It's a party, come on in!" she said, waving me into the house and stumbling to the living room. Mary flopped down onto a couch. Clearly, she had been drinking for at least a few hours.

"Mary, what are you doing?"

"I'm sitting on the couch. What?" She hiccupped.

"I know you went to Graham's house."

"Who's Graham?"

"My boyfriend. You know him: twice as tall as you are, black hair, brown eyes, enjoys *hiking*?"

"I don't know who you're talking about." She reached for a short whiskey glass, but I bounded over and swiped the glass before she could get to it. Mary almost fell flat on her face trying to grab it out of my hand.

"No fair, you're taller."

"Mary, you're wasted."

"Whatever, Laura. You're just a prude."

"I'm not falling for that trap. I don't care if you're drunk. I'd just prefer it if you didn't go out of your way, and risk spraining an ankle, to seduce my boyfriend. You two have nothing in common, and he's clearly not interested in you."

"You're delusional. I'm not interested in your weird magic mountain man."

"Then why were you at his house *throwing yourself* at him earlier, hmm? Why did he have to call the cops to bring you home?"

"That didn't happen."

"Is that really what you're going with?" I was fuming. All the sympathy I had accumulated for Mary flew out the window. I didn't know why she was drunk, and frankly, I didn't care. She wasn't going to steal another boyfriend from me, and I was not going to give up my life in Pine Lake.

"It didn't happen. You're just paranoid because you *know* Graham would be way more interested in me than he *ever* would be in you." Mary squinted her eyes and swayed on the couch.

I was sure that this scene was playing out very differently in her mind.

"Fine," I said. "I'll take it up with Tony when he gets back. I'm sure he'd be happy to know all about your visit to Graham."

Mary immediately sobered up. "Don't tell Tony, please. He's going to get so *mad*. Which is stupid because it's not as if he doesn't cheat, but to him it's like this big... this... weird... it's a thing." She was spinning on the couch, trying to find the words, but was dead serious. "He's not dangerous or anything. I mean, I can deal with Tony. But I don't want to." Mary dropped her head in her hands and started sobbing.

Her reaction caught me off guard. I didn't know what to say.

"Tony left me alone, and I got paranoid and angry," Mary continued. "I still don't have my medication. They keep going *missing* somewhere, and now Tony's all mad again and just like... please don't tell him." She looked up at me, and her gaze was so pathetic that I couldn't be mad anymore.

I went to the kitchen and poured the whiskey down the sink. By the time I came back to the living room, Mary was snoring into the couch cushions. I covered her with a blanket and left.

28

M y head was spinning, and there was no sign of it stopping.

I needed to make a list. Sometimes, when it felt like my life was spinning out of control and I didn't know which pieces of it to put together, I made a list. Kind of like a to-do list, but rather than putting my tasks in order, it was putting my thoughts in order so I could start to understand them.

1. Brian was not the man I thought he was.

This didn't have to extend to Graham's theories; it boiled down to Brian's behavior. When I first met him, Brian had seemed like a charming, intelligent man with a deep love for the community in Pine Lake. I honestly couldn't understand why a guy like him was single — even said so, more than once.

The more I got to know him, the more I realized that the

charm was a veil for manipulation, and the intelligence was proof of how controlling he could be. If you peeled back the layers of Brian's charming veneer, you got a narcissist with an ego that would never make room for caring about another person. No matter how good he was at flirting, and how much chemistry we had, I knew Brian was not the person who would make me happy.

2. *Graham's theories.*

I still didn't know what to think about this. If I wanted to jump into the paranoid side of my brain, it made sense. Pine Lake constantly had *drama* going on. For the residents who loved to gossip, it was a source of perpetual entertainment that someone was always arguing with their neighbor about something.

I thought back to a few months ago when two neighbors had been fighting over who poisoned the other's lawn — it went unresolved, and now the two barely spoke. If you were close with one house, you could not be close with the other. They drew lines in the sand, and everyone who knew them had to pick a side. Drama like that didn't happen in other small towns, not the way it did in Pine Lake.

His theories did make sense in a way. The question was, could they be accurate, but also wrong? Was it possible that he had the wrong suspect in mind when it came to who was causing all the drama? Who was manipulating everything? After my most recent conversation with Shelly, I was really starting to wonder if she might be the one behind everything. After all, she had been arguing with Brandy before she suddenly died.

3. Tony and Mary.

Tony and Mary were a mess, and it was best I just stayed out of it.

To my delight, the past few days had been fairly peaceful. Tony came home, and he and Mary had been living in relative bliss. I kept my promise not to say anything, and in return, Mary cheerfully greeted me like nothing had happened between us and we were still on the road to being civil neighbors. The flowers from Brian kept coming, except now, he'd started hand-delivering them. Every time he came by, he found a reason to come inside and ask me to dinner. Every time I said no, I had to come up with more and more creative excuses because for some reason, Brian just couldn't take "no" for an answer.

I had just ushered Brian out of my house for the third time in as many days when my phone rang. My plan was to go back to my list, trying to parse what was true and what was false, but I noticed it was Graham calling. I remembered that I hadn't apologized to him for Mary's behavior, or checked to see if he was okay, so I answered.

"Graham, I'm so sorry I haven't called. I've been meaning to—"

"Mary came by a minute ago wearing nothing but a bathrobe," Graham interrupted. "She just stood on the porch and, uh... dropped it. Before I could say anything, a guy came running up the path screaming, and then Mary started screaming, so I slammed the door and locked it. The screaming got quieter, so I think they've gone back down the path." He took a moment to catch his breath. "I just wanted to warn you, in case that was Tony and you're next on his list."

It was like someone had slapped me across the face and said, "Smile! You're on our hidden camera show!" I didn't know whether to laugh, scream, hide, or do all three. Tony and Mary were listed as "stay away." I had avoided thinking about them so I could stop myself from acting on any impulse I had to investigate the motivations behind their actions.

The motivations were always toxicity, and getting involved just gave me a headache, nightmares, and panic attacks. I ought to have listened to Dr. Delgado in the first place and just moved away from Pine Lake with no forwarding address. Maybe even changed my name so they couldn't find me.

Tony and Mary arrived home about an hour after my phone call with Graham. It definitely wasn't an hour-long walk, so I assumed they stopped to either make out or scream at each other. I stayed hidden in the house, reading a book and pretending I didn't exist. Someone knocked on my door at one point, but I ignored them.

Turned out it was Brian, trying to coax me out on a date, but I could think of nothing worse than getting caught in the middle of Tony, Mary, *and* Brian.

Hiding from the couple didn't stop me from hearing them. They were screaming at each other so loudly that I could make out their argument even though my windows were closed. The gist of it was that Tony accused Mary of cheating on him, and Mary denied it. She then turned the argument around on Tony and listed the names of the women she *knew* he had slept with since they'd got to Pine Lake. If her list was correct, Tony had been putting in the work to get around. He might even be more prolific than Brian.

Tony called Mary paranoid and crazy — which I found unfair. As an impartial listener, I thought Tony should at least take into account the fact that Mary was unwillingly off her medication. Mary called Tony delusional, claiming again that he'd moved them to Pine Lake so he could try to get me back. That brought them back to the top of their weird cyclical argument. I cringed every time I heard my name, which, unfortunately, came up a lot. I decided to put on headphones to drown them out. It was getting late anyway, and I needed to go to bed.

An hour or so later, there was banging at my door so violent that I thought it might be an earthquake. I knew it was probably the demonic duo, and at first, I thought I could ignore it.

But a minute later, both of them were on their deck, screaming at me to open my front door.

"Hi, guys," I said, meeting them on my porch. "How's your night?"

Behind them, our neighbors had stopped pretending they weren't watching. People had stopped on the street or were watching with glasses of wine and cans of beer from their windows. Great.

"Did Mary try to seduce your boyfriend?" Tony demanded.

"Did Tony try to sleep with you when we came over for dinner?" Mary interrogated.

I just looked between them, unsure of whom to answer first.

"Laura, I already caught Mary showing up to your lumberjack's house in nothing but a bathrobe. Unless they're having an affair *already*, then she's on a mission to steal your boyfriend."

"Well, you probably know a lot about that. I think you can judge the situation for yourself," I said.

Mary snorted. "See, Tony? You can't exactly be trusted."

"Mary, maybe now isn't the time to get up on your high horse," I said. "You are right though. Tony did try to sleep with me that night you guys came over for dinner, and that was why I asked you two to leave."

"Hah!" Mary screamed and pointed a finger in Tony's face. "You're no better than me, are you?"

"Right. You are *both* determined to ruin my life," I said.

They turned and gave me a look like *I* was somehow the villain.

I held my hands up in surrender. "Listen, I don't want anything to do with this. Whatever this argument is, it's between the two of you. Yes, I am dating Graham. Yes, Mary has tried to seduce him twice now, and yes, Tony tried to get me to sleep with him. Do whatever you want with that information, but please make sure to do it *off* my lawn, or I will call the cops."

With that, I slammed the door in their faces. I didn't feel bad or guilty, and I didn't second-guess my decision. I had closed the door on two toxic people and walked away from it.

They did the same. I could hear them yelling as they walked across my lawn and back into their house. It was far too easy to track Tony and Mary via their argument. I could hear them as well as I'd been able to hear Brandy and Shelly arguing a while back. It was muffled but still loud. I put my headphones back on and went upstairs.

As soon as my head hit the pillow, the headphones beeped and turned off. I had forgotten to charge them, and the battery was dead. All I could hear was Tony and Mary, who still had the energy to keep going after hours of screaming at each other.

I fell asleep listening to their argument, hoping that something would happen to end this toxic cycle.

29

I had a hangover the next morning. I knew for a fact that I wasn't the only one who felt that way.

As I dragged myself to the Rise N' Grind, I could see neighbors in their hoodies and robes, struggling to take out trash bins and do gardening in the morning sun. Tony and Mary's fight had gone on into the early hours of the morning, and I imagined that some of my neighbors had hosted an afterparty.

No one felt very good, least of all me. I got a lot of sympathetic stares on my walk to the coffee shop, which I used as my office. Even the tech bros who were regulars had heard about the fight.

"I hear you really put them in their place. Good on you," Tod said as he handed me my coffee. "This first one's on me. I know you might need it this morning." He winked. Tod was probably at one of the gossip afterparties and was nursing a hangover himself. Not that you'd ever know: he was far too young to feel that sort of thing.

"Thanks, Tod," I said as I went to the small table that

faced the wall. The fewer people I saw today, the better. I had charged my headphones overnight so I could be sure they would last me the whole day.

After days of thinking about nothing except my problems and the dramatic coincidences plaguing Pine Lake, I was ready to get back to work. Andrea Caldwell had finally disposed of her cheating husband, but she was on the verge of getting caught. I wanted to get the climax of the novel finished today so I could give my editor a positive progress update.

Before I even opened my computer, I felt a heavy hand land on my shoulder. Brian had found me the second I was out in public.

"I must have some kind of radar on me," I joked.

Brian didn't laugh; he just gave me another sympathetic stare. "I heard about what happened last night. I wanted to come over and apologize, again. I wish I had known—"

"It's fine," I said, cutting him off. "Honestly, you couldn't have known, could you?" I tried to bore my eyes into his skull to find out the truth — had Shelly told Brian to rent the house to Tony and Mary after learning about them from Celene? Was she the real reason they'd moved to Pine Lake? I wanted to ask him, but I wondered if he'd tell me. Did he suspect it was Shelly who was causing all this drama in town? If he did, why did he keep her on staff? It didn't make any sense.

I didn't get any answers to my unasked questions, but I did receive an awkward hug.

"I think I've figured out a way to make it up to you."

I inwardly cringed. "Is it dinner, again?"

He shook his head. "I'm going camping this weekend — in an RV, nothing too rustic — to bathe in the mountain springs at the Sequoia Spring Park. Why don't you come with me? The natural heat will relax your muscles, and the purified water will help with dehydration. You're obviously stressed out and not sleeping, because your hair is thin, and your skin is a little sallow."

Thanks for your concern about my sallow skin, Brian, but I think I'll pass.

A weekend away where I couldn't get rid of Brian was exactly what I *didn't* need. Besides, I was pretty sure I was already in a relationship with Graham, and I wouldn't go away with anyone else, let alone Brian, while I was involved with someone. That would make me as bad as Tony.

"I don't think so." I smiled up at him as brightly as I could. "Maybe you could take another one of the ladies on your roster."

Brian's face froze. He could not compute. Brian was the jock who always got the girl. He was not the guy who got rejected, and he did not understand how to deal with this.

"I need to get back to—"

"I'm offering you a trip to an expensive hot springs spa, and you don't want to come?"

"Yes." I sighed. "I don't feel well, and I don't think I'm going to be feeling better by this weekend. I want to relax and unwind, but I need to do it alone, not with someone who... will be expecting me to chat and be charming."

I wanted to tell him that not only was I already seeing someone but also that I couldn't relax and unwind with someone I didn't trust. However, a little voice in the back of my mind told me it was best not to play those cards just yet. Brian was too emotionally volatile, like my father was, and I knew I had to be careful what I said to him, or I'd wind up in a stalker — well, more of a stalker — situation than I already was with him.

"Fine," Brian said, cooling suddenly. "I'll take someone else who appreciates being pampered."

"Have fun," I said as I pulled on my headphones.

Brian blinked at me and backed away.

The man truly could not compute rejection.

EARLY THE NEXT MORNING, Graham called. "Laura, I truly hate to bother you, but I need your help." He sounded desperate.

"What's happened?" I asked, suddenly concerned.

"I'm in jail."

"What? Why?"

"Mary was murdered. And I'm the prime suspect."

30

M ary was dead. It was a strange feeling. I remembered the day Brandy died, how I'd broken down and cried in the middle of my lawn. I had barely known her, but her peaceful nature had informed the first two years I lived in Pine Lake.

With Mary, all I felt was shock. Up until three years ago, Mary had been a huge part of my life. She had been there for every milestone and every accomplishment. It was why I'd chosen her to be my maid of honor. Though it didn't seem that way from her recent behavior, there had been a time when Mary was my biggest cheerleader. To know that she had been murdered, and that our last conversation was during an all-out brawl between her and Tony, made me feel numb inside. I sat on the back deck, staring at her house, waiting for her to come outside and for this to be nothing but another nightmare.

Instead of waking up from a nightmare, I had to go and pick my boyfriend up from jail. Mary had been found in Graham's yard, so he was obviously the investigation's prime suspect. He'd managed to bail himself out and find a lawyer, who was pretty confident everything would be fine.

As I drove Graham home, he told me what had happened. A runner had found Mary that morning. A fallen tree was in the runner's usual path, so she took a different route where the houses were shrouded by trees. When she stopped on a hill to catch her breath, she glimpsed Mary's blonde hair — in stark contrast to the underbrush that was hastily thrown on top of her. Her body was at an odd angle, like she had been picked up and dropped on the spot. The worst part was that she was found in Graham's yard, just under a window.

When the police went to break the news to Tony, he slammed the door in their faces. They rang the doorbell again, this time asking him to go with them. Someone told the cops about the hours-long fight he'd had with Mary, so they wanted to bring him in on suspicion as well. He'd punched that police officer in the nose, which would likely lead to additional charges.

"Laura, I swear it wasn't me," Graham said as we arrived at his house.

I didn't say anything. I just stared at the spot in his yard where they'd found her. Police tape wrapped around trees, and evidence markers poked out of the ground.

"She kept coming over. For three nights, I heard banging at my door, and if I looked out the window, it was always Mary. One night, she brought a bottle of champagne and sat on my deck drinking it, taunting me from outside. That night, I didn't answer the door. I figured she'd get tired and go home—"

"Graham, please stop," I said, turning to him and putting a finger over his lips. "I don't think you killed Mary. But I do need you to stop talking about her like that. You don't" — I winced — "*didn't* know her like I did. You only knew her for a moment. I would argue that you knew her in her *worst* moment. Right now, I don't want to remember her that way, okay?"

Graham nodded, and I moved my finger. He gave me a kiss on the forehead and stepped out of the car, then bent down and looked at me. "If there's anything I can do, please don't hesitate to ask."

I tried to smile, but I think it came out looking like a grimace. I watched Graham go inside, trying to avoid all the police tape as he did. When his door closed, I drove home.

Tony came by later that night. It took him a little longer to be released on bail, since he had assaulted a police officer. I found out later that his lawyer had managed to get them to drop the assault charges, on account of Tony being "overwhelmed with grief." I was sitting on my back deck with a glass of wine, which was getting warm as I stared out at the lake. My mind was finally empty. I guessed it didn't take Brian's hot springs to get my mind to stop reeling; all that needed to happen was the brutal murder of my ex-best friend.

Tony appeared on his deck and waved at me. "Mind if I join you?"

In that moment, I thought it might be okay. Tony was the only person who knew Mary as well as I did, so I thought he would be best equipped to help me process the shock.

I let him in, and we walked out to the back deck.

"I had to tell her mom from jail," he said. "She was my one phone call."

"Does she think you did it?"

Tony shrugged. "Of course. But her mom never liked me very much."

"Yeah, her mom was always a bit of a snob," I said.

We clinked glasses and laughed.

"*Mrs.* Casden felt that her precious daughter would end up with a banker or a prince or something. Not an architect turned web developer, whose job she couldn't explain to her high-society friends."

"She only ever liked me because of my dad. Once I made it clear that *the* William Whitmore wasn't going to be turning up at any society function that I attended, I was straight onto her blacklist."

We both laughed. Mary's mother could give anyone psychosis within a few minutes of meeting her. She was the snobbiest woman I had ever met — and I grew up around New England WASPs. When Mary and I first became friends, we bonded over how our uptight mothers had given us anxious tendencies and trauma from dealing with narcissists. I laughed thinking about Mary's uncanny mimicking of her mother, how she was able to make it seem like she was clutching an *actual* set of pearls even though there was nothing around her neck.

That was the thought that made me break down.

I bent over, crying a very ugly cry. My mouth was open, and I just started howling as tears slowly streamed down my face.

Tony came over and wrapped his arms around me, pulling me upright and nestling my face in his neck. "It's gonna be okay. You're going to remember the best parts of her," he said as he rubbed my back.

I moved away, and Tony slowly caressed my arms. I froze to the spot as his hand traced over my shoulder and

neck, up to my lips, where he pulled my chin closer to him
—

Wait — *what is he doing?*

I grabbed my wineglass and brought it down on Tony's head, kicking him backward as I did. "Tony, what the *fuck* are you doing?" I screamed.

"What am *I* doing? You just smashed a glass on my head! I could need stitches."

"You're fine. Whatever's wrong with you isn't on the surface, that's for sure."

"What is *that* supposed to mean?"

"Mary's barely in the morgue, and you're trying to shove your tongue down my throat." I pushed him toward the door. I wanted him out of my house — *now.*

"Laura, you don't understand. I regretted being with Mary from the moment it happened; you just wouldn't listen to me when I tried to reason with you. But now that Mary's out of the picture—"

"They found her body this morning. How *dare* you say she's 'out of the picture.'"

"But now we can bond. We were bonding. I could feel it between us, you know — you wanted it."

I took Tony by the arm and threw him out the door and onto the lawn. "Tony, you can take that bond straight to hell. Don't you *ever* come near me again."

"You can say that, but you'll change your mind. Laura, we're meant for each other."

"You aren't meant for anyone but a garbage pickup!" I shouted and slammed the door in his face. That was when I started to really cry. I hadn't ever felt that alone in my entire life.

I spent all of Sunday either in my bed or on my couch. It

was all starting to sink in. I started to receive phone calls from former friends who were finally apologizing for ever believing Mary, and people who still thought I was evil, but deserved to be consoled, nonetheless. I let their voicemails play out. I didn't even answer when Celene called.

The only productive thing I did was email Dr. Delgado to make an appointment for the next day. I knew for a fact that I would need the impartial advice. That, and he also might be able to help me sort through all of the conspiracies I was embroiled in.

Late on Sunday, my doorbell rang. I immediately assumed it was Tony, so I just went up to the door and told him to go straight to hell.

"Well, *that* wasn't the greeting I was expecting."

It was Brian. Brian who had been on a weekend vacation at a hot spring with some woman, and who probably hadn't heard that his tenant had died. I opened the door, and there he was, with a bouquet of flowers, of course, and a bag of artisanal bath salts.

"You look like you've been through hell," he said.

"Mary died," I blurted out.

"Mary who?"

"Mary Casden. My neighbor? My ex-best friend, your tenant? She died."

Brian blinked at me like he didn't believe it. It was probably how I'd looked all day on Saturday.

I led him inside and sat him down on my little hallway bench. I took the flowers and the bath salts out of his hand and left them on the floor by my shoes. "Brian, are you okay?"

He nodded. "What happened to her?"

I hedged my reply, not wanting to tell him I knew what

happened. "I don't know exactly. Someone hurt her." I frowned, wondering who could have strangled her. I doubted it was Tony, and I knew it wasn't Graham. Could it have been Shelly? If Graham's conspiracy board was right about all the manipulation and the deaths, then she was certainly capable — of course, Graham thought it was Brian who was behind it all, but he'd been out of town...

"Where did they find her?" he asked, breaking through my spiraling thoughts.

I hesitated to tell him the truth. I didn't want to implicate Graham any further, and telling Brian anything basically meant that you were telling the whole town. I didn't want to start a game of broken telephone featuring Mary's strangled body under Graham's window.

"I don't know," I said. "A runner found her, so it wasn't at home."

Brian looked at me curiously. He could probably tell I was lying, and I didn't have the energy to persuade him that it was the truth. What did it matter what I said? He would have to talk to Tony at some point, and Tony had absolutely no problem throwing Graham under the bus.

"How are you feeling, Laura?" he asked.

"Numb. She was my best friend for a long time."

"I'm glad I brought you some bath salts. It seemed like a relaxing gesture, and you can use it now more than ever."

"That may be true, but I can't accept a gift like that. Thank you, though." I picked up the flowers and gifts and handed them back to Brian.

He used my hand to help himself up, then wrapped himself around me, the bath salts and flowers hitting my back, and nuzzled my neck.

I pushed him off and backed away, mentally thinking

about the nearest pointy object I could threaten him with if he came any closer. "I don't need a hug from you, especially not one like that."

"I didn't mean to— oh God, I'm so sorry, you must think I'm a creep," Brian said, taking a step toward me. "I promise that I just wanted to give you a hug and offer my creature comforts. Let me draw you a bath, maybe pour some wine. You deserve it after everything Mary has put you through."

Was there something in the water in Pine Lake? This was turning into a zombie movie, where all the men were motivated by sex, and they were using death to get it.

"Brian, you have to leave before I kick you out of here," I said, pointing at the door. "I have had enough unwanted attention from friends back home trying to console me. The last thing I need is a bath and whatever you are calling your 'creature comforts.'"

Brian put his hands up in surrender. "Fine, I get it. You're in shock, and you want to be alone right now. I personally would never want to be alone when my 'best friend' died, but okay, to each their own." He stepped back and walked out the door with the gifts I refused. "You be careful, Laura," he said as he closed the door behind him.

Yes, I would be careful, careful of the creeps who thought your former best friend dying was a good time to hit on you.

31

I had tried calling Graham a few times, but he wasn't answering his phone. It was pretty unusual for the fairly steady man, so I decided to go over there and see if he was okay. It couldn't be comfortable living next to a crime scene, with state police traipsing in and out of your home, questioning your every move on a night you probably don't remember because it was so boring. I should know, I'd written that scene many times before and was in the middle of writing it again now.

> *Andrea Caldwell stared at the yellow tape enrobing her husband's car. The police officer had just asked her, again, where she had been that night. Her alibi was airtight, there was no reason for anyone to suspect her, but she froze when faced with the car that her husband had died in.*

It was a stressful time, even for those who were innocent. I decided to bake some cookies. Even if Graham didn't want to see me, the cookies would be comforting enough. I couldn't help but wonder if Graham was as innocent as he seemed. He was gentle, but a very large man. It would have been easy for him to strangle Mary and then leave her in the underbrush. But if that were the case, why would he leave her under his window? Wouldn't he know that it would make him the prime suspect? What if Mary had just pissed him off one too many times and he lost control?

What if he cast a spell on her?

I shook my head at that last thought. I wasn't sure whom to trust, but I also had heard Graham talk enough about ceremonial magic. Whenever you cast a spell, you had to be prepared for it to come back to you threefold. So if you cast a spell to harm someone, you'd better be prepared for a long trip to the hospital yourself. So killing someone would be even worse in Graham's book, I figured. No, Graham wasn't behind Mary's death; everything in me told me he was innocent.

I finished the cookies and set out to deliver them. I had to climb over a mountain of bouquets to do so. Brian sent one first, and then Tony sent a bigger one to compete, so Brian reacted with an even bigger bouquet, which meant in the span of *one day* I had received about twenty deliveries of flowers. At one point, I got a call from Katie to make sure it was okay to keep receiving them at home.

"This next one's going to be about three feet tall — do you have the space for it?" she asked excitedly. I'm sure she was itching at the prospect of creating the floral sculpture.

"Sure. My deck is going to be beautifully decorated for the next couple of weeks."

"Great. I have an idea planned for a replica of Pine Lake, with regional flowers depicting the town."

She hung up before I could change my mind and say no to her floral Pine Lake. It might be beautiful, but it certainly wouldn't persuade me to go on a date right now. I was truly beginning to think that all men were governed by a certain piece of anatomy located far away from their brains.

Graham's house was quiet when I arrived. I guessed the bulk of the investigation had been completed over the weekend. All that was left was some police tape blowing in the wind and boot prints through Graham's herb garden. The house seemed sad to look at, its peace disturbed by death and policing.

I knocked and at first heard shuffling, though no one came to answer the door. I knocked again and noticed the curtains in the nearest window moving a little, like someone had peeked through them and moved away. I knocked again, resolved to just leave the cookies and go home, when an older man with graying curly hair and thick glasses opened the door.

"Are you Laura?" he asked.

"Yes, who are you?"

"I'm Arthur, Graham's attorney. Are those freshly baked cookies?" he asked, staring down at the still-warm plate in my hands.

"Yeah, I baked them for Graham. Figured he might want some comfort as he has to go through this investigation and all that. Is he here?"

"Graham is here," Arthur said, directed more at the cookies than at me. "But unfortunately, I can't allow him to speak with you. He's very stressed. I'm sure you understand why, and I feel it is in his best interest if he takes a step back from socializing with you for a moment. We don't want it to seem as if there was, um... motivation for Graham to take aggressive action. I think if anyone were to see you here—"

"But there's no one around. Who's going to know if I come by with a plate of cookies?" I protested.

Arthur looked at me over his glasses. "I think we both know that in Pine Lake, everyone knows when you've visited the site of a murder with a plate of cookies for the prime suspect." He took the cookies and went back inside, closing the door in my face.

Well, that was that. My prospects were the two men who didn't care if the police thought it was suspicious that we'd start a relationship right after my best friend was murdered. Two men who truly only thought of themselves and their needs. I turned around and started walking back, ready to face my fate. A porch full of flowers and the prospect of despicable men.

I turned onto my street to a scene that was all too familiar and unwelcome. Neighbors out on the porch, their attention on my house. What could be happening now?

It was a fight on my front lawn.

32

Of course it was a fight. What else could it possibly be?

Tony and Brian were having a shouting match on my front lawn while Katie was putting some finishing touches on the sculptural bouquet depicting Pine Lake. The bouquet was at least four feet wide and almost as tall as I was. Had it not been the physical embodiment of two men I didn't want, fighting for my affection at the worst possible time in my life, I would have been ecstatic.

"Are you kidding me, dude?" Tony shouted at Brian. "Laura doesn't want some sculpture. It isn't even *for* her, it's just for you to show off how much money you have."

"It isn't about money; it's about affection. I'm proving to Laura that I'm here for her, unlike you," Brian yelled.

"You barely know her. I've known her for years. Laura is the love of my life, and I won't give up until she knows that my feelings for her are real. I've been waiting for this moment for years; she knows it. She practically told me as much the other night."

Brian scoffed and ran at Tony. Katie screamed and ran to her sculpture, protecting it from the incoming blowout.

But the blowout didn't happen. Brian grabbed Tony by the shoulders and brought him in for what looked like a hug. From the angle I was at, I could see that Brian was whispering something in Tony's ear.

Tony turned white as a sheet. Brian released him, and Tony just stared at Brian for a moment, all bravado completely gone. Tony looked around at the flowers, at Katie, and at the neighbors who had come out to watch the show, then hurried away into his house.

What had Brian said to Tony to cause a reaction like that? Did he threaten to evict Tony if he didn't back off? Still, that wouldn't have caused Tony to run away — if anything, he would have made sure the whole neighborhood could hear that Brian had to resort to threats in order to get the girl.

Brian calmly sauntered over to Katie, helping her straighten up the bouquets. He picked up a selection — the ones Tony sent, I assumed — and shoved them into a garbage bag that he had in his car. Brian smoothed down his shirt and waved Katie away. She took a few photos of the flowers, then hopped in her car and drove away. Brian, meanwhile, sat on my bench with a satisfied smile.

In that moment, all I wanted was to go home and crawl under the covers. I contemplated walking around for an hour and coming back when Brian was gone, but Brian was willing to threaten someone for dominance over my affections. He would have no problem waiting for me to get home.

I took a deep breath and walked the last block to my house. "Brian, fancy seeing you here." I pretended that I hadn't seen anything, plastered on the biggest smile I could, and mustered up all the chipper feelings I had.

"Laura, I thought you were home, since you weren't at the Rise N' Grind, and you weren't anywhere else in town. You were baking, and then you were gone."

His words had me stopping in my tracks. "How did you know I was baking?"

"I can still smell the freshly baked cookies. The scent lingers. I need to know your recipe."

"I think there's a candle you can get in town that has the same scent."

Brian laughed. "That's not the same as real freshly baked cookies." He wiggled his eyebrows in the direction of Katie's sculpture. "What do you think?"

"I think Katie is too talented for her own good. I don't even know how I'm going to get it inside."

"Well, that's why I'm here. I can help." He smiled and stood up from the bench, slinking over to me.

I didn't want his help. If I couldn't get that thing into my house, I was prepared to call Katie and tell her she could display it in her shop. I stepped backward, tripping on the top step. Brian rushed forward and grabbed my waist just before I fell, pulling me up and into his arms. He leaned down to kiss me, and I managed to dodge his lips, so all he got was my forehead. I squirmed out of his arms and hurried toward my door.

"That's fine. I think it's nice on the lawn. That way the rest of the neighborhood can enjoy it as well. Seems a shame to have all of Katie's work go to waste and just die in my living room. Bye, Brian."

I stepped inside and slammed the door before he had the chance to follow me inside. Brian banged on the door and rang my bell a few times, but I ignored it. I went up to my bathroom and drew a bath, willing myself to ignore Brian's anger coming from downstairs.

I sat in the bathtub, let the water rise around me, and started crying. It came out choking, sobbing, big fat tears, like my eyes were sweating from the stress of the past weekend.

What was going *on* in Pine Lake? What had happened to my utopia? How could I possibly continue living here like this? I suspected that Brian wasn't going to let up until I became his girlfriend. Tony probably wouldn't either, unless Brian followed through on his mysterious threat and stopped him. To top it all off, Graham wouldn't speak to me. His lawyer was nice enough, and I guessed it was true — probably bad visibility to be seen with the deceased's best friend turned enemy in the days after her murder. I wouldn't write a character that stupid.

Speaking of which, my book was in shambles. My anger at Tony and Mary had been the motivator for so long, and my changing opinions of them had led to a winding, confusing plot, which my editor would have a hard time parsing. I could already feel the rewrites in my fingers.

This bath wasn't working. I got out and got into bed, wrapped in a towel, too tired to change and too wired to go to sleep. I stared at the ceiling and waited for the night to pass and for the sun to rise on a new day.

I woke up the next morning after only getting maybe thirty minutes of sleep to Celene calling me from the road.

"I'm coming up for the day. I think you need it."

"What time did you wake up this morning?" I asked, wondering how she could be such an early riser.

"I woke up at five, had a coffee and breakfast, and hit the road at 5:30, so I'll be there about 7:30."

"When is 7:30?"

"Half an hour from now. Wake up, lazybones." The phone clicked off.

I stood by the fact that waking up later than 7:30 a.m. did not make me lazy.

When I answered the door, Celene was out on my lawn, inspecting Katie's sculpture and taking photos.

"Is this supposed to be the town?" she asked.

I nodded, covering my yawn with my arm.

Celene squealed. "I'm sorry, I know this is probably triggering for you. I'll stop being excited, but I *have* to send some pics to my crafting group."

Ahh, yes, the crafting group. That reminded me that I still had questions for Celene about the crafting group and how — *if* — she knew the same Shelly as I did, or if I was somehow mistaken about whom exactly we'd run into that weekend.

I ushered her in before Brian's radar went off, and he appeared at my door. Celene wrapped me in a big hug, and I started sobbing again. She led me back to bed and tucked me in, and I slept for another couple of hours.

When I woke up, Celene was sitting in my living room, knitting, and watching a documentary about birds.

"I went to get a coffee and ran into your neighbor Carl. You should talk to him more; he has absolutely no idea what's going on in town, gossip-wise. But we did talk for a while about the birds around Pine Lake. He even let me look through his binoculars at some red-throated speckled something."

Maybe Celene would fit in here better than I ever did.

"Celene, I need to talk to you. A serious talk, not about Mary, but about Shelly."

"Michelle Blanchet, who is really this Shelly Blaze, who also claims we didn't run into her on the weekend?"

"Yes. How do you know her again?"

"From my crafting group, I told you. You know the one I've been a part of for, like, five years? Anyway, I don't know why she is using two names, or why she would have said she wasn't part of my crafting group, unless she's hiding something or is embarrassed."

"I don't think she's embarrassed. I do think she's hiding something, but I don't know what it could be." I rubbed my forehead as I tried to process everything. "I know you already told me, but can you tell me again what you talked about?"

Celene put down her knitting and shifted in her seat.

"Celene? Please tell me. What did you guys talk about?"

Now she got up and wandered around my living room, adjusting knickknacks and fluffing pillows, clearly avoiding the question. "You have to understand, I had no idea she knew you or that this would be interesting to her in *any* way."

"Okay."

"And you have to promise not to judge or get angry because — again — I didn't know she knew you or that this would affect you in any way." Celene was suddenly very serious.

How bad was this going to be?

"Celene, please just tell me what you told her about me."

Celene took a deep breath. "So this woman appeared in the group about six months ago. She said her name was Michelle Blanchet and that she had just broken up with her boyfriend of a few years and was looking for a group of gals to commiserate with because she was stuck in a small town and didn't want to feel like everyone was talking about her like some little wounded gazelle. All she said was that she was supposed to get married, and that the wedding was off." Celene paused to check my reaction.

I nodded at her to continue.

"We all welcomed her in, and I told her about you. I promise that I didn't say your name. Just that *my friend* had gone through the same thing, and she was doing really well now. As encouragement for the girl, you know? Anyway, we kept talking. We chatted on the phone sometimes, and she asked about you. You know, things like, 'What did your friend do to get over the guy? How is she doing now?' that sort of thing."

"Did you ever tell her specifics?"

Celene bit her lip and sat down. "Eventually, she came to the virtual knitting groups, and she stuck around. She said she felt like she could trust me, and she started sharing details about what had happened with her. She said that the reason she kept talking to me about it was that she trusted me and felt like my friend — you — and she had gone through the same situation."

I had to wonder if this was some of Shelly's master manipulation tactics that she'd used on the rest of the residents in town. Had she gone to such extremes to garner information on them too? I bit my lip, waiting for Celene to continue.

"I remember her saying stuff like, 'It's so crazy that I met you at this time in my life, just when I needed it.' She really played the heartstrings, you know? I don't remember when, but she started asking more specific questions about you. It wasn't that often. Remember, this whole thing has been happening over the past six months or so. Anyway, about four months ago, we were kind of gossiping about her ex and his new girlfriend, and she asked me your ex's name."

"And you gave it to her?" I asked.

"Well, yes," Celene responded. "She suggested we look him up on social media and laugh at him. At the time it was just... funny. Trash-talking Tony and Mary, giggling over their cringe social media posts, that sort of thing."

It was my turn to stand up and walk around. I went to the kitchen and got a glass of water, just for something to do. I wasn't mad at Celene. I understood what she'd done, but the problem was it was *my* ex, and this was all now coming back to bite *me* in the ass. Not Celene. And I had to wonder if it had even gotten Mary killed. It wasn't something I wanted to voice though. I didn't want Celene to feel guilty about it... I stopped.

Something suddenly occurred to me. Maybe I had it wrong, but also right. Maybe Shelly was behind the craziness in town, or maybe all of that was just conspiracy theories. Maybe everything that had happened recently was because she was jealous of me? I'd seen the way her face lit up when she spoke of Brian... could that be why she'd done all of this digging into me and my life prior to coming to Pine Lake? How had she even known how to find Celene for that matter? Had I mentioned her to Shelly at some point? I sighed. Probably.

Celene had followed me into the kitchen. "I didn't think it was a big deal, Laura; please don't be mad at me."

I nodded. "I know it didn't *seem* like a big deal, and I'm not mad at you, in fact her even tracking you down is probably my fault, so no, I don't blame you. However, look at where all this gossip has gotten me. Hell, where it's gotten Mary. I think Shelly's been stalking me because she's jealous of my relationship with Brian. What if she was trying to frame me for Mary's murder?"

"That is insane. Who would do that, and how was I supposed to know that she even lived here?" Celene demanded, obviously still trying to defend herself, but I was already past it.

"I—" I started, but she just continued on.

"She never said. And she went by Michelle, not Shelly. And, oh God..." Celene looked sick to her stomach. "Oh Mary..."

"I know." I didn't want to push, but I kept going with my thoughts. "This is what gossip gets us into. It seems so harmless at first, and then it blows up in your face, just like that dinner you practically forced me to have with Tony and Mary." It was a low blow bringing that up, but I was trying to prove a point about gossip and work through some of my thoughts.

"Hey!" Celene yelled.

She rarely ever yelled. When Celene yelled, it was deep and solid, like an ancient mountain was yelling at you. It made me stop in my tracks.

"I made a mistake, but there is no need to throw it back in my face. I'm on *your* side, remember? You were the one who wanted to keep living in Pine Lake, so I gave you the best advice I could. I'm not a psychic, Laura. I get that you want to blame someone, but I'm *not* the one pulling the puppet strings here. I couldn't have predicted that Tony and

Mary were going to blow up at dinner, and there's no way I could have known that the woman I knew as Michelle Blanchet worked for and is obsessed with your landlord-Realtor-mayor-wannabe boyfriend, Brian Oliver."

I blinked. Celene was right. I shouldn't have faulted her for her advice. I had asked for it. This was all on Shelly's head. Maybe. What I did know was that Celene wasn't the one masterminding this cyclone of drama, and I had obviously underestimated Shelly's intelligence when it came to manipulating those around her. With that kind of talent, it was a wonder she was settling for working for Brian. That only made sense if she really liked him in a romantic way.

"You're right. It was a low blow for me to bring that up. I'm sorry, Cece."

"It's okay," she said, and pulled me in for a hug. "You know who we really need to go after though, right?"

33

Celene and I waited in my car, baseball hats pulled down low, for Shelly to finally leave the office for the day. When she did, we waited for her to be about half a block ahead of us before getting out and following her.

Shelly turned and started walking toward the boardwalk, right in the direction of my house.

"What is she planning to do?" I whispered to Celene.

"I don't know, but at least it's not a surprise," she answered.

We kept following Shelly until she got to the same stretch of boardwalk where I'd confronted Mary when *she* was the one stalking me.

That was when I heard Celene boom, "Michelle — Shelly! Blaze or Blanchet or whatever your name is, we need to talk to you."

Shelly froze in her tracks. She slowly turned around, and I could see her gulp. She made a move to run.

Celene just held out her hand. "Don't even. You think we won't catch up to you?"

Shelly barely squeaked out a response.

We motioned for her to come over to us, and Celene and I sat her down on a bench.

"Why did you ask me all those questions about Laura?" Celene took the reins of the interrogation.

I was very impressed. I'd never heard Celene's mom voice, and it was enough to make a boxer quake in his boots.

"I don't know what you're talking about," Shelly whispered, staring at Celene's feet.

"Tell me right now: why were you asking me questions about Laura, and what were you doing on your way to her house?"

Shelly broke down in tears. Not the kind that would tug at our heartstrings and let her go, the kind that proved she was as terrified of Celene's anger as she should be. "Okay! Whatever! Brian told me to ask about what happened with Laura's ex. It's not even a big deal; he just wanted to know so he could get on her good side when they started dating. He asked me to find out what her ex's name was, and if he was still with the woman he'd cheated with; that's why I got you to gossip about them. You were right; they're total cringe." Her voice turned flippant.

"So you got all this information from Celene and then you told Brian?" I asked, confused. That didn't make any sense. I was still very suspicious of her. "When was this?"

Shelly shrugged and looked down the street, avoiding my gaze.

I glared at her. "Did you tell him Tony's name before or after he and Mary moved here?"

Shelly continued to hesitate.

Celene gave her a firm nudge. "Answer, Laura," she said, in a vaguely threatening tone.

"Before."

"Why did you contact Tony and Mary and encourage them to move here? What did you think you were going to accomplish?" I demanded.

Shelly looked taken aback. "That wasn't me. When I found out they were the ones Brian had rented Brandy's old house to, I told him that it was a bad idea and you'd be mad."

"You're lying. Brian wouldn't rent to them if he knew who they were."

Shelly shook her head and then got angry, stepping up into my personal space. "I tried to tell him not to contact them and bring them here, but Brian never listens to me anyway. He's so, like, basically obsessed with you, and you don't even care. I *love* Brian. You don't deserve him at all," she shrieked at me.

I took a step back, my eyes widening. I had originally thought Shelly was this somewhat apathetic young woman who worked for Brian because she was bored. It had only dawned on me recently that she had stayed all these years because she liked him, but to know she was in love with him, that blew my mind. She'd been with him long enough to see what a bad romantic partner he'd be, so how any self-respecting woman could want to be with him was beyond me.

I frowned, thinking over everything she'd said and then about Graham's conspiracy board. I was missing something. "So what, you do all this manipulation to, what... help Brian's business because you think it will make him love you?"

"I don't know what the hell you're talking about. I didn't do anything," Shelly insisted.

"Really? What were you doing tonight? Why were you going to my house?" I asked, not bothering to keep the disdain from my voice.

She removed a small envelope from her bag and handed it to me. "Brian told me to drop this off for you."

Frowning, I opened the envelope. Inside was a fridge magnet shaped like a bear that was holding a heart. I rolled my eyes. The guy just wouldn't take no for an answer. When was he going to get it through his head that I wasn't going to date him?

"Why did he give you this to give to me?" I asked, still feeling suspicious.

Shelly shrugged. "I dunno. He was mad that the flowers weren't working to win you over, and I told him maybe you don't like flowers. So he said to give you this." She gestured toward the object in my hand.

I turned the magnet around in my hands. If Shelly hadn't just told me that Brian *did* know who Tony and Mary were when he rented to them — of course she could be lying, but that just made me more confused because why lie about that? — the gesture might have charmed me. It was cute, it was simple, and I always needed more fridge magnets, so why not use it? It didn't mean I had to date him.

Shelly turned to Celene. "You have the magnet, so can I go home now?"

Celene looked at me, and I nodded. We released Shelly and sat down by ourselves. She pulled out her phone and hit the off button.

"Did you record that?" I asked, gesturing to her phone.

Celene nodded. "I thought I'd better get everything on

record in case she confessed or something, but she didn't really, did she?"

I sighed. "No. Either she's really a great liar, or she isn't the one behind all of this. Maybe it's just a conspiracy theory about all of this, and it's all a coincidence?"

"Maybe." She bumped her shoulder into mine and glanced at my hands. "What do you think this means?" Celene asked, pointing at the magnet.

"I don't know. All I know is that Brian has had me in his sights for a long time, it seems, and he isn't a man who is used to not getting what he wants."

"Do you think Shelly was telling the truth and he's the one behind Tony and Mary's move here?"

I shook my head. "Honestly, I don't know what to believe anymore. But I need to somehow find a way to put all this together."

CELENE LEFT THAT NIGHT, but not before helping me put together a chart of all the strange coincidences that had happened between me and Brian.

I woke up the next morning and stared at what we had put together. It wasn't as elaborate as Graham's map, but it was starting to look that way.

I held the fridge magnet in my hand and looked at all the times that Brian had happened to appear in the same place that I was, or had come by unexpectedly when he knew I would be home. I thought about that moment when he knew I was baking cookies and claimed it was because the smell lingered in the air, but I couldn't smell a thing.

Graham had mentioned that Brian used secret cameras; he had found one pointed at one of Brian's properties. Was it possible that Brian was spying on me, or was I just being paranoid? The list was extensive, and reading the comments I remembered Brian making — there was a time when I had been impressed about how well he knew me. He knew what kind of foods I liked. He knew the exact wine I liked to drink without asking.

The more I stared at the magnet, the more the paranoia took hold. I started looking around my house — how many times had Brian come over to help install something or repair a part of the house that I thought didn't need a repair? I always deferred to his expertise and his excuse that when we transferred ownership of the house, he wanted it in perfect shape.

Something about the magnet was bugging me. I turned it this way and that, and I started to wonder. Was it possible that it was bugged? Was that how he knew the things I liked before I'd ever mentioned them to him? Obviously not with this magnet since he'd just given it to me — or could it be? My skin began to crawl at the thought, and suddenly I had to know.

I brought the magnet over my head and slammed it down on the hardwood floor. I saw a spark in the glass eyes of the bear, and I knew that my gut instinct was right. The magnet wasn't a sweet gesture or a sign that Brian was scaling back — I had a really bad feeling it wasn't just a listening device, it was a camera so that he could watch me in my own kitchen.

I bashed the magnet against the floor until it finally cracked on the side. I grabbed a knife out of the wooden block holder and used it to slowly pry open the face of the magnet. There it was — a tiny camera, the kind you might get at a spy shop or for a nanny cam, placed between the eyes of the bear.

I paled as I stared at the thing. He'd just given me this one... was it possible there were others? How many cameras existed in my home? How many microphones were embedded in the walls of this place?

What else in my house was secretly a camera?

34

I started in the bathroom, terrified that Brian had seen my naked body without my knowing. I unscrewed every lightbulb, took the door off the medicine cabinet, and knocked on it to check if it was hollow. Sure enough, it was. I pried open the medicine cabinet and found a two-way mirror with another spy camera inside. I couldn't believe it — there was no boundary Brian wouldn't cross. I felt sick to my stomach at how violated I felt.

After that, I checked every vase that came with a bouquet of flowers from Brian. I looked in baseboards and behind picture frames. I even took apart the robot vacuum he gave me. There were cameras and microphones in everything. I packed them all into a bag, not even caring that Brian would likely be notified that his precious spy cams were now unplugged and offline.

I got ready and almost stormed out of my house when I remembered —

The fancy coat hooks that seemed far too heavy for their size. They were in the entryway, the same place where I had kissed Graham for the first time. The next morning, Brian had appeared at my door, fuming that I had been cheating on him. I should have known. That was how he knew that Graham was at my house, not through his stupid gossip network. I ripped the coat hooks out of the wall and threw them in the bag.

There was only one person who could help me now, and I wasn't going to give up until we could talk.

Graham didn't answer the first few times I knocked, so I tried calling. He still didn't answer. I resorted to plan Z. I climbed up onto his deck and banged on the window. I could see him in his hallway, looking shocked and confused.

"I know your lawyer told you not to see me," I yelled, hoping he could hear me, "but this is important!" I held up the bag of cameras and microphones that I had pulled out of my house. "This is about Brian!"

Graham took one look at the bag and bounded across his living room to the door. He ushered me inside and pulled the curtains shut. "Just a precaution."

He wrapped his arms around me. I could smell his after-shave, and his sweater was warm. He must have just taken it out of the dryer. It was the closest we had been to each other in a week, and all I wanted to do was pull him down toward my lips and—

"What did you find?" he asked.

Right, business. I came here on a business matter.

"Cameras, microphones, you name it. My house was full of them."

"Seriously?" He gasped. "I thought you didn't believe me."

I put my hand on his chest and looked up at him

earnestly. "I believed you, but I thought it was Shelly behind it, not Brian." I shook my head. "Let me explain?"

He gestured toward the sofa, where we sat down.

"So, I was really suspicious of her, because of her fight with Brandy and some other odd interactions, and then I found out that Shelly had been pumping my best friend for information about me for months. She's been posing as a member of my friend's crafting circle and claimed that she wanted advice after being left by her boyfriend right before her wedding. So my friend Celene started off giving her advice based on me, but eventually Shelly pressed and—"

"She got all the information about your ex and passed it along to Brian?"

"Yes. Graham, it's true. It's all true." I blew out an exhausted breath. "I still thought she was behind it all, but when Celene and I confronted her, she gave me a fridge magnet and said it was from Brian. I didn't want to believe it, but Celene and I started writing stuff down, kind of like you did—"

He smiled and nodded.

"And I started seeing all these coincidences, and then I looked at this magnet he had sent her over with, and... that led to finding all of these." I pointed at the bag, shaking my head. "He orchestrated it all, Graham. He knew about Tony and Mary before they moved here, I told him who they were, but he went and found them, got to know them because of that, but he also knows more than what I told him in person. I think he was the one who killed Brandy. See the notes Celene and I made—" I reached into the bag and pulled out the chart that we'd made, thrusting it into his hands, "this is every 'coincidence' where Brian appeared where I was working or hanging out. Along with the things he knew about me before I told him. It's uncanny. This is only possible if he was following me or watching me in my house."

Graham started looking through the chart. "The thing is, we live in a really small town. A judge would look at this and say that there aren't very many coffee shops in Pine Lake, so why *wouldn't* Brian go there? Again, he may have known Tony's name, but it doesn't prove that he orchestrated the couple's move. There has to be something more concrete."

"I have Shelly on record. Celene recorded us interrogating her on the phone. It's proof that Brian told her to gather information on me."

"We need proof that he did it maliciously, that he did it to manipulate you and the world around you."

I slumped into a chair. I had thought Graham would be excited, that we could start working on a way to take Brian down, but he was acting as if he didn't care about my problem and wasn't satisfied I had finally proved to him that his theory that Brian was controlling the town was true. And what about all the cameras and listening devices I'd pulled out of my house? Weren't they enough?

"I know what we could do," he said finally, "but it isn't exactly ethical. You can't tell Celene about it."

"I won't. What is it?"

"I think I can hack into Brian's network. It isn't very secure. I can probably remotely access their files, and — maybe — we can find some kind of evidence."

"How did you find this?"

"One of Brian's former residents sent it to me. She was the only one who ever believed my conspiracy theory and told me that someone could hack into his network via the portal he uses for his tenants to report repairs and stuff like that."

"I know that network. I've never used it because Brian always guessed—"

"Of course. It's a two-way street. He can always access your computer history if you have the application installed, but he didn't realize that *we* could access his email as well. I never tried it because I didn't know what to look for, but now—"

"—if we search Tony's name, maybe we can get proof that he persuaded Tony and Mary to move."

Graham and I had moved closer and closer in our excitement. We were so close that I could smell his toothpaste, and I felt oddly intoxicated by it. Graham didn't need to use magic to cast a spell on me; his whole body was already attracting me.

We ran to Graham's office. I logged into my profile on Brian's tenant network while Graham searched his notes for how to hack into the system and access Shelly's or Brian's email.

"I found it. May I?" he asked.

I stepped away from the computer and let him work his magic. He followed the notes exactly — he wore little red reading glasses, the kind you buy at a drugstore, and followed each step with a finger on the page.

Laura, get it together. You two are busy cracking a conspiracy theory.

"I got it. This is Shelly's email... Brian's password reset requests go into this inbox. If we request a password reset..." Graham did so.

We waited a minute, and the request appeared in Shelly's inbox.

Graham set up Brian's new password. "I think 'Con5piracy' is a good one, don't you?" he joked.

I smacked him gently on the shoulder. "We don't have time for jokes right now, magic man, just pick something easy to remember."

We managed to get into Brian's email, and Graham searched Tony's name.

Jackpot.

Highlighted were about a hundred emails between the two, starting from about four months ago — right around the time that Celene said she and Shelly started stalking Tony's social media together.

Brian had emailed Tony as a real-estate agent, showing him the "utopian opportunities available in Pine Lake Mountainside Community." Tony, to his credit, mentioned that he knew someone who lived there — I knew my mother had to have told him — and might not be interested, but Brian persisted. He sent Tony email after email, promoting the town and the opportunities here. He mentioned the community of retired tech billionaires — showing that he'd somehow found out Tony's job was now in the tech space.

Finally, there it was:

Hello Tony,

I would like to make you aware of an upcoming opportunity available at 68 Lakeside View. One of our elder community members is ill and may not survive much longer. We are in negotiations for me to purchase her property, and as we've been in communication for the past little while, I wanted to offer you the property first. It offers beautiful lakeside views and a close-knit commu-

nity. It is my understanding that you and your partner have come on some difficult times socially, and I am sorry for that. However, here in Pine Lake, we would be more than happy to welcome you into our fold. Let me know what you think.

Always,

Brian

Did Brian orchestrate Mary falling out with her friends to push them to move to Pine Lake?

"So Brian knew about Mary's mental state?" Graham said. "Do you think it's possible he contributed to her mental issues before they moved here?"

"Maybe. I mean, look at what he's done." I frowned as I stared at the email.

Hesitantly, Graham asked, "Do you think he was stealing her medication so she would go off the rails and cause more drama here?"

My blood ran cold. "Based on everything we've seen and read, and all the cameras I've found at my place, I think it's very likely."

35

G raham made herbal tea and set a cup down in front of me. "It'll help calm us down. Marshmallow root, rosehip, lavender, and a little honey for sweetness."

"I think I need something a little stronger. Got any spells that might work on me?"

Graham laughed. "Have you heard of the Shoticus Tequlius spell?"

"I don't think I have." I smirked.

"Ahh, well, first you lick a pinch of salt from your wrist, and then you drink the fermented nectar of the agave plant in a small glass. After that, for the spell to reach maximum potency, you squeeze the juice of a lime onto your tongue," he said, standing up from his desk.

"Maybe we should try that?"

We laughed as we each had a shot of tequila.

"Oh, I haven't done that in a while," I said, my face screwed up from the strong alcohol.

"Me either. I think I'll stick to my calming tea," Graham said.

"What do we do now?" I asked. "Should we go to the police?"

Graham shook his head. "I don't know what they'd think about our messy notebooks and conspiracy theories. Besides, even though we printed out the emails, we didn't exactly acquire them legally."

"Do you think we could get Tony on our side? He could prove that Brian orchestrated the move — after all, the emails were sent to Tony. If he prints them out, it's a whole other story — one without any illegal hacking."

I hadn't thought about Tony since the fight on the lawn.

"Graham, I think that you and Tony are in danger," I said, remembering how Brian had whispered something that made Tony's face lose all its color.

"Why?"

"Brian wants me as his girlfriend, and he will stop at nothing to get there. I know he threatened Tony — I don't know what he said, but it made Tony literally run away from him. If Shelly told Brian that I came after her and forced her to admit that she got Tony's name from Celene, and then a day later all of Brian's cameras go offline, he's definitely going to follow through on his threat."

"You think so? But Tony isn't that much of a threat."

"Brian thinks so. Tony's been sending me flowers, trying to get me to talk to him so we can rekindle our relationship." I saw Graham's face fall. "It's not going to work, trust me. I think Tony is trash, but I'm afraid Brian is under the impression that Tony is still his competition."

Graham took a long sip of his tea. "Brian is going to eliminate anyone who stands in the way of your affections for him until there's no one left to turn to except Brian Oliver."

"I can't believe I'm going to say this," I said, "but we have to go save Tony."

A fog had started rolling in. It was the first day in recent memory that the sun wasn't out on Pine Lake; fitting for our mission to go save the man who, for years, I'd hoped would just disappear off the face of the earth.

Graham and I hopped in his car, but the fog made the short drive even longer than if we'd just walked. Finally, we made it to Tony's house. The door was open, but the house was completely empty.

"Tony!" I called out. "Tony, are you here?"

"Tony!" Graham yelled. "Hello? Anyone home?"

He wasn't there. The house was empty, but the sliding doors to the back deck were open. I noticed there were strange footprints that almost looked like blood leading from the kitchen out to the back deck. Tony had been cooking pasta — there was a pot of tomato sauce all over the floor, and a pot with noodles was about to boil over. He couldn't have gone far. Graham dutifully turned off the stove, and we crouched low to the ground, following the footprints out to the deck.

On the far end, leading away from my house, was a staircase leading down the boardwalk that surrounded our houses. It must have been new, a nice addition in Brian's renovation. The saucy footprints continued down the steps, onto the boardwalk, which was covered in mist. As we crept down the stairs, we heard strange choking sounds getting louder and louder.

Brian had his hands wrapped around Tony's neck. His usually perfectly done hair was messy, as Tony kept batting at his head, trying to get Brian off him. Tony had already started to lose color, and his kicks were too weak to stop Brian.

"Brian!" Graham boomed behind me.

Brian turned his head, his hands still on Tony's neck, as the camera on Graham's phone started flashing.

I followed suit, taking photos as manically as I could, creating an amateurish strobe effect as we ran at the two men.

It worked. Brian put his arms up to cover his face, dropping Tony to the ground. Tony started coughing and dragged himself away from Brian.

"You two are going to regret this," Brian said, pulling out a gun.

36

B rian stood at the bottom of the stairs. There were two ways out of this situation that didn't involve Graham and me getting shot. We could run up the stairs and risk getting hit from behind, or we could jump the stairs and risk breaking an ankle on the boardwalk below.

I made the choice for us. I hoisted myself over the railing of the stairs, slapping Graham's arm so that he knew what I was doing. He followed suit, and we jumped onto the board-walk below.

I turned to the right, figuring the best thing to do was to run to the end of the boardwalk, where there was a small dock. A couple of residents kept little rowboats for fishing, and beyond were the woods. If we could just get to the trees, it would be harder for Brian to aim at us, and we might have a chance to call the police.

Behind, I could hear Brian laughing. "As if I'm not going to chase you!" he yelled.

The fog kept rolling in over the lake, obscuring our view

of Brian. He was too close for comfort, and his first shot landed right at Graham's feet.

"He's got a silencer on the gun. No one's going to hear it go off."

My stomach churned. I felt like I was in the last pages of one of my novels — Andrea Caldwell being chased by the very hitman she'd hired, unaware that her husband had hired the same man to kill her. Living the scene was not nearly as enjoyable as writing it. In reality, I didn't know where to run that would be safe. The hasty plan to run into the woods flew out the window as I desperately tried to avoid Brian's aim.

"It's a good thing you're such a poor shot!" Graham shouted into the fog. He made a sudden turn down one of the docks.

I squealed as I almost slipped and fell into the water.

"It's a good thing your weak little girlfriend is so loud!" Brian shouted behind us, shooting at the rowboat, which I'd almost fallen into.

Graham grabbed my arm and pulled me in front of him.

I stopped short — we had reached the end of the dock. There was nowhere left to run except into the lake itself.

Behind us came Brian's slow, heavy footsteps. His body was a dark mass in the dense fog, but it was enough. I could feel the rage pouring off him. It gave me a flashback to when I was a kid, as my father would approach me and my mother when he was angry.

"Brian, why are you doing this? Why do you care?"

"You came to *my* town thinking you could say no to me, and now you're asking me *why I care?*" Brian's voice was too calm and slow. He was no longer fighting: he was stalking his prey.

"We know what you've been doing," Graham said. "We have evidence that you installed cameras everywhere, and that you strong-armed Tony and Mary into moving here."

Brian clapped slowly. "Congratulations. The town freak finally has proof that I'm a maniac. Well, too bad you won't survive to tell anyone. Even if you did, no one would believe you."

"Why not?" Graham asked.

"I have Shelly planting evidence at your house as we speak. When she's done, the police will be convinced that Tony framed you for killing Mary, *and*, thanks to your silly girlfriend here, they'll know that *you're the one* who has been secretly bugging Laura's home. And then after killing the two of you, Tony will be so full of remorse, he'll take his own life. Meanwhile, I'll be the one mourning the woman I fell in love with."

"You're delusional," Graham muttered softly, but I didn't think Brian heard him.

"You really did have this all planned out, didn't you?" I asked.

"You can't just have plan A; you have to have a plan B, C, and D. That way, when some flighty girl like you, *Laura*, decides she doesn't want to go along with your plan, you'll know exactly what to do next."

"What did you think I was supposed to do?" I glanced at Graham, then back to Brian.

"You were supposed to be happy that I'd saved you from Tony and Mary. You'd realize you still felt trauma from them, and then I'd be there to console you. I've spent years studying you, Laura. Or hadn't you noticed that I knew exactly what to say to you and exactly how to make you *want* to flirt with me? Then when I killed Mary, and

Tony started hitting on you, I'd be there to save you from him."

I felt sick at how Brian casually mentioned murdering Mary.

"But you had to go off with this warlock elf guy and ruin my whole plan," Brian continued.

"Warlock elf?" Graham repeated.

Brian ignored him and said, "I must admit, I never thought you'd go for Graham. I thought I had spread enough rumors about him that you'd be afraid of him. But you are one stubborn woman. Always independent, always needing to go off on your own; you can't just choose the option that is right in front of you."

"Maybe because that option was trying to force itself on me. Is that what this is all about? Because I wouldn't date you?" I roared. "That's pathetic."

"Of course it's not about you dating me. What do I care about you? This is about the town, don't you see? Pine Lake is my baby. You all think you make your own decisions, but I'm the one orchestrating it all. You think this plan has been going on for the past six months? Absolutely not. I have plans that span years in the future. Everything I do now is planting a seed for what will come."

"What do you mean?" I asked with another glance at Graham. I wanted Brian to keep talking.

"I convinced Tod to open up the Rise N' Grind because I knew it would create a hip hangout spot for the younger residents. That gave a pocket for a new group of women to start gossiping with each other, more women to spread the rumors I wanted everyone to hear, *and* it gave me ammo against some of the retirees. In a few months, there will be a blowup, and the town will split into two — young vs. old."

"What about Brandy?" Graham asked.

"Did you kill her too?" I added.

"I had to. When I sent Shelly over to the old woman's house to convince her to sell it to me, she refused."

So that was what Shelly and Brandy had been arguing about. I couldn't believe that Brian had monologued like an evil villain in a Bond movie. He truly was a puppet master. He believed Pine Lake was his property, the people in town were his playthings, and he made Shelly do his dirty work.

Brian lifted the gun and pointed it at me. "No matter, I can just get rid of you. You will be just another Pine Lake tragedy. Your deranged ex-fiancé murdered his girlfriend and framed your boyfriend; then when you rejected him, he killed you both and then himself. At your funeral, I'll pick the woman who comes up to me first, and she'll be my wife."

"Your wife? You thought I was going to *marry you*?"

"If you would've just stuck to the plan, then yes. You *were* going to marry me. Now, I'm going to have to kill you."

37

I died and waited for the white light people tell you about. I wondered why my life didn't flash before my eyes. It would have been nice to revisit some of those memories.

As I patiently waited for the white light, I heard someone calling my name in the distance. That was strange. I had never heard about this before. I wondered if it was an alternative to the white light. I didn't really believe in an afterlife, so maybe this was what happened instead. I hoped it wasn't the devil, who was calling me down to hell. I didn't think I had done anything truly heinous in my life. Purgatory, maybe, but nothing worthy of being sent to the fiery pits of the underworld.

"Laura, wake up!"

I felt a cold hand slap me across the face. Slowly there was light, but not very much. There was a blurry figure and the smell of lake water all around me. The figure slowly came into view — it was Graham. "Are you visiting me?"

"What do you mean?" Graham asked, staring deep into my eyes. "Laura, are you okay? Are you hurt?"

"Are you having a seance? Am I dead?"

"No! You're alive, you — are you sure you're okay?"

"I blacked out—"

"I threw an oar at Brian, and it hit him on the wrist. He shot at you, but I think the bullet hit the water. I don't know. You fell and hit your head on one of the mooring posts" — he gestured to Brian — "and I knocked him out before he could get at you."

Behind Graham, Brian lay unconscious on the side of the dock. One of his arms hung in the water, and the wind had started rocking the dock a little bit.

"Graham, you have to move him. He's too heavy—"

Just as I said it, Brian's weight took him over the edge of the dock. His body hit one of the boats, and it flipped over, turning Brian into the water.

Graham scrambled to the dock. "I can't see him. It's too dark."

"I can jump in—" I winced as I stood up. There was a bump on my head for sure, and I might even have a concussion. My vision started to clear, and I realized that Graham's arm was hanging awkwardly in his shirt. "What happened to your arm?"

"I fell back into one of the boats when I threw the oar. I think I dislocated my shoulder. It's okay, I can probably pull him back up with the other." Graham started taking off his shoes, getting ready to jump in.

"Graham, stop! You'll drown!" I screamed, but he didn't hear me.

Graham jumped sloppily in the water, screaming with pain as his dislocated arm hit the surface of the lake. He went under, but almost immediately came back up, struggling to tread water with his one good arm. "I can't find him. The water is almost black. This part of the lake is deeper than I thought. Aren't docks supposed to be in shallow water?"

"Let me help you." I slowly got up and jumped in after him.

Graham was right, the water was deeper than I expected, and the lake was almost black. I swam down to the bottom, my head throbbing. Brian's unconscious body was bobbing eerily back up to the surface, and I managed to grab him by the arm. I pulled him, kicking myself toward the shore that led to the forested area of town, away from the dock. Without Graham's help, there was no way I could pull him onto a boat, so the rocky shore would have to do. It wasn't going to be comfortable for Brian — if he was even still alive.

Not that Brian deserved any comfort or consideration. He had murdered Mary and Brandy and shot at me because I wouldn't be his wife.

Not now, Laura. You have to get him to shore; then you can start analyzing what Brian said.

I dragged Brian's limp body to shore, turning him on his side and slapping his back, hoping he would wake up. It was no use. In the time it took to find him in the murky lake, he had drowned, died.

I stood up and slowly started walking back to where Graham was struggling to climb the small ladder up to the dock from the water. I grabbed his good arm and helped to hoist him up the last step.

"Thank you," he said.

"You're welcome," I answered.

We sat on the dock for a moment, looking back at Brian's body.

"All your notes, your theories," I said, "they were all right. Brian was playing with this town like it was a dollhouse, and he would stop at nothing to make sure everything played out according to his plan."

"Do you think he really thought about this stuff years in advance?" Graham asked.

I shrugged. "I don't know. If he did, does that mean I'm somehow in Pine Lake because of him?"

"I guess we'll never know," Graham said.

We sat there like that for a little while longer, shivering in the fog and staring at Brian's limp body. My head was throbbing, and I was sure Graham was in excruciating pain, but we were both too tired to do anything.

Suddenly, I remembered that we had left Tony at the bottom of the stairs. I grabbed Graham's bad shoulder, causing him to cry out in pain.

"I'm so sorry, I just — Tony!" I stood up and ran back to the stairs behind Tony's house. It was hard to find because the fence onto his property was disguised from this side of the boardwalk.

"Tony," I called out, "are you okay?"

"Yeah," said a groggy voice. The part of the wall that led to his house creaked open. "I'm fine. Just sore." Tony's voice was croaky, and he could barely speak above a whisper. "I called the cops. They're coming."

"Brian's dead."

"I know. I caught it all on camera." He pulled out his phone. "Gotta keep my gal safe." He smiled and reached out to touch my cheek.

Just when I had started to feel sympathy for him again,

Tony managed to squash any good feeling I had for him by hitting on me at an inappropriate time. I mustered some strength to bat away his arm.

"If you're feeling like keeping me safe, why don't you go up and get us blankets? Graham dislocated his shoulder, and I had to jump into the lake to try to save Brian."

I turned and stumbled back to Graham. "Tony's fine," I said. "He's just fine."

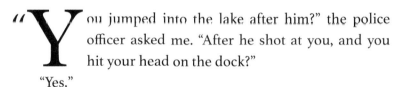

38

"**Y**ou jumped into the lake after him?" the police officer asked me. "After he shot at you, and you hit your head on the dock?"

"Yes."

The police officer stared at me through squinted eyes. "Why?"

"I didn't want him to die. I thought I might be able to pull him out. Graham certainly couldn't with his shoulder dislocated," I said.

The police officer just nodded and made a note in his book.

Graham and I were at the hospital. I'd insisted we be kept together, so they opened a curtain between our two little cubicle areas in the ER. If the police wanted to interview us, they could do it with us together. Graham's shoulder was dislocated, and he'd fractured his wrist fighting Brian on the dock. I had a nasty bump on my head, but luckily, no concussion. We were both being treated for hypothermia.

Jumping in the lake and then having to sit, wet, in the fog, landed each of us a thermal blanket and an IV, just in case.

A nurse cleared her throat, and the police officer looked behind him.

"Just a minute—" he started to say.

But the nurse cut him off. "No more minutes; you've already had ten. These people need to rest. You can interview them later."

The police officer rolled his eyes and sighed.

The nurse put her hands on her hips and glared at him. "What use will they be if they wind up unconscious again? You won't have anyone to do your job for you, and you'll have to actually investigate something in this town. Get out before I call hospital security."

The officer stared at her for a moment before realizing that there was no way he could stare down a nurse. She was far too powerful for him. He stood up and closed his notebook. "Make sure you don't go anywhere. When the hospital discharges you, you can go home, but don't leave town."

"Am I going to be arrested?" I asked.

"Probably not. The video your friend took is pretty damning. It shows Mr. Oliver pointing his gun at you, and Mr. Silverton knocking it out with an oar. Don't quote me on it, but this seems like a pretty clear-cut case of self-defense. I think you'll be fine, but you don't want to piss off the department. It's best if you rest at home, not at a spa somewhere." He turned, sped past the nurse, and exited the room.

"Are you feeling warmer now, sweetheart?" the nurse said as she fluffed my pillow and measured my vital signs.

"Yes, I think I'm okay. When do you think I'll be able to go home?"

"Well, the hospital wants to keep both of you here overnight for observation. You had quite a chill out there. As for going home — that might take a little longer." She leaned in and whispered to me, "I heard the officers talking. It seems your house, and that of your ex-fiancé, is a crime scene. You might need to find somewhere else in town to stay for a while." She winked and glanced over at Graham, who was fast asleep.

The nurse was right. It was impossible to live in my house as it was dusted and investigated for evidence that Brian had been spying on me. I had already turned over all the cameras I'd found in the house; now it was a matter of figuring out if he had done anything else. My house wasn't the only one — every property that belonged to Brian was being turned inside-out in the search for evidence of his manipulations. For once, there wasn't just one person to watch; it was going on all around us.

Graham invited me to stay with him during the investigation. We checked with the police and his lawyer, Arthur, to make sure it wouldn't put us under any more suspicion, but based on what they had already uncovered, it was becoming even more clear that we had acted in self-defense.

"It's a good thing you're here," Graham said. "It takes me an hour to type out an email with just one hand." His right hand was still wrapped in a cast, and his arm was in a sling, and would be like that for at least six weeks.

I had to email *Goosh* to let them know I couldn't keep up with my advice column for the next month or so. When I explained why, my editor said in a hushed tone, "Are you going to turn that into a book?"

"I honestly hadn't considered that, Lindsay."

One long phone call later, during which Lindsay basically planned out my memoir for me, I was officially on sabbatical. I could spend the next few weeks transcribing Graham's Dictaphone notes and writing his emails for him.

Our lives came together quite easily. Celene was very happy when I told her that Graham was also a morning person, and he did a modified sun salutation every morning to start the day. I started doing it with him, and Graham joined me in my evening tradition of a glass of wine by the lake.

It had been a long time since I'd lived with someone, and it took a lot of getting used to. For example, I was no longer used to having conversations during the day. The beauty of living alone was that you didn't have to talk to anyone all day — of course, that was also its biggest downside. My conversations with Graham spanned from debates about what kind of reality television was worth watching to teaching one another about our preferred genres to write in.

We got closer every day. We didn't share a bed, but when I woke up in the middle of the night from a nightmare, Graham would come to my room and rub my back until I fell back asleep. Sometimes, we cuddled, and I would melt into his warm body, breathing in deeply his warm, woodsy smell. I wanted him, badly. I had been thinking about it since the hospital. I was wound so tightly, and I wanted to unwind with Graham. I wanted to feel his arms around me, and I wanted to feel his lips all over my body. He still only had one good arm, and when we cuddled, he had to rest his slinged arm on my waist, so I could often feel the tickle of his fingertips on my stomach.

Our days were often interrupted by updates on the investigation. The police brought Shelly in for questioning, who immediately started "singing like a canary," as the detective put it.

Shelly was truly heartbroken over Brian's death. She knew all about his many plans for the town, down to where he kept his records with information about all of the townspeople. Those records also showed that Brian had done his research into Tony and Mary as well and had actually caused problems for them in the city. He had made it so they would have to move to Pine Lake because the opportunity was too good to pass up. Brian had spread rumors about Mary, rumors about Tony sleeping with her friends, making Mary even more unhinged than normal.

With Shelly's help, the detectives discovered the stash of medication that he'd taken from the mail office so Mary wouldn't have it and would go even more crazy.

I had to wonder why Shelly had helped him with everything. Did she think she could somehow make Brian have an affair with her or leave me for her? He never would have. He'd probably have killed her before he allowed her to blackmail him. Brian knew that his power in town came from a clean image. Maybe Shelly knew that deep down and kept working for him just to stay close to him.

"What's going to happen to her?" I asked the detective.

"Oh, we contacted her family. Funny, they had barely heard from her the past few years. It seems Brian Oliver had told Shelly that they disapproved of her, and she was convinced that they never wanted to speak to her. Her mother was sweet. She'll take care of her."

Brian's manipulations knew no bounds. Something that I kept thinking about from his bizarre monologue was that he had studied me and knew just how I wanted to be flirted with and how I would react to his behavior. This was beyond creepy. I wondered if he knew my father or had somehow studied him, played to my "daddy issues," and then tried to be the right man to resolve them.

When I brought this up with my therapist, along with everything else that had gone on, he put up his hands in surrender.

"Laura, I think this might be above my pay grade," he said, and we both laughed.

With all that had gone on, I had been too stressed to even call my therapist up to that point. Dr. Delgado had finally called to check up on me after I'd missed various appointments. He recommended I see a trauma specialist for a little while before coming back to him.

"You've been through a lot, and I suspect the sense of being manipulated and feeling violated because of Brian spying on you will be with you for quite some time. Someone who specializes in trauma will be able to help you navigate the next few months better than I can," he said when we were finally able to reconnect.

"But I like you. I want my appointments with you," I whined, even though I knew what he'd said was true.

I had spent months in a paranoid spiral, often questioning my own judgment and the behavior of those around me. I needed someone who could untangle my knots one by one before going back to Dr. Delgado.

"Think of it as taking your car to a collision center before getting it back on the road," he said. "Eventually, you'll have to take it to a mechanic again, but right now, you need to take it to someone who can make it drivable again."

After we hung up, Graham chuckled. "That was a good

analogy. I like the idea of therapy being like maintenance on a car," he said, wrapping me up in his good arm.

"I didn't realize how much it was like that until Tony left me. But right now, I don't need therapy, I need a long bath and maybe a massage."

Graham purred, and I felt it on my cheek. I burrowed myself farther into his embrace, wrapping my arms around his neck.

"A bath and a massage? That sounds very luxurious."

"It is, and you know what's even more luxurious?" I asked.

"What?"

"A bath, a massage, a man who smells like a woodsy candle, and maybe a cuddle?" I whispered into his stubble.

A beard suited him. It added to his character as a mountain mystery man.

Graham let his hand drop to my waist and gave me a deep kiss. I had been waiting for this, and in my excitement, I dug my nails into his back. I thought he would pull away, but instead, he pulled me closer, and I could feel his heartbeat against my breast.

"Who needs a bath?" he whispered. "Why not just the massage?" He bit my ear.

I melted into him, pushing him onto the couch. "Who needs the bed when we can get cozy on the couch?" I lay on top of him and bit his lip, running my fingers through his hair.

We kept kissing. Graham slid his good hand under my shirt, and in one smooth motion, he flipped my body beneath his. His soft lips grazed my neck, and he took off my shirt in one swift movement. His lips traced down my body, over my breasts, and down my stomach.

When he got to the button of my jeans, he looked up at me and said, "Who needs any of it when I have you?"

We made love twice. Once on the couch and then, after taking that luxurious bath, again in Graham's bed.

That night, I slept peacefully for the first time in months.

39

That night was the first of many that I slept peacefully in Graham's arms, but it was one of our last in Pine Lake.

There wasn't much of a trial when it came to the *State versus Brian Oliver* over the deaths of Brandy and Mary. The defendant was dead, and it was clear from all of the video footage that his death was an accident that happened in the course of self-defense.

"Even if they didn't take the tapes into evidence," Arthur, Graham's lawyer, argued, "we still could have entered that Brian was clearly stalking you, Laura, and since you pulled him out of the lake, it was clear that you were not interested in his death. You wanted him to live and face the consequences of all of his actions."

It wasn't exactly how I would have worded it, but it would do me just fine.

Graham and I were exonerated, and we could move on with our lives. Neither of us were interested in living in Pine Lake anymore. While the community was starting to heal in the absence of Brian Oliver — old rivalries made peace with one another, and conflicts that were bubbling to the surface managed to resolve themselves before boiling over — I still felt traumatized and under observation everywhere I turned. I wanted to move back to the city, where I could be anonymous. Another face in the never-ending crowd of strangers.

There was the unfortunate matter of the house. Technically, mine belonged to Brian's estate, and since he was *technically* a criminal, his assets were in limbo. The community of Pine Lake launched a lawsuit and petitioned that since Brian's psychopathic obsession with controlling the town had fallen mostly on his tenants, they should be given the option to purchase the houses they lived in.

"Do I do it?" I asked Graham after the lawyer told me what would be happening. "Purchasing this place was always my plan."

"It might be nice to have a property up here, in case anything happens," he said. "Not that I'm planning to break up with you, but I know you might want to have something to fall back on."

I decided to give it some thought. Thanks to the agreement I had with Brian — one that I now realized played right into his fantasy of me falling in love with him — I had just enough money to make an offer on the house. It would be nice to have lakefront property, be like the Carters next door, and only come during the summer holidays and perhaps at Christmas. I could easily rent it out to someone, make sure to let them be, and only check in if there was a problem.

I was visiting the city, trying to get myself reacquainted with the pace of life there after being in such a secluded town for a couple of years. I met Celene for coffee and discussed it with her.

I had barely finished my thought when she blurted out, "I'll rent it from you."

I blinked in surprise. "Really? You don't want to live in a small town, do you?"

Celene blushed. "Well, these past few months you've been trying to heal yourself and your poor head, get over that psychopath and what he did to you. So I haven't said anything because I didn't want you to think I was being some kind of *narcissist*, and I wasn't sure how you felt about the town, plus the people in the town—"

"Celene, spit it out."

"I'm dating Carl."

"The birdwatcher?"

She nodded. "We started talking one day when I came to visit you, and then the next time I was down, I stopped by to tell him about a rare bird that I'd seen in the city. Basically, we started texting, and then we talked on the phone, and I guess he was a little clueless about the whole Brian thing since he spends half his time online — and then I found out that he was the guy who'd founded and developed the app I use, *Crafters*."

I sat there with my jaw hanging open. I'd forgotten that Celene had met Carl. I should have had a clue when I'd caught her watching a bird documentary. Come to think of it, Celene would be the perfect fit for Carl. Extroverted enough that he wouldn't be a loner anymore, but so nerdy that he'd never fault her for her crafting obsession.

She blushed harder. "Anyway, we've been kind of getting more serious, and it might be nice to live in the same town for a while and properly date."

"What about your job? And your family?"

She shrugged. "My family won't be that far away. And my job has let me go remote for now, but I might quit. I want to see if I can lead some workshops at the crafting store here. You know, knitting peace in your community."

"That sounds wonderful. I'm happy for you and Carl."

"He sent in a video, you know. He was looking for birds that only come out in fog, when he saw you, Graham, and Brian on the dock. He filmed the whole thing and called the police too, which is good because apparently when Tony called, his voice was so hoarse that they thought it was just a prank. So the police had videos of the whole event from two different angles."

"I wondered where they got the other video footage from," I said with a smile.

Celene was so proud of her nerdy boyfriend. I felt happy that I could pass along my place to her and give Celene a new start with Carl.

"WE SHOULD CLEANSE THAT HOUSE," Graham said as we started unpacking.

I was using the rent Celene was paying me to finance a mortgage on a small townhouse in the city. Graham bought the house next door. Living together was great for a while, but I needed my own space to feel alone in. I was much more sensitive to being watched these days.

"What do you mean?" I asked.

"Before Celene moves in. We should go up there and do a cleansing ritual."

"I already cleaned it. And the police practically gutted the place to make sure there were no more cameras."

Graham took me in his arms — his sling was off, and he was starting to get more mobility in his fingers. "I meant cleanse the aura, you know? Burn some herbs and perhaps cast a spell of protection. I left Celene some crystals. I assume she'll know what to do with them."

"I don't know, but that does seem right up her alley," I replied. "I think we did what we could. We scrubbed that house from top to bottom, preparing it for its new resident. When I was doing it, I made sure to think about the upcoming brighter days the house would see, and I tried to infuse that into my actions. To some, actions with intentional thoughts behind them are a sort of spell. You don't need the ceremony of herbs and tinctures to cast protection over a space."

Graham beamed. "Have you been reading some of my books?"

I shrugged. "Maybe I've skimmed a few," I whispered into his lips and gave him a light kiss.

"We should order a pizza before we do that. I need to regain some of my energy," he said, going into the other room to order from the nearest place. "I hope we figure out which of these 'best pizzas in town' is the actual best pizza. Maybe I'll cast a searching spell to find out."

"No spells. I would rather find out by trying. I don't need to divine my future with you."

Graham walked back into the room and smiled. "True, there's no need for us to act as if we have a fate or destiny. Now we know for sure there's no one manipulating our decisions."

A part of me — a very, very small part — was glad that Brian had had a master plan. Without it, I didn't know if I would have bonded so strongly with Graham. If I hadn't had

Graham's steady presence, it would have been easier to go back to Brian because who would I have compared his behavior to? Tony's?

"Why are you looking at me like that?" Graham asked.

"I'm just sorta glad to have been played like a fiddle, you know? It's like we were set up by a matchmaker."

"A deranged matchmaker."

"Hey, not everyone can be good at their job. He was just trying his best to create a utopia. Even Rome had to fall before civilization sprang back up."

Graham threw his head back and laughed. "So, do you think there's someone in this city plotting our future together? Do you think they have a five-year plan?"

"I don't know, but I hope they have a plan B now that we're in town." I kissed him again and pushed him in the direction of the kitchen. "Please go order a pizza before I eat *you*."

Graham walked off, and I felt my phone buzz in my pocket. I was expecting a call from Celene to tell me she had arrived at the house, but when I looked, I saw it was a friend request on one of my social media accounts. I opened the app and saw:

Tony Ellison, 38, wants to connect.

I quickly looked out the window. There was no sign of him. This time it was truly a coincidence.

I blocked the notification and went back to unpacking boxes.

THANK YOU FOR READING

Did you enjoy reading *The Lake House*? Please consider leaving a review on Amazon. Your review will help other readers to discover the novel.

ABOUT THE AUTHOR

Theo Baxter has followed in the footsteps of his brother, best-selling suspense author Cole Baxter. He enjoys the twists and turns that readers encounter in his stories.

ALSO BY THEO BAXTER

Psychological Thrillers

The Widow's Secret

The Stepfather

Vanished

It's Your Turn Now

The Scorned Wife

Not My Mother

The Lake House

The Detective Marcy Kendrick Thriller Series

Skin Deep - Book #1

Blood Line - Book #2

Dark Duty - Book #3

Printed in Great Britain
by Amazon

42320490R00162